RESTORATION

THE REVELATION SERIES

FINALE

RANDI COOLEY WILSON

Copyright © 2015 by Randi Cooley Wilson. All rights reserved.

No part of this publication may be reproduced, distributed or transmitted in any form or by any means, including photocopying, recording, or other electronic or mechanical methods, without the prior written permission of the publisher, except in the case of brief quotations embodied in critical reviews and certain other noncommercial uses permitted by copyright law. Please contact the author directly for usage opportunities. This book is a work of fiction. Names, characters, places, and incidents are a product of the author's imagination or are used fictitiously. Locales and public names are sometimes used for atmospheric purposes. Any resemblance to actual people, living or dead, or to businesses, companies, events, institutions, or locales is completely coincidental.

Published by Secret Garden Productions, LLC
Editorial editing by Kris Kendall at Final-Edits
Copy editing by Liz Ferry
Cover Design by Bravebird Publishing
Cover Photo ©Mayer George
Book Formatting by Indie Formatting Services – Jeff Senter

Restoration (The Revelation Series, Finale)/ Randi Cooley Wilson
Printed in the United States of America
Second Edition January 2016
ISBN-13: 978-1511847445
ISBN-10: 1511847441

ALSO BY RANDI COOLEY WILSON

THE REVELATION SERIES
REVELATION
RESTRAINT
REDEMPTION
REVOLUTION
RESTORATION

THE ROYAL PROTECTOR ACADEMY
VERNAL
AEQUUS
NOX

For The Readers,

Thank you for taking this journey with me

"The world shall burn; and from her ashes spring New Heaven and Earth, wherein the just shall dwell."

John Milton, Paradise Lost

AUTHOR'S NOTE

Goodbyes are never easy. They are often painful and full of sadness. Stepping away from these characters, and this story, is no exception. A few years ago, the voices of Asher and Eve infiltrated my head in a spellbinding way. I was captivated by their demand to be heard and moved by the story they asked me to tell. Never did I imagine, in all my wildest dreams, that they would enthrall your hearts and souls in the same way as they mesmerize mine. For that, I'm so grateful. In writing this series I have found my literary voice. My love. My passion.

So, here we are, at the final chapter on Eve and Asher's journey. And what a journey it has been. I hope you have enjoyed each and every moment, as I have. May this story live forever on these pages and inside each of your hearts! I dedicate this one to you.

Thank you, for embracing this series.
Thank you, for loving these characters.
Thank you, for taking this journey with me.

Randi Cooley Wilson

PROLOGUE

Life is an unwritten book, full of empty pages, waiting to be filled with our story. Each moment is a poignant chapter. Some we'd like to revisit. Others we would rather skim over. Yet every instant has a purpose, a reason for our being. I don't know if I believe all of the written words defining my journey but I will say this: every beginning has an ending, and every ending, a beginning. — Eve Collins, *The Revelation Series*

1 The End Begins

The mist is breathtaking as it creeps hauntingly onto the property, bathing the lush landscaping in bluish-gray hues. I allow myself to succumb to its magical allure, as I take in a deep cleansing breath, filling my lungs with the damp, cool air.

My gaze drops to the pad of paper sitting on my lap. With my index finger I trace the numerous sketches of a circular, barbed-wire dragon I've drawn over and over again, in shades of black and gray. I know it means something. What . . . I don't know.

With a rough exhale, I place the notebook and pen next to me on my favorite bench under the old oak tree and brush my bare feet across the dewy blades of emerald grass. The world is still. Silent. Embodying a sense of calm and peace. Somehow, in this moment, I know my mind needs the tranquility.

Vaguely, I hear a voice in the back of my head. It speaks to me in a soft murmur. Whispering words of protection and love. My memories sit locked in a jar, inside my mind. It's painful to try to release them.

I knit my brows and allow my gaze to roam over the landscape. I don't recall how I got here. Or why my feet are bare. I'm not even sure where *here* is.

The warm breeze picks up and my hair lifts and twirls in the wind. As I attempt to get control of the wild strands, my hand brushes over the wound on my head, beneath my hairline. My fingers linger on the bandage. Something else I don't remember.

Curling my feet under my legs, I cover them with my long, white, cotton dress and study the quiet grounds. I'm unsure how I know this, but there was a heaviness that used to inhabit my chest. Now, it's gone. I think it pleases me to feel numb.

I think . . .

Unlike the other days when I've sat in this very spot, today, a strange loneliness begins to seep into my soul, a revelation that produces an eerie emptiness deep within me.

My heart feels vacant.

Something isn't right.

I'm not right.

Confusion sets in again, causing me to shake my head slowly, trying to remove the cobwebs that have wrapped their intricately woven, tangled maze around my memories and thoughts, holding them hostage.

The balmy breeze picks up once again, carrying with it the familiar and comforting scent of bubble gum. *Odd.* With curiosity, my gaze lifts and focuses on a shadow beginning to form within the mist. I watch in awe as an outline of a person emerges from within the darkness. I keep my eyes glued to the unknown figure.

I'm not afraid. The petite silhouette comes closer and I reach my hand out awkwardly to touch it, but at the last minute show restraint and pull away.

"Are you okay?" the shadow asks, with concern laced in its recognizable voice.

My heart stops when I hear the words. There's silence, as the figure waits for an answer. I open and close my mouth, trying to form intelligent words, but am stunned into silence by what I'm witnessing.

The being sighs in disappointment at my temperament and begins to slowly edge closer to me. I think it believes I'm scared of it, so it's treading lightly, so as not to startle me.

The dark shadow breaks through the heavy mist and comes into focus. For a moment, I can only stare in disbelief. My body is frozen in place. I can't pull my gaze away from her.

Memories float through me like a movie. Snapshots of cherished moments. The locked jar releases just enough to help me understand who and what I'm seeing. I swallow hard when recollection hits me. My eyes blink unhurriedly.

"I think I'm having an outlandish dream," I whisper, trying to find my voice.

"No shit." The dark outline says with sarcasm dripping from her lips. "Same one?"

My gaze lifts, locking onto a pair of chocolate orbs, staring warmly at me.

"Oh God," I exhale on a weak breath.

"I feel like we've had this conversation before," the amused voice quips.

The ghost kneels in front of me, enfolding my hands in one of her own and using the other to tuck a strand of hair behind my ear. The apparition smiles and it makes me want to cry.

"I'm here to help you find your way back, Eve Collins." She speaks in a low, lulling tone.

"I'm lost?" I question her in a soft voice.

"Yes. It would seem that you are in need of redemption," she confirms.

I pause for a moment. "I don't . . . I don't think I'm supposed to be here," I offer, mystified.

"You are supposed to," the spirit assures. "Everything happened the way it was meant to."

Her words trigger something inside of me and for the first time in days, I feel. Emotion floats through my veins almost painfully. My heart and soul fill with a surge of grief and my eyes begin to sting with a rush of tears.

"Aria?" I choke out.

"Hi, Eve," my deceased friend and college roommate utters quietly.

"I-I d-don't understand," I stumble. "How are you here?"

Aria tilts her head, squeezing my hand in reassurance, while I stare at her pink pixie hair.

"I promised you that I would see you on the other side," she explains. "I guess Kingsley College is your version of the other side." Aria crinkles her nose and stands, looking around.

After a moment, she sighs dramatically and plops

down next to me on the bench, fidgeting with her frilly pink dress. Once she's content with her appearance, she crosses her black fishnet-stocking-covered legs and swings her pink combat boots across the top of the grass without a care in the world.

"The other side?" I repeat, trying to work through what she's talking about.

Aria turns to me, smiling with mischief, and my chest tightens. I've missed her. Her small hand lifts and with a gentle touch she brushes the hair away from my wound. Warmth soars through me as I feel the cut heal itself under the bandage. Freaked out, I flinch away.

"There, all better," she murmurs.

My forehead creases. "It's gone?" I cry out, touching the bandage. *Holy shit.*

She nods and bites her bottom lip. "Killer superpower, right?"

"Totally," I agree, exhaling. *What the hell is going on? I have to be dreaming.*

"You know, Eve, you could have healed that yourself," she suggests.

My eyes slide to hers. "That's crazy. I'm pretty sure I can't heal myself, Aria."

Amusement crosses over her features as she leans back, blowing a pink bubble with her gum, then popping it dramatically. "Yes, you can. You have some amazing gifts, Eve." Her voice trails off while she looks in the distance at nothing in particular.

"Gifts?" The word is full of incredulity.

"You hit your head. It's why you can't remember anything." Her tone is flat.

"How?" I inquire. "I don't remember." The statement hangs in the air. *A head injury would explain why I'm talking to my dead friend and sitting barefoot in a campus quad.*

"I'd like to say it was because you were drunk and face-planted at a frat party," she counters, with an underlying sadness in her statement.

"That doesn't sound like me. It sounds like you," I shoot back.

We both smirk at the same time, knowing that Aria face-planted more than once at a few frat parties during our first semester together due to her alcohol-induced state.

"Fun times," she answers.

I tilt my head back and close my eyes. "If that's not how it happened, then how?"

Aria releases a pained sound from her throat. "You fell, from a pretty high place."

I drop my chin, open my eyes, and follow her line of sight to the empty parking lot near Lexington Hall, curious as to what has caused her face to pinch like a beautiful, angry fairy.

"I fell?" I repeat, attempting to get her attention.

She clears her throat. "Hotness with the really cool car was supposed to catch you. That was the plan anyway. But with your stubbornness, down the toilet everything went."

I shift my gaze back to hers. "I'm not following. *Hotness* was supposed to catch me?"

"Gage Gallagher," she states slowly, as if I should know who that is.

I shake my head, letting her know that I have no idea what, or whom, she's talking about.

Aria frowns. "I guess falling from a cliff and hitting

your head on rocks will do that."

My jaw drops. "I fell off a cliff?"

She blows and pops another pink bubble. "More like you were dropped."

"Oh. My. God. What dumbass would throw me off a cliff?" I exclaim.

Aria laughs and my gut rolls. It's been so long since I've heard it.

"I've missed you, Eve," she expresses with a tinge of sorrow.

"Me too." I watch her for a few bewildered moments. "I'm sorry. I can't remember what happened to you. I just know that you're no longer with me and that I miss you like crazy."

"It's for the best." Aria begins to pick at the black, chipped polish on her nails. "Someday, the memory will return. When it does, just know I would do it again, without thought."

"Well, that's not cryptic or anything," I tease.

Aria laughs. "Obscurity is my middle name."

"I thought it was Gertrude?" I bump her shoulder.

She tosses me an annoyed glance. "You can't remember anything, at all, and yet somehow you can recall my god-awful middle name? You suck, Eve Marie Collins."

I shrug. "Maybe I have selective memory?"

"Clearly," she banters in the easy way we used to.

We sit in silence for a bit, while I scan the campus, trying to recall pieces of my life.

"Being here, with you, does that mean I'm dead?" I ask with caution.

Aria shifts on the bench in reflection and chomps on

her gum in an irritating cow-like manner that used to make me want to strangle her. After a few quiet moments she grabs my notepad and traces the dragon I've been sketching obsessively for hours on end.

"From darkness, comes light. Does that mean anything to you?" Aria asks.

I let the weight of the words embrace me but I have no connection to them. "Should it?"

Aria sighs. "Yeah. It should." Her voice sounds deflated.

"I'm sorry. I don't remember." I bite at the inside of my cheek in a nervous manner.

"You're not dead. We're in a realm that you've created. To heal," she whispers.

I pull in my brows and stare at her in doubt. "That's absurd. People can't create realms."

"No, Eve, *people* can't. *You* can," Aria states. "Sometimes, when a being realm jumps, or dream walks, they lose themselves within the safety of the world they've created." Her gaze slides over the lush landscape. "Maybe that's why you've chosen Kingsley's campus as your healing realm. You went back to the beginning. Before—" she stops abruptly.

"Before what?" I encourage.

Her finger taps on my sketch. "This."

My eyes shift downward to the dragon. "Aria, I don't even know what *that* is."

"It's home," she states matter-of-factly.

"Home?" I reiterate on a whisper.

"Home, Eve," she confirms in a slow drawl.

I inhale and study her face. Memorizing every piece of

it. I don't want to forget her again.

"How are you here?" I ask again, with tears filling my eyes. "Don't misunderstand, I love and miss you but how the hell are you here? I know you're dead. Is this a dream?"

Placing the sketch pad back down, Aria throws a sly smirk at me. "I'm your guardian."

"My what?" I ask, puzzled.

"Guardian angel. I've been assigned to you by Michael, since inception," she says guiltily.

I nod once, buying time because dead Aria sounds crazy and I'm not interested in pissing off spirits. "So if you're my guardian angel," I clarify slowly to appease her, "Who is Michael?"

She arches a dark eyebrow at me. "Don't be condescending, Eve, it's true. Michael is my boss. The warrior of Heaven, archangel Michael," she describes with a dip of her chin.

"I don't think I know him," I play along. *Crap. Ghost Aria is batshit crazy.*

Her lips tilt. "Believe me, you two have met before. One might even say you two are so close you share DNA."

I throw her a stunned glance. "I know an archangel?"

Aria laughs. "Holy shit, this is fun. Yeah, you do, Eve. And stop whispering to yourself in your head about my sanity levels. I hate when you do that and it's starting to freak me out."

"By the grace," I murmur and she stills. "You're crazier now than when you were alive."

"Repeat what you just said," Aria demands.

I lift my brows at her odd expression. "You're crazier—" I begin but she cuts me off.

"No. Before that, what did you say?" She pins me with an insistent stare.

"By the grace?" I wave her off. "I have no idea where that came from. Just like I don't know how I got here." I motion to the campus. "Or why I feel the need to draw two hundred pages of dragons. Or why I'm talking to my deceased best friend." I hold her gaze.

Aria just continues to watch me with a perplexed look. "You and I were childhood friends, before college. Did you know that?" Her chocolate irises study my expression.

"Were we?" I ask with skepticism lining my tone. *I must have really whacked my head.*

"You've known me in the present as Aria, but from ages one to eighteen, I was your friend . . . Courtney," she explains in a gentle tone.

I release an odd laugh. "Courtney? My childhood friend, since preschool?"

"Yes." Aria shifts on the bench in irritation.

"Crap. Someone must have slipped me something. Did I drink at a party?"

Aria ignores me and continues. "The Angelic Council assigned me to protect you at your birth. Elizabeth and Michael felt it was important you have a normal childhood, hence why I took on the façade of Courtney. It made it easier to guard you. Besides, they thought if you grew up experiencing a mundane life, you would have a solid understanding of, and compassion for, mankind. Skills to help you restore the balance when the time came to face the revolution."

Elizabeth. Strangely, at the sound of my aunt's name, a tortured pain builds in my chest.

Restoration

My lips part slightly. "Aria, no offense, but nothing you're saying at the moment makes any sense. I mean, you're trying to convince me that up until I was eighteen you were someone else. By the way, Courtney attends Stanford now and looks nothing like you." I hold her unwavering silent stare. "You're using words like archangels, the Angelic Council, and protection. You sound insane," I point out. "Restore the balance? Revolution? Do you need my help to get your spirit to Heaven or something?" I ramble.

Aria spits her gum angrily into her hand before placing the pink wad under the bench.

"Hey, that's littering," I scold.

She rolls her eyes. "It's a realm that you've created. In. Your. Mind. Eve."

"Meaning?" I ask tersely.

"Meaning it's not real. It's in your head. YOU are trapped your head." Her voice is heated.

"Dream or not, don't litter," I chastise. "It's bad for the environment."

"Realm. Not dream," she corrects in annoyance. "And for the love, try to focus."

"Whatever," I retort, not wanting to fight with my dead best friend.

"The Angelic Council granted you divine protection until age eighteen, at which time I was to be removed as your guardian. When your birthday came, Michael and Elizabeth were not ready to tell you about your bloodline because they felt you were unprepared. They'd hoped you would get settled in at college first. Make sense?" she asks, hopeful.

"Ah, no, Aria. It doesn't," I reply.

"The council didn't call me back right away. Michael

assumed they'd changed their minds. Just to be sure though, he hired," Aria pauses and searches for the words, "outside protectors. When you started having your nightmares, Michael allowed me to stay on, until the council officially removed me. We sent your childhood *friend*, me, as Courtney, off to Stanford, and I took on my true form as Aria, so I could attend Kingsley College with you," Aria says. "As your guardian."

She's lost her mind. I smile awkwardly. "So, you were Courtney, and now you're Aria. Back from the dead, to bring me home." I laugh-snort.

Aria narrows her eyes at me. "Don't freak, but your sass has asked for this."

In an instant, she morphs into my childhood friend, and my jaw falls.

"Holy shit," I exhale.

A few seconds later, she turns back to Aria. "See. Courtney and Aria."

I press my fingers into my temples to ward off a migraine that is coming on too fast.

"What the hell, Aria!" I shout.

"I'm sorry. I figured I could just explain and you would understand how this works, but for the love, you are so stubborn," she blathers on.

"I'm just confused. Ghosts morphing into my old friends isn't helping," I bite out.

She exhales and nervously bounces her legs up and down. "I wish I could tell you *everything*, Eve. Just show you your memories, but I can't. It's against the rules."

"What rules?" I ask harshly.

Aria stands abruptly and darts her hand out for me to

take. "Come with me."

I frown at the gesture.

"You can trust me," she huffs.

I stare at her for what feels like an eternity.

"Take my hand, Eve, and let me guide you home."

"What if I'm not ready to go home?" I pin her with a glare. "If I've created this *realm*, as you say I have, then there has to be a good reason I'm still here, right?"

"You're hiding. I'm sorry, but you have to see this through," she replies in a stern tone.

We stare at one another for a moment in a standoff before I reluctantly give in.

Aria snaps her hand toward me again. "I promise, your journey is almost over."

After a minute of silence, my shoulders sag. "Fine," I murmur, placing my hand in hers.

She wiggles her eyebrows at me. "Close your eyes until I tell you to open them."

"Aria." I sigh.

"Just trust me, Eve. I've got you, I promise."

I swallow at her familiar words and do as I'm told, sliding my eyelids closed. Warm gushes of air hit me, and instantly, I feel myself dissolve, evaporating into thin air. I shiver at the thought.

Aria whispers in my ear a few seconds later. "Go ahead, open your eyes."

I blink my lids open and take in the thriving gardens. Gone is Kingsley College. In its place is a backdrop of natural beauty in the form of exquisitely colorful flowers and flourishing vegetation, with paths guarded by tall, white birch trees and a crystal blue lake. The sun's golden rays illuminate the floral oasis, bathing us in warmth and pure light.

Twirling in a circle, I take everything in. My gaze lands on a marble bench, sitting under a blooming cherry tree. A few of the pink blossoms have fallen elegantly onto the white stone and dirt ground. A ping of recognition hits me, but then it quickly vanishes.

"How in the . . ." I trail off.

Aria shrugs. "It's a perk of being a guardian angel."

"Where are we?" I question in awe.

"Wiltshire, England." Aria's voice is barely a whisper. "You're home, Eve."

"Home?" The word falls out of me like it's a foreign sound.

"Siren?" a deep, masculine voice full of anguish says from behind us.

I turn and come face-to-face with the most beautiful set of full, kissable lips I've ever seen. I lift my gaze and meet the tortured expression of the very attractive owner of said mouth, which is pulling into a sexy smile and literally melting me from the inside out.

Twinkling indigo eyes are outlined in long, thick, dark lashes, fanning perfect cheeks. Feeling my own cheeks heat under his gaze, I pull my eyes from his and instead take him in.

The top of his hair is long and dark brown, styled in sexy, messy pieces. My fingers twitch, itching to run through the soft strands. *Wait, how do I know they're soft?* He dips his chin at me, and a small frown line appears between his distinguished brows.

The sudden urge to smooth out the worry line and

comfort him overwhelms me. Instead, I stiffen my stance, trying to control the urge to curl myself into his muscular arms.

The intimidating man clenches his five-o'clock-shadowed, chiseled jawline in response to my silence. Watching me, he anxiously runs his hand over a striking Celtic cross tattoo on the inside of his right forearm. I study the movement and swallow my increasing desire when I notice two black leather bands, one on each of his wrists, adorned with onyx.

I try to compose myself as my gaze roams over the body covered in a white t-shirt, worn jeans, and black motorcycle boots. *Holy shit. I know who this guy is.* I inhale and pull air into my lungs before I pass out and embarrass myself.

At the sharp intake of air, I catch his scent of smoky wood and leather.

"See something you like, siren?" he asks, half-amused, half-confused.

We hold one another's gaze for what feels like an eternity. I get the impression his question is a game that he and I play. For whatever reason, I don't know the rules this time.

I drop my eyes and turn to Aria. "Why is the hot guy from my architecture class here?"

After an awkward silence beats between the three of us, the good-looking guy speaks.

"The guy from her architecture class?" his smooth voice repeats, pronouncing every word.

I snap my gaze back to his, curious as to why his brows are knitted and he looks like he's ready to light the world on fire at the sight of me. At his expression, I'm hit with déjà vu.

"Aria?" The striking man looks to her for confirmation.

"She doesn't remember, Asher," Aria offers as a form of explanation.

Asher's deep, intense stare lands on me again. Pain. Guilt. Sadness. They all cross his beautiful face before he nods once to her in understanding. "Then I'll help her to."

I narrow my eyes at him. "I don't need your help. I don't even know you, pretty boy."

The Adonis prowls toward me and lowers his voice to a sensual tone. "You know me."

My heart slams against my rib cage at his intensity. "I don't," I whisper.

"No?" he asks, looming over me.

"No," I barely manage to choke out.

Asher cups my face with his hands. They're warm, strong, and at the same time, demanding.

"Ilem jur pri tú-tim, ew tú-tim pri pos-tim ali ide in-zen, mání, vas-wís, ew ter-ort. Esta-de ai esta Ilem de, Ilem pos-tim in-saengkt pri, tú-tim," he says, staring deeply into my eyes.

"Asher St. Michael, do not push her," Aria warns.

Asher ignores her and steps even closer to me. His nerve-racking presence, and something else I can't quite place, causes me to shudder as goose bumps appear all over my skin.

"Cold?" his deep, cocky voice taunts me in a familiar way.

"Stop," I mutter the plea. My head begins to fog and a

dull throb forms behind my eyes.

Aria tries to step to my side, but Asher holds up a hand, stopping her from moving.

"Do I make you anxious, Eve?" he continues, allowing a thumb to trace my bottom lip.

With every word he emits, a heaviness fills my chest. My vision blurs and I sway slightly. Gentle yet strong arms wrap around my waist, holding me steady.

"I've got you, siren," he whispers.

Asher's minty breath blows over my lips, causing them to part and breathe him in.

"I . . . I don't know you," I speak softly. *Do I?*

"Tas ámotas." Asher's voice is a sad plea. His gentle hands clasp either side of my neck while his thumbs tilt my chin upward so he can brush his mouth over mine in a tease.

I release a small whimper at the light caress.

"I will protect you, always," he promises across my lips.

I squeeze my eyes shut as they begin to fill with water. The visions and his words are too much. I shake my head in terror when a searing pain makes itself known on my lower back.

"Please stop," I beg.

"No. I gave you my word. I would pull you from the darkness and always bring you home." He ignores my request, not backing down. "You're home. Now come back to me."

"I don't . . ." I stutter a bit, not sure what's happening.

"It's okay, Eve. It's just your memories coming back," Aria explains gently.

I step away from Asher. My body is trembling, and it

feels like my heart and soul are splitting inside me. "Stop!" I say firmly. "It's too much. I don't know you!"

His expression falls. After a moment, he nods and takes a step back, giving me space.

"Eve." Aria comes into my sightline. "It's okay. You're safe. Asher will protect you."

"I don't remember him, Aria," I bark automatically, not really meaning it. There is something familiar and safe about him. I do feel protected. I just can't work through the haze and lack of memories in my head. *Crap.* I rub my lower back. *Why the hell is it pulsing?*

"You do. And it's time that you do," Aria says, squeezing my hand. "Hey, hot stuff." She looks over her shoulder. "Show her the gargoyle protector tattoo, would you?"

My eyes shift between Aria and Asher. "Gargoyle. Protector. Tattoo," I repeat.

Unsure, Asher studies my dead friend for a brief moment before locking eyes with me and grabbing the hem of his t-shirt. With one tug, it's off, and I'm left breathless at his raw beauty. I swear, his perfect chest and stomach just made me lose IQ points by staring at it.

"Look at his heart, Eve," Aria prompts.

My gaze shifts to his chest and my breath escapes through parted lips. Tattooed over Asher's heart is the black, circular, barbed-wire dragon I've been sketching. Silently, I walk around Aria toward him. He stiffens, watching every one of my moves as I approach.

I lift my hand to the tattoo, and with my index finger, trace the design. Asher's eyes slide closed, blissfully. As soon as I make skin-to-skin contact, my lower back begins to throb like a heartbeat, syncing with his.

Images flash through my head in rapid succession. Vows of protection. Promises of forever. Murmurs of adoration. Declarations of love. Asher devouring me, kissing me like I'm the air he breathes. A tattoo on my lower back that matches his perfectly. A mate mark.

"What the hell?" I whisper, and quickly remove my hand, as if his skin shocked me.

All the images dissolve immediately at the abrupt end of my contact with him.

I step back and feel Aria's palms on my shoulders. "Asher is your protector, Eve."

"My protector?" I repeat, confused.

"Yours," Asher states in a firm and resolved manner.

"Wait." I spin to face Aria and scan her face. "I thought you were my guardian?"

"I am, but you are his. And he is yours," she responds in riddle.

"Won't you be with me now?" I ask.

Sadness glides across her face. "I was called back. It's why I saved you from Deacon that day. My assignment had ended. Plus, I thought it would be cool to go out with a bang." She winks. "Isn't that right, Ash?"

"Yes," Asher answers her with softness in his voice.

Panic floats through me. "So you're leaving me? *Again*? And who is Deacon?"

"My assignment is over," she attempts to soothe me. "I can't stay."

"And him?" I motion toward Asher.

"Asher is your protector." Her tone is gentle but firm.

"Wait," I shout. "I can't do this without you, Aria."

My eyes sting with tears.

Aria tilts her head at my emotional state. "You're very special, Eve," she speaks softly. "I know it feels like the weight of the world is on your shoulders, but I believe in you. If anyone can bring us all restoration, it's you."

"Restoration from what?" I ask in a small voice. "And why him?"

"You are our savior, and he is yours," she retorts.

I watch her, watching me. "I think you've said that to me before, right?"

A small smile pulls at her pink lips. "I have. I meant it then and I mean it now."

I swallow the painful lump in my throat. "Aria—"

She interjects and snatches me in a tight embrace, stroking my hair to calm me. "Listen, let's not do mushy-gushy friendship stuff."

I half-sob, half-laugh, in response to her favorite line.

"Promise me that I'll see you again?" I implore.

"When the time is right, I promise," she assures and smacks my ass, startling me like she used to. "We're done, hot stuff. My girl is all yours again." Aria nods behind me to Asher.

Asher steps forward, looking lost. His hands are shoved in the front pockets of his jeans.

"Thanks for reaching her when I couldn't," he says to Aria.

"You keep her in one piece, or I will end your existence myself, gargoyle," she warns with a pointed look before her expression softens. "Tell Leo I send my love to him."

"I will. On both accounts," he answers sincerely

before pulling her into a quick hug.

She turns to me. "Have fun saving the world with your badass gargoyles, Eve."

I pinch my features. "I don't want to say goodbye to you again."

My guardian takes my face in her palms and wipes away the tears staining my cheeks.

"I'm part of your story, always," she declares in a soft voice.

I sob and squeeze my eyes shut. When I reopen them, she's gone. My heart twists painfully at losing her all over again.

Asher steps in front of me, looking shy and devastated. It's almost as if he's taken on my pain and sadness as his own. I watch him work his throat as he attempts to swallow. One of his hands lifts, and with the back of his knuckles, he brushes away my tears.

After allowing me a few moments to grieve, Asher silently leads me to the bench and we sit. He takes my hand in his and turns it over before placing one of the pink flowers from the tree into my palm. A memory of him doing this before hits me. *We were sitting on this same bench and he was sharing a story of his mother.* I inhale sharply at the vision.

"The darkness can be overwhelming," he speaks quietly.

My lids flutter at his words. They're the same ones from my memory.

"You are my place of peace." His voice is low.

Asher closes my hand around the blossom and my heart becomes heavy in my chest.

"You are the light to my soul," he continues.

My body begins to hum and fill with warmth as his leans closer.

"You are my purpose."

Strong hands cup my cheeks and my eyes slide shut.

"Open your eyes, siren," he demands.

My lids blink open and meet Asher's intense gaze.

"You are my everything."

Asher moves his mouth toward mine and my breath hitches.

"You. Are. My. Forever," he whispers across my lips.

And I breathe him in.

"Come back to me," he insists, placing his hand over my heart.

Just as his lips touch mine, everything goes black.

2 After the Storm

The heaviness pushes down like a stone on my chest while life returns to my body. Warmth rushes within my veins, and a tingling sensation caresses my skin. I cling to the light energizing my soul and the oxygen invigorating my lungs. Everything aches. My limbs. My heart. My mind. It all hurts, causing my body to tremble from the inside out.

A strong hand curves around my cheek. The fingers belonging to it slide down my face and trace my jaw. Slowly, warm fingertips brush over my throat and across my collarbone. A large palm settles over my heart and stays there, absorbing each beat.

"I'm here, siren," a gruff, familiar voice laced with

exhaustion and heavy emotion says.

My soul lifts in recognition. I will my eyelids to open, but they refuse.

"How is she?" A second known voice cuts through my coma.

"I don't know. After her fall, I placed her in a stone state healing sleep. She drifted out of it and built her own realm, then locked me out," Asher replies sadly. "Michael allowed me to call upon her guardian to retrieve her."

Long fingers stroke my hair, leaving a scented trail of cigarettes and spice with each brush. "You are fiercely stubborn, love." The second voice chuckles.

Asher exhales a frustrated breath, and I attempt to get my eyes open, unsuccessfully.

"Would you stop fucking calling her love, Gage," Asher bites out.

"She needs rest to heal, dark prince. Don't rush her recovery. My guess is when she wakes, and recalls the memory of her guardian, her anger will make you wish she was back in a stone state," Gage warns. "Her reaction to McKenna's actions will be bad too."

Even though I can't see Asher, I can feel the tension radiating off him in waves. Unable to console my protector and mate, I allow myself to drift back into a peaceful sleep.

Hours later, my eyes finally open. The soft light from the candles and fireplaces help guide my returning sight. After a few tries, they fully adjust, allowing me to see that I'm still in Asher's stone state bed, in the chamber at La Gargouille Manor in Wiltshire, England.

As I sit up, the cool, black silk sheets glide down my bare arms and pool onto my lap. I roll and stretch my neck from side to side, working the kinks out. Then I straighten out my tank top and matching sleep shorts, assessing how I feel, which is completely normal.

Nothing seems out of place except this itchy bandage below my hairline. I rub at it and sigh in aggravation before my focus shifts and my eyes fixate on Asher, standing shirtless in front of one of the lit fireplaces.

Sitting straighter, I admire the black dragon tattoo covering his back. The London clan's family crest rolls over every muscle, adorning his beautiful and exposed skin.

The way the fire's shadows dance across his skin, the dragon almost seems to come alive off his physique. I inhale an appreciative breath. Asher St. Michael, prince of the gargoyle race, emanates darkness, power, and raw beauty.

My legs swing over the edge of the bed and I slide out. Once my bare feet touch the floor, I stalk toward him, like a predator. I know he senses me. He knows I'm awake, yet he hasn't turned to face me. If he's waiting for me to approach, he thinks he's hurt me somehow.

Once I reach him, I place both my palms flat onto his back, over the dragon. Asher's skin twitches under my touch, and his body visibly trembles. I breathe in his scent and press my lips between his bare shoulder blades, where I know his raven wings are concealed.

We stay in this position for mere seconds before Asher turns and our eyes meet. Warm hands capture mine, placing my palms on his chest, so one hand is over the protector tattoo.

Asher flattens my fingers to his body, like he's willing me to become one with his skin. He's staring so deeply into my eyes, for so long, the intensity actually takes my breath away, and at the same time, intimidates me.

"Hey," I speak quietly.

"Hey yourself, siren." He matches my quiet tone.

"What's wrong?" I question, sensing his distress.

"Now that you're awake . . . nothing," he replies on a shaky breath.

Asher studies me with adoration before leaning down and kissing my forehead. When he pulls back, he runs his thumbs under my eyes in a light brush, savoring what he seems to see.

"Indigo. Thank fuck," he exhales.

I wrinkle my forehead. "My eyes have been indigo for a while now, Ash."

Fixated on my face, Asher dips his chin, coming to an internal understanding before speaking in a stern tone. "Let's keep it that way, yeah?"

My hands slide up to cup his jaw. "Always. It means I'm yours."

The gargoyle's jaw clenches. "How are you feeling?" His fingers brush over the bandage.

"A little confused, but physically fine," I respond. "What happened?"

Asher watches me for a moment. "What's the last thing you remember?"

I step out of the safety of his embrace and face the fire. "County Kerry, Ireland," I begin. "We were at Domus Gurgulio Castle to meet with the Royal Gargoyle Council of Protectors." I turn back to face Asher.

The flames warming my back do nothing to soothe the chill that runs through my veins when my eyes meet Asher's cold expression.

"Go on," he pushes.

"Um, I remember Lord Falk accusing you of failing to protect the supernatural realms, because of the priestesses' deaths. Then he wrongly blamed you for Lady Finella's betrayal and beheading. I also recall the council saying that you've disregarded your oaths because of our mate bonding." I blink slowly and swallow. "And you accused Lord Falk of treason. You said he provided our traitor with safe haven." I stare at Asher.

He nods once. "And."

I tilt my head and scrunch my face. "And what, Asher?"

"It would seem my father, the king of the gargoyle race, has risen from the grave."

I inhale. "Right. Garrick appeared in the council chamber," I recount.

Asher runs his hands over his face and through his hair while releasing an exhausted breath. "Yeah, siren. He did. For the record, it's true. My father is the traitor."

I step toward him to provide comfort, and then stop when realization hits me.

"Wait, you baited the council because you knew Garrick was the conspirator?" I accuse.

Asher holds my gaze. "The traitor assumption was only a theory."

"All this time . . . you knew he was alive?" My voice sounds dejected.

Asher backs away from me and sits on the side of the bed. He motions for me to come to him, and after a brief moment of contemplating smacking the beautiful right off him, I go.

He positions me between his legs, probably so I won't run away, and wraps his large hands around my waist before looking up at me through sooty eyelashes.

"I've known about my father being alive for a while, Eve," he says quietly.

Suddenly, all the air in the room is gone. "How! Why the hell didn't you tell me?"

Asher works his jaw. "We have a lot to discuss as it relates to Garrick St. Michael."

My mouth falls open at his confession. "Did Callan—" I quickly correct myself. "I mean, do he and Keegan know too?"

Obviously Keegan knew since I told him that day in his office. *Holy. Fucking. Shit.*

He nods once. "My brothers and I all knew," Asher states. "Dear old dad's traitorous involvement with the dark army was just a hypothesis." He pauses. "Until now, of course."

My eyes shift to the bed, trying to make sense of everything. I study the silk sheets and strewn pillows. Ironically, Asher's stone state bed is spelled to bring mates together, yet it feels like it's always the place my deceit rears its ugly head, threatening to tear us apart.

I swallow and slide my gaze back to his. "I knew too, Asher," I admit in a guilty tone.

"I know you did," he responds without missing a beat.

I arch a brow. "You did?"

"You confided in Keegan," he points out. "There are no secrets within this clan."

"Keegan told you?" I bite my lip. "Of course he did. Are you pissed I didn't tell you?"

Asher pauses for a moment and studies my face before speaking. "You did. In your own way, the day we were in the gardens. I knew when you were ready, you'd confide in me."

He shrugs and I sway. "I can't believe you knew and didn't say anything."

"Maybe you should sit down. We have more than enough time to discuss my asshole of a father when you're feeling up to it."

I blow out a long breath. "I didn't know how to tell you without destroying you. I asked Michael for confirmation after Morgana mouthed Garrick's name to me in the park, before she died. I was protecting you, Asher. I didn't want your world to implode."

"I know," he says in a quiet murmur, squeezing my waist in reassurance.

"I went to Keegan for help. I thought . . . I thought he would be the only one strong enough to handle it. Oh God. He knew the entire time I was confiding in him?" I question.

Asher's expression turns regretful. "Yes."

"Was this all a test? To see where my loyalties were?"

"No. My brothers and I had theories. Your admission to Keegan confirmed what we already assumed to be truth. None of us wanted to believe it, but your words solidified it."

"I'm sorry, Ash."

His lips tilt slightly. "You are forgiven for protecting me, siren."

I step closer and run my hands through his soft hair before tugging gently, forcing his chin to lift. "You'll forgive me that easily, gargoyle? What's the catch?"

"No catch." His eyes hold mine. "There is only my unconditional love for you. Eve, there is nothing you could do that I wouldn't forgive. By now, you should know this, yeah?"

I hold his unwavering gaze before nodding my understanding.

"I love you. I really do," I whisper in relief.

"Because I'm awesome?" he teases suggestively, offering me his sexiest smile before grabbing my waist and yanking me down next to him onto the bed.

After a small laughing fit and a quick brush of his lips, we both shift so that we're lying facing one another, propped on our elbows. Asher picks up a strand of my hair, twirling it absentmindedly, and I stare at the Celtic cross tattoo, a reminder of his oaths.

"Are you really ready to come to terms with Garrick's return?" I inquire in a serious tone.

"Keegan, Callan and I have been dealing with our father's resurrection for a while now. Was it a fucking shock to see him—alive? Yeah. But I'm okay. We all are. What happened in that council chamber reminded us of who we are and what we're meant to do."

"And me?" I watch with fascination as he wraps and unwraps my hair around his finger.

He tugs the strand lightly, getting my attention. "You didn't run. You trusted my brother and showed loyalty to the clan. I don't like that you kept it from me, but I understand the need to protect. So it's that fucking easy, siren. End of discussion."

I gawk for a second at his sincere expression before letting go of my guilt.

"How's your head?" Asher asks as his eyes dart to the bandage.

"Fine," I assure him.

"Do you remember my father taking you from the council room?"

I scan my memories. "Yeah. Garrick held me over the cliff, right?"

Asher's expression darkens. "He fucking did, and he will pay for it, on my word."

"Oh. My. God." I grab his face and scan him for injuries. "The dark army was going to attack. I knew you wouldn't reach me in time, and I released the light energy. Are you hurt?"

Asher's hands wrap around my wrists, pulling them away. "I'm fine, siren."

"I watched you and Gage tumble through the air to the ground," I recount, worried.

"Your energy knocked the wind out of us, like it did with McKenna that day in the training room. Other than a few singed areas on our clothing, we're both fine."

"How is that possible? It destroyed the dark army." I state in confusion.

"Michael seems to think it's because of our Celtic tattoos. They symbolize our loyalty to the Spiritual Assembly, which is not a dark entity, in turn protecting us."

"What about Gage, though?" I counter. "I thought he didn't align with either side."

"Gage took the oath when he agreed to protect you. He hides his tattoo on his calf."

I take in a sharp breath. "Garrick dropped me. He let go. I fell, Asher."

Sadness and regret pass over Asher's face. "I know, siren."

"I don't remember anything after that." I dig through my mind.

"Gage and I planned to distract my father. McKenna was behind him, ready to run the Angelic Sword through him. When she did, I was supposed to catch Garrick and Gage you. However, you beat us to the punch, catching us all off guard when you released the light source, pushing Gage and I away. When Garrick dropped you, Kenna dove to catch you. She did, but not before you cracked your head on a sharp rock." He winces and brushes his fingers over the bandage.

"So I've been healing?" I motion to the tousled bed.

"You lost a lot of blood." He pulls me closer, forcing my hands to curl around the back of his neck. "I had to put you in a stone state healing sleep. When I went to dream walk to you, you had locked yourself in a realm that you created. Do you recall?"

"Aria." I swallow hard as the images hit me.

"She's your guardian and agreed to go in and retrieve you." He leans his forehead to mine. "I didn't want you to find out about her that way, but I couldn't get through to you."

"Aria is my guardian angel," I repeat with astonishment in my tone.

His fingers dig into my hair. "Since your creation."

"You all knew," I accuse. "You didn't think it was important to tell me, Asher?"

"You know how this works. Initially, we weren't allowed to tell you. Then, the Angelic Council called her back, ending her assignment, and we took over your protection."

"Heaven kills off guardian angels when their assignments are over?" I challenge.

"Aria knew you were in danger and stepped in, knowing her time with you—her assignment was over," he says. "That's why she did it. To protect you, siren."

"I knew she got to me way too fast," I recall. "Were you ever going to tell me?"

He pulls back to look at me. "On the plane to England, but you were so sad and tired. After a while, you dealt with her death and put it behind you. At that point, the clan didn't feel it was necessary for you to know." Asher brushes the strands of hair that have fallen forward off my face. "I'm sorry for not telling you earlier."

I squeeze my eyes shut. "I finally got to say goodbye to her, properly."

He offers a sad smile. "I'm glad. Everyone should get a chance at a final goodbye."

"I guess we're even. I didn't tell you about Garrick, and you didn't tell me about Aria." I grimace. "I hate to admit this, but I'm starting to think we really do need couples therapy."

Asher releases a light chuckle. "I knew the moment I met you that we would, siren."

"Clearly, we have communication issues," I retort.

"Don't leave out our abandonment and anger issues," he adds in a light tone.

I take in a deep breath. "In my right mind, I never would have shut you out of the realm."

Asher swallows loudly. "I was going fucking insane.

You had this vacant look. My heart completely stopped when you told me you didn't remember me." His voice trails off.

I cup one of his cheeks with my hand and lean forward, planting a soft kiss on his lips.

"We promised each other we'd face this together. You running, scares the shit out of me." He exhales. "But I've gotta tell you, siren, you forcing me out of a realm that you've created and trapped yourself in, with no memory of us . . . I've never been more terrified in my life. Don't ever fucking do that again, yeah?"

His words hit me in the gut. I've hurt him, again. "Never," I vow.

Asher leans forward and allows his lips to lightly caress mine, sealing my promise to him.

"How is everyone else?" I inquire.

"They'll be relieved once they learn you're awake." He releases a ragged breath.

"Let's go say hi then." I start to move off the bed, but Asher stops me.

He crawls over me, straddling my body. Holding my eyes, his fingers circle around both my wrists, lifting and pinning my hands over my head before he presses his weight into me so I'm trapped on the bed. With an odd expression, he sighs heavily.

"In the spirit of being honest, I need to tell you something before we go upstairs," he says.

"Okay." My tone is lined with caution.

"You're going to be pretty pissed off when I tell you this. Hence the need to restrain you."

Crap. I chew on the inside of my cheek. "You have my

full attention."

"After you hit your head, you lost a lot of blood. So much so that you almost bled out. We needed to perform an immediate transfusion to save you." He frowns.

"Are you saying your blood is running through my veins, Asher St. Michael?" I seduce.

Asher's signature sexy smirk appears on his lips. "Fuck, that sounds hot."

I wiggle my body underneath his and he growls at me in annoyance. "Siren," he warns.

I giggle. "All right, continue."

"If I had infused you with my blood, it would have completed the bond." His tone drops.

"So?" My face contorts, wondering why that would be an issue.

"So, I didn't want to make that choice without your consent."

At his admission, my heart soars. Then I realize, if he didn't save me, someone else did.

"Then whose blood saved me? Callan? Keegan? Abby?"

Asher swallows and shifts focus. I squirm under him to get his attention again.

"As long as they are not blood sharing for a protector bond, only a mated female gargoyle can transfuse without tainting their mate bond. Or a non-mated male," he explains slowly.

My heart sinks. "Are you saying that Gage infused me with his blood?"

Asher pins his dark gaze on me. "You think I would let another male create a blood connection with you? Let alone Gallagher. Not in this fucking lifetime."

"Then, who?"

"McKenna."

"McKenna!" I repeat in a shout. "Where the hell was Abby?"

Asher flinches. "Abby wasn't able to share."

"What? Why not?"

"I can't say."

I groan in annoyance. "You should have just completed the bond with me. I don't care. I want to spend forever with you, Asher. Anything would have been better than McKenna."

"I didn't want to take that decision from you because of potential death." He smirks. "Good to know, though, that a forever with me is preferred over McKenna saving your life."

"You do realize she is never going to let me live this down," I whine.

"Oh, I'm counting on it." He winks. *Damn gargoyle.*

Asher releases my wrists once he's decided I won't harm him. Instead, I narrow my eyes.

"Did you think I was going to plunge my daggers into you when you told me?" I quip.

"Callan told me to guard my loins, but I know you love your daggers," he banters.

"You suck, gargoyle." I push at his chest.

Asher places his hands on the bed, one on either side of my head. He leans down, pressing his body against mine. "Can I tell you something, siren?"

I swallow and nod, attempting to get a grasp of the sensations running through me.

The tip of his tongue darts out to wet his lips. "Your mouth looks incredibly sexy when you say the word *suck*."

Asher's breath is seductively warm and minty across my lips, causing my body to go on alert. Summoning all my willpower, I place my hands back on his chest and push lightly.

"Aria told me that this journey is almost over. Yet, it feels like the calm before the storm." I sigh. "Why does it feel as though we're just beginning?"

His expression falls. "Because we are."

"What do we do now?" I ask, biting my lower lip.

Interlacing our fingers, Asher pulls me off the bed into a standing position. His lips quirk into a knowing grin as he steps into my space.

"Now, siren, we brace ourselves for an epic battle."

3 Blood Ties

The swooshing sound of air catches my attention as Asher and I step into the training room. Abruptly, Asher's hand darts out in front of my face, plucking an arrow out of thin air, a breath away from landing right between my eyes. *What the hell?*

My breath hitches at the sight of the sharp point he's holding a hairline from my face.

"I guess my blood does nothing for her reaction time," McKenna says unenthusiastically.

"For fuck's sake, Kenna. Are you insane?" Asher barks out, snapping the arrow in half.

McKenna rolls her eyes as a twanging sound from the

bow's string echoes through the room. She's loaded another arrow, aiming at my heart this time. "Catch it, blood of Eden."

"What?" I ask, annoyed at her games.

"Catch. It," she repeats slowly, eyeing me as she looks down the arrow's body.

"McKenna," Asher warns, but I step in front of him.

"Aim and shoot, gargoyle," I taunt.

"You don't have to do this, siren," Asher states from behind me.

I hold up a hand to quiet him. I know this is some sort of McKenna test, and if I don't allow her to execute it, I'll never hear the end of it.

"Aim. And. Shoot," I repeat.

A smirk forms on McKenna's lips as she pulls the arrow back and releases it. Within seconds, the weapon flies toward me, floating through the air. Strangely, when I focus on the tip, everything around me slows down, including the arrow. Even though it's only been seconds, the slow motion allows me to reach out and snatch it before it hits me.

"Holy shit," I breathe out, astonished I did it. My widened eyes flick to McKenna's before I walk over and drop the arrow at her feet. "You missed, cupcake," I drop my voice.

"Way to go, cutie," Callan cheers, forcing my attention to the other side of the room.

I smile at his excited manner before catching Abby's sympathy-marked expression.

Furious, Asher storms up to the beautiful, blonde gargoyle warrior who is currently seething at me. Keegan steps between his brother and mate.

"What the fuck was that about, Kenna?" Asher growls around his eldest brother.

McKenna narrows her eyes at him. "I was testing her blood connection."

Asher slides his glance my way before returning his attention to McKenna. "Explain."

"As cousins who share blood ties, Abby and I have a link to one another's feelings. Just like you and your brothers do. Now that my DNA has been mixed in with the blood of Eden's, Abby and I have opened our connection with her," McKenna points out. "We're blood tied."

I watch Abby carefully. Her expression has contorted into one of guilt and pain.

"Sorry, Eve. I sensed your heart rate increasing out of fear, so I slowed down the air in the room so you'd catch the arrow," she admits.

"There are truly no boundaries in this family." Abby and McKenna can now sense my emotions. *Fabulous.*

"Guess you're truly clan now," McKenna sneers.

I force a casual shrug. "I've always wanted to be blood sisters with you, Kenna."

She scoffs. "Don't twist it. I saved your weak life out of duty. Nothing more."

I step around Asher toward her. "Nothing says family bonding like a gargoyle protector saving a human charge." *I need to stop taunting her before she really does snap me in two.*

McKenna moves around Keegan and looms over me. "Like I said, you're nothing more than an assignment."

"I love you too, cupcake," I snip.

McKenna just death stares me down. "Fuck off, blood

of Eden."

Abby gets in between us. "Girls, please."

At her proximity, the strong scent of vinegar hits me and I scrunch my nose.

"Why do you smell like pickles?" I ask Abby.

She looks at me sheepishly. "Callan made me a fried pickle sandwich earlier."

"Ew, why?" I question, taking a step back. The scent of garlic and dill is overwhelming.

Abby rolls her beautiful sapphire eyes. "Don't ask," she replies, blowing her long red strands of hair out of her face as she moves away from us. "It's something new he's trying."

I turn to Callan. "You're pickling now? What happened to baking? Or the chili cook-off?"

"Pickles are a very underestimated food, cutie," Callan argues.

"Baby, they're a condiment, not a food," Abby counters.

"What?" He squawks, clearly in disagreement with his mate. "Pickles are most certainly a food, babe. It's a preserved cucumber. A cucumber is a food. Hence, pickles are food."

Abby sighs and places her hands on her slender hips. "Pickles are used to add flavor to food, which, Callan Thomas St. Michael, is the very definition of a condiment!"

"I hate to say it, Callan, but relish is made from pickles and it's a condiment," I add.

Asher comes up behind me and pulls me into his arms. "Don't get involved, siren."

"But it's true," I defend.

Keegan clears his throat. "I hate to put an end to another. . .fascinating clan food debate, but now that Eve is feeling better, we have more important things to discuss."

"What could possibly be more important than discussing my pickle?" Callan admonishes.

We all stare at Callan. His expression becomes marred by confusion at our shocked silence. After a few seconds, he offers us his megawatt toothy grin, catching on.

"That came out different than it sounded in my head," Callan admits.

"What else is new?" McKenna bites back.

Abby wraps her arms around Callan's waist. "It's okay, baby. We all love your pickle."

"Speak for yourself," I mumble.

Callan's eyebrow arches before he grabs Abby, dipping and kissing her inappropriately.

"By the grace, get a fucking room," Asher exhales.

Callan points at his brother. "What's wrong, Ash? You want a piece of my pickle?"

Asher scowls. "What the fuck is wrong with you? No, I don't want your pickle."

"If everyone could rein it in, we have a summit to convene," Keegan states pointedly.

Asher turns me in his arms so I'm facing him. "We need to meet with the other clans, to alert them of my father's resurrection and strategize what our next steps will be."

"So we're going to London then?" I inquire, knowing the flats in London are where the clan likes to hold meetings.

Asher scans the room before returning his focus to me. "No. London isn't safe. My father has access to all our homes. We'll stay in Wiltshire, just long enough to convene with the other clans. Then we'll head back to Massachusetts. It will be safer in the States."

"We have two days. That's it," Keegan reminds Asher.

"Why only two days?" I interject.

"Tadhg is watching Garrick. They're in Egypt at the moment. He'll be there for the next two days, amassing an army, after which . . . well, we don't know," Asher explains.

"You think he'll come here?" I ask.

"Without doubt, Eve," Keegan answers. "Garrick St. Michael is not someone you want as an enemy. His will is strong. As are his motives. Unfortunately for you, you're the target."

"Oh," I exhale.

"Yeah, 'oh,' blood of Eden," McKenna mimics.

"We should begin outreach to the clans immediately," Keegan suggests.

"Let's roll," Callan replies, and everyone begins to make their way out of the room.

"Hey." I tug on Asher's shirt so he's forced to look at me. "Give me a minute." I motion my head toward McKenna's retreating back.

A small smile forms on his perfect lips. "Are you sure you want to poke the bear?"

"I need to," I reply.

He places a kiss on my forehead. "This time, watch out for flying fists, yeah?"

I narrow my eyes. "Excellent reminder."

Just as McKenna is about to leave, I cup her elbow, forcing her to face me. "Hold up."

Angry eyes scowl at me as she yanks her arm free, with little effort. "The next time you touch me, blood of Eden, I'll snap your neck and leave you for dead," she threatens.

I roll my eyes. "As much fun as that sounds, all I need is a moment of your time."

She grits her teeth. "What do you want?"

"To say thank you," I deadpan.

She stares at me, unblinking. "I knew saving your human life would bite me in the ass."

"Yes, well, I have that effect." I attempt to rein in my anger.

"Are we done now?" she asks, clearly irritated.

"I mean it, McKenna. Thank you," I repeat sincerely.

She blows out a long breath through her perfectly glossy lips. "You're welcome," she answers in an aggravated tone. "For the record, it's our duty to protect one another in this clan. I guarantee it won't be the last time I save your pathetic life, and I don't want to braid one another's hair and share our innermost secrets every time it happens. Understood?"

I think that might have just been her version of a welcome hug. Suddenly, I'm feeling all sorts of warmth and love from the ice queen. I smirk knowingly.

"I understand, McKenna. You think of me as family."

"How hard did you hit your damn head?"

"You just admitted that you're planning to keep me around, and dare I also say, you offered to protect me again. As. You. Would. Family," I speak each word slowly.

"By the grace, you're dense," she mutters under her breath.

"So I'm growing on you then?" I tease.

McKenna steps around me, attempting to leave the training room.

I smile, unable to help myself. "Good talk, cupcake."

"Fuck off, blood of Eden," she throws over her shoulder on her way out.

I could have sworn her tone was laced with the tiniest amount of amusement. McKenna can deny it all she wants, but she's saved my life twice, stood by me when Asher was hurt, and subtly protected me on a number of occasions, which can only mean one thing.

McKenna McIntyre St. Michael likes me.

☙❧

I study the circular driveway from my spot on the upstairs landing. The open window allows the spring breeze to pass freely, bringing with it the smell of freshly cut grass. I watch McKenna and Abby greet each supernatural being as they arrive. Each ethereal warrior smiles graciously and stands with a poise and elegance I find myself envious of.

Surprisingly, Keegan was able to secure everyone's attendance for this morning. I guess when the royal gargoyle family requests an audience with you, your schedule clears and you arrive quickly and without question.

After a few moments of gawking, I turn to see Asher coming up the staircase, carrying a handful of rolled up maps. With great dramatics, he tosses them on a nearby table.

"What are those?" I ask with a puzzled expression.

His lips tilt in a wicked smirk. "Apparently, siren, you're using one of your newest powers and manifesting escape plans."

"What?" I whisper to him, shocked that I would do what he's accusing me of. "You can't be serious," I state, rummaging through each floor plan. It's true. There are five layouts of the manor, staring at me. "I must have unknowingly done this in the shower," I explain. "I was thinking of how much I'd rather be anywhere but at this summit."

Asher arches his brow in a cunning way. After a moment, he saunters over to me and deliberately leans into my personal space, running his fingers down my cheek and over my jawline. His eyes soften and his fingertips brush across the necklace he gave to me.

"You're on edge." It wasn't a question.

"Clearly," I reply, motioning to the blueprints. Lifting my eyes, I fall into his stare. "Walking into a room full of supernatural beings tends to end poorly for me. You know, given our semi-bonding and my divine bloodline and all."

He smiles down at me. "You can relax, siren. Everyone at this meeting is an ally."

I pin him with a hard glare. "Isn't that what we thought about Lady Finella? Or your father? How about the countless others who have deceived us recently?"

He studies me thoughtfully. "This meeting is important. We need to strengthen our alliances within the protector and supernatural communities so we have a fighting chance."

"I know," I exhale.

Asher slides his hands around my waist, pulling me to him. He breaks our connection by dipping his head to my neck, lightly kissing and nipping his way back up to my lips before claiming them in a searing kiss, sending tremors rippling through me.

My body becomes pliant as he glides his lips slowly

and sensually across mine, ceasing all worried thoughts I have.

With a growl, he pulls away, allowing us to breathe. "I will protect you, always."

"I know," I whisper.

"Do you?" he asks, frowning while scanning my face.

"I do," I reply in a firm tone.

"We are stronger together, yeah?"

"Yes," I declare.

After a moment, he releases a breath and dips his chin, stepping closer to me.

"Will Gage be joining us?" I question, changing the subject.

"After he takes care of a business matter in Paris," he replies, gazing into my eyes. "You are mine to protect. No one can take that from me, except you. Are you planning to, siren?" he asks with sternness in his voice.

I tense. "To what?"

"To take it away from me?" Asher holds me tighter to him, searching my face.

Something inside my stomach drops. I inhale and trace the spot just above his heart, where the protector tattoo is. "Never," I promise. "I will never, of my own accord, leave you again, Asher. I swear. I am yours, forever," I respond, trying to reassure him.

"Good. Then stop manifesting escape routes and let's go greet our guests." He smirks.

With my heart drumming rapidly in my chest, I nod my agreement. Asher links our hands and guides me downstairs. A few moments later, we step into the conference room and my gaze roams over the gargoyle clans with a combination of awe and trepidation.

Callan steps into our sightline and I can't help but notice his T-shirt.

"Family drama: the gift that keeps on giving," I read out loud.

"Too soon, cutie?" Callan's eyes twinkle.

I attempt to hide my grin as Asher pushes at Callan's shoulder to get his attention.

"Keegan is going to have a shit fit when he sees that." Asher points to Callan's shirt.

"He already has." Callan shrugs. "Besides, it's clever and witty. Like me."

Asher sighs and motions his chin into the room. "Let's get this over with, yeah?"

We push our way between the numerous bodies to stand by Keegan. Asher clears his throat, gaining the attention of the murmuring room. Everyone quiets, turning their attention to us. Asher clutches my hand in a show of unity not missed by anyone.

"Thank you all for coming on short notice," Asher begins. "If you're not already aware of the recent supernatural happenings, let me brief you. It's come to light that Lady Finella, Queen of the Fae realm, was mated to Asmodeus, King of the Nine Hells. Together, they conspired against and slaughtered our revered Priestesses. In the process, the Eternal Forest has fallen, its life essence gone with the priestesses." Asher's tone is solemn.

"Whit has become ay th' fairy, yer highness?" Griff, or Griffin, the leader of the Scottish clan of gargoyles, and McKenna's relative, asks in a gruff and heavily accented voice.

Asher turns his attention to the large, Viking-like man, whose long gray beard and mustache hit the middle of his broad chest.

"The Angelic Council has sentenced and executed her," Asher answers.

"By th' grace," Griff responds, his blue eyes saddening. "It was th' will ay fate 'en."

Asher nods once, his gaze meeting mine. "It has also come to light that Asmodeus is working with Deacon, leader of the Declan clan. The half-demon, half-gargoyle's mate, brother, and mother all cease to be," Asher adds. His expression hardens before he returns a sharp glare to the room. "There is a royal bounty on Deacon's head. Meaning, when he is captured, no mercy is to be shown. Only a slow, painful end to his pathetic existence."

At Asher's words, low rumblings roll through the group.

My focus glides over Asher's stiff body. It's at moments like this, when he is ferociously protecting the ones he loves, that I'm reminded of how dark he can really be. Sometimes I forget that at the core, he's supernatural royalty and a fierce gargoyle warrior.

"Ye'ur askin' us tae kill one ay our own. By torture?" Sean, Griff's second in command, poses in a heavy Scottish brogue.

"Asking?" Asher ponders the word. "No," he growls, looking between the group leaders. "It's a royal decree. Deacon has come after my clan. My kin. My mate," he says slowly. "In our world, he has declared war on my family. It's personal. An eye for an eye, brother."

The tall, muscular Scotsman runs a frustrated hand

down the dirty-blond braid in the middle of his head. I study the tattoos adorning the skin on either side of his shaved skull.

After a moment, he meets Asher's hard glare. "Ah dinnae loch it, yoong prince."

I guess McKenna's stubborn and disagreeable personality traits run in the family.

"Your likes and dislikes are not my concern, Sean," Asher bites out. "My word is final."

Griff steps in between the two gargoyles, placing a large hand on Sean's chest in an effort to pacify the agitated protector before turning to Asher. "Yer wuid es noted, yer highness. When we find hem, th' Scottish clan will brin' Deacon tae ye, strugglin' fur his last breath. On our honur as protectors." Griff nods his head respectfully to Asher.

"Thank you for your kinship, Griff," Asher answers sincerely.

"Why are we really 'ere, Asher?" Thomas, the second in command of the Irish clan, inquires. "What 'tis da real reason for dis summit? Aside from askin' us ta torture an' kill our own." His leather jacket groans in protest as he crosses his lanky arms over his chest.

I study Asher's Adam's apple as he works hard to swallow. The slight break in his regal, authoritative composure is only evident to me. "It would seem we have an undead gargoyle king, working with the dark army in an attempt to destroy all that we've built," he responds.

Silence falls across the room as each gargoyle allows the weight of Asher's words to sink in. Abby meets her cousin's eyes with sadness as Thomas's brows rise in understanding.

"Christ, son. Are ye sayin' Garrick St. Michael is alive?" Angus, leader of the Irish clan, and Abby's uncle, questions. "By de grace."

Asher turns his attention to the heavyset, older, bald man whose face is hidden behind a long, thick red beard. "And unlike Deacon, if you find my father, he is to be brought to my brothers and me alive. We claim ownership of his existence. It's our birthright to cease it."

Suddenly, everything turns into mass chaos. There is shouting and barking. Asher releases his grip on me to help Keegan and Callan attempt to gain some control. My eyes slide to the back of the room and I watch as Gage silently slips in, keeping a safe distance.

He's studying the drama with disdain marring his expression. Our eyes meet for the briefest moment before he turns his attention back to Asher, with a small tick in his jaw.

"ENOUGH!" Asher shouts and the room stills.

"An' what o' da council, yer highness?" Thomas challenges Asher.

"The council is not to be trusted. They harbored my father, even when they knew he'd placed human lives in danger. As king, my first decree will be to dismantle it," Asher counters.

"Christ, lad," Angus barks. "Are ye mad?"

Asher's stance becomes more rigid and threatening at Angus's words. He steps closer to the gargoyle leader. "Are you questioning my authority, Angus?"

"Ye're plannin' an uprisin'. Against de council!" Thomas exclaims.

Asher cocks his head to the side. "I am doing what is needed for the sake of our clans' futures. And to ensure the safety of humans and protect my mate," he admonishes. "Your king, our leader, whose priority it was to protect mankind, decided to side with the enemy in an attempt to keep our race safe. My father had an innocent human woman raped, tortured, and murdered for no other reason than to make a point."

I watch Gage visibly flinch at Asher's reminder of how his mate, Camilla, was tortured.

"Garrick used human life to control and manipulate, with the council's blessing. That is not honor. That is not loyalty. That is not the behavior worthy of a king of the protector race," he continues. "We are gargoyles. It is our calling to protect those who can't protect themselves. Through duty, honor and loyalty." Asher stands taller and lifts his chin to the silent room. "I am your next king. You will show allegiance to my clan, the royal family, and my mate, your future queen. AM. I. CLEAR?" he barks at the stunned faces.

After a few uncomfortable moments of everyone's eyes darting around, Gage steps forward. Without a word, he casually swaggers over to Asher, stopping within a half-foot of reaching him. With every silent exchange between the two, my breath hitches.

Both warriors stand tall, full of respect for one another. Something I've not seen before. Gage slides his gaze to me and tilts his head as if I'm already the queen and he's acknowledging it, then he turns back to Asher and silently takes a knee, bowing his head.

"The Paris clan offers its allegiance to the royal family, as well as the future king and queen of our race." Gage lifts his gaze and meets Asher's with a steel resolve. "In the name

of Camilla Valeria Marquez Gallagher." *Holy shit.*
It would appear that Gage Gallagher just picked a side.

4 Broken

My steps echo in the silence as I weave through Notre Dame's chapel. The flying buttresses hover so high above me, it's almost as if they're trying to reach Heaven. I continue to make my way down one of the two empty aisles, noting the delicate forms of French Gothic architecture. Honey-toned sculptures and majestic stained glass windows adorn the sacred *"Our Lady of Paris"* cathedral.

As I pass through the grand gallery, I inhale, trying to feel a divine connection to something—anything that will give me the courage and strength to pull him from the darkness. It's futile. After the protector's declaration, I know he is spiraling in self-loathing.

I trudge up the three hundred eighty-seven stone stairs of the north tower, then cross the narrow walkway to the south tower, passing the chimera and gargoyle statues before squeezing my way up two wooden corkscrew staircases, leading to the viewing platform.

Stepping onto the balcony, I exhale a sigh of relief when I see what I've come in search of. He's perched on a stone ledge with his grey wings on display and a cigarette hanging off his perfect lips. I slowly approach him so he won't disappear in avoidance.

"This seems a bit cliché for you, Gage," I quip in a soft tone.

The bad-boy gargoyle doesn't acknowledge my presence. Instead, he hides behind his lit cigarette. The early rising sun's shadows cast him in a combination of darkness and light.

Uninvited, I take a seat next to him on the ledge and try to hide my fear of the fall below. Instead, I study the beautiful red and orange hues of sunrise, engulfing the city of Paris. We sit in comfortable silence for a few moments, basking in peace on the historic building.

"Where is your protector?" Gage asks in a flat tone.

I tilt my head, admiring his profile. "Sitting right here, next to me."

Gage's entire body becomes stiff as he turns his head to face me. "Love," he sighs.

I hold his sea-green gaze. "Don't say anything to dispute that you are my protector, Gage, because your actions will refute your words." I inhale. "Plus, you have wings and you're sitting on top of Notre Dame. I'm pretty sure that screams stereotypical gargoyle protector."

Amused, he twitches his lips before returning his focus to the sun-kissed city below us.

Restoration

"Asher's still convening with summit members," I blow out an exaggerated breath.

"War strategy is a necessary evil." He sighs. "How did you get here?"

"Nassa wanted to practice teleporting candle magic skills. So here I am."

Gage's shoulders slump. "Christ. I should have known the sorceress was involved."

"After declaring your allegiance, she's worried about you. Honestly, so am I," I admit.

"Your concern is misplaced."

I allow the endless silence to stretch between us until it becomes suffocating.

"Why are you here?" I dangle and swing my feet. "Seeking divine intervention?"

He snorts. "Not in this lifetime."

I shrug. "Perhaps in the next then."

Gage takes a deep inhale of his cigarette before putting it out and throwing the remains over the side of the church. "Not likely, love."

"What is it with you supernatural beings and littering? You know, it's probably your fault humans are experiencing global warming," I accuse, pointing to the falling butt.

He ignores my remark. "Do you know how many times this cathedral has been restored?"

My brows furrow and I shake my head.

"Numerous. Camilla was part of the last round of restorations, cleaning and repairing the old sculptures. Christ, she loved this place. At least twice a week, I'd wake up in the middle of the night and discover her missing, only to find her here, immersed in the calm she found by restoring the church's sculptures." He offers me a heartbreaking smile. "It's ironic really. She spent more time with the stone gargoyles than she did with me. The real thing."

"You protectors aren't easy to love. Sounds to me like she found solace in her art," I offer.

"It's why I didn't question where she was the night she was killed. I'd woken up in a cold sweat. My body felt empty and my heart hollow. It was as if my soul left me. And I knew. I knew she was gone. Even still, my mind wouldn't believe it to be truth," he trails off.

I reach over and take his hand in mine, offering him a reassuring squeeze.

"I got dressed to come here, and I kept telling myself that once I walked into the cathedral, Camilla would be sitting on the floor, like she was every other time, piecing back together all the things in the statues that she couldn't fix in me. Strands of her long hair would be falling out of the messy knot she'd put it in. Her sparkling eyes would find mine, and she'd smile at me like she always did, in that way that made me feel as though I was the only man alive." He swallows and hangs his head. "My delusions were destroyed the moment I opened my front door and found her bloodied and distorted body lying lifelessly on the ground."

My eyes slide shut, forcing away the tears threatening to fall. Gage lifts our intertwined hands and rubs at his chest, trying to relieve the pain and emptiness that I know is settling in.

"I miss her so much," he exhales. "It's hard to breathe without her. The scars she's left behind actually seep with loneliness and tear at me." His voice cracks with emotion.

I reposition myself so I'm straddling the ledge and take

his face between my palms. "I can't imagine the layers of pain her death causes you to fight through on a daily basis."

A lone tear slides down his face, dropping on my hand and crawling across my fingers.

"Camilla was my one piece of truth in a world stained with dishonesty."

I release my hold on his face and gently wipe away the water streak from his cheek.

"It's beautiful that you come here to remember and feel closer to her."

He releases an abrasive laugh. "Beautiful? No. Ironic, that this is the place I see her face glowing with life and marred in death. Where my reality and memories collide. Where I am incapable of letting go."

I swallow a painful lump through my tight throat, and a tear escapes my own eye.

Gage sniffs harshly. "Don't waste your tears on me or Camilla. It's pointless."

"I'm sorry I didn't believe you about her death," I respond sincerely.

He levels me with a sad expression. "As I told you before, you can't understand what you don't know. There's history you can't appreciate because you are not from our world."

"Until recently, I had no idea your world could be so cruel," I counter.

He shrugs a dismissive shoulder. "There is darkness in everything that is light, love."

"I still can't believe Garrick is alive," I mutter.

"When the bastard spoke of Camilla, in the council room, it was all I could do not to rip his heart out, right there, in front of everyone," he growls.

"Did you know he was alive? I mean, before you found that piece of paper with his name on it? The one you threatened me with in Paris?" I ask, knowing he most likely did.

He pauses before meeting my eyes with a cold stare that could pierce through stone.

"Garrick St. Michael is a conversation you should be having with Asher, not me."

My heart begins to race and I blink slowly. "I'm choosing to have it with you, Gage. You're the one who keeps telling me to get all the facts, so I can make informed decisions. How am I supposed to do that when everyone constantly keeps me in the dark?"

He sighs and pulls out another cigarette, lighting it. With a deep inhale, he relaxes his shoulders and traces his lower lip with his thumb in contemplation. "Once upon a time, Asher and I were the best of friends—brothers. Our fathers were close allies. I have no siblings, and over the years, the London clan became a second family to me." Gage looks off into the distance and shakes his head. "As we got older, our fathers grew more and more distant. They became obsessed with ruling their clans and saving our race. After Camilla's death, I went to Asher and his brothers with my theories of Garrick and my father's involvement. For a long time, they didn't believe me. It's understandable. They were grieving the loss of their parents, and without proof, there was no reason to assume the king was alive." Gage drills his gaze into mine.

"Until I gave you a reason?"

"Until you gave us confirmation," he corrects. "Asher

witnessed firsthand the devastation Camilla's death caused me. After losing my mate . . . I lost it, love. I became unhinged. Broken. The London clan attributed my 'conspiracy ranting' to my grief. Right before Asher took you on as a charge, I was able to convince him of his father's past involvement in Camilla's death. Ironically, it was Deacon who provided me with that evidence. Asher and I suspected Garrick was still tied to Deacon somehow. His resurrection was only a theory, that is, until you scribbled his name on a piece of folded paper and gave it to Michael."

"How did you get hold of the piece of paper, Gage?"

"It's not your concern, love."

"I thought you and Asher weren't close anymore." I say. "Sounds like you two still are."

He inhales another round of nicotine and lets it out on a long breath. "There are layers of causes and betrayals, spanning over many years, that have led to Asher's and my distance."

"Yet, he trusted you, and only you, with my protection?" I point out. I watch the line of smoke coming off the last of Gage's cigarette. "Explain why Asher chose you, over his family, to protect me when the council removed him," I demand quietly.

Gage puts out his cigarette. "When Deacon gave me the proof I needed for Asher to believe his father and mine were working jointly, we started to piece together their plan. Knowing it would take longer for Keegan and Callan to come to terms with Garrick's involvement, Asher and I agreed to keep it quiet while I did some recon. When Asher was assigned as your protector, it was the perfect platform for me to infiltrate the Declan clan and get into bed with the dark army. Aside from my non-allegiance to the councils, the strain between the London clan and me allowed me into Deacon's graces without question."

"This entire time, you've been working with both sides?" I clarify.

"I volunteered to work for Deacon in order to gain confirmation, then filter information to Asher," he continues. "So, yes. I guess I was working with both sides."

"And me?" I accuse. "Was I just a pawn in this game you two are playing?"

"You, love, were an unexpected complication."

"Complication?"

"I watched Asher's reaction to you, that day at the coffee shop when we first met. His feelings for you were clear as day," Gage states.

"I remember you telling him you were both on different sides," I remind. "Why?"

"It was my way of warning Asher. My only intention that day was to introduce myself to you. To see just how much of a distraction you would be for him. Uncharacteristically, Asher allowed his feelings to override his head and he showed up. His overprotective, misplaced emotions were written all over his face. I didn't agree with his newfound affection for you. I needed him to focus on what he and I were trying to accomplish and not be distracted," he says. "Telling Asher that Deacon said hello to Michael was code. I had been accepted into the Declan clan's fold. The rest of my words were a reminder of the consequences if Asher didn't put duty, honor and loyalty above all else, even you."

"Meaning if he fell in love with me, I would end up

like Camilla?"

"Asher never meant to fall in love with you. When he did, the panic set in. His awareness of what Camilla's death did to me, along with his understanding of just how dangerous the Declan clan and Garrick are, caused him to fight his feelings. When the council removed Asher, he turned to the only protector he knew would guard you with his life. Given my history and inside knowledge, he felt you would be safest with me since his brothers were unaware of our infiltration plan."

"I thought the clan didn't have any secrets?" I murmur, slumping in annoyance.

"Some undisclosed information is necessary. Even amongst family," he retorts.

"This entire time, you've both been playing everyone, including me? Why didn't you and Asher just tell everyone? Why all the need for secrets and lies?" I say, defeated.

"You didn't need to know. It would have been too dangerous," he responds. "If you are planning to be in his life, then you need to learn that protector and royal business, at times, will not be a place for you to intervene."

I curb the desire to punch him in the nose at his misguided, and frankly annoying, remark. Instead, I watch the sun fully come up over Paris. "Did Abby and McKenna know anything?"

"They were in the dark too. I'm sure by now they've been enlightened," he answers.

I exhale. "I thought you didn't pick sides, Gage. All this time, you were on Asher's side."

"Make no mistake, the London clan and I are not on good terms. Don't misunderstand my part in this for anything more than it is. The only side I'm on is Camilla's, even in death. The dark prince and I will continue to work together to bring Garrick, Deacon, and the dark army down. That's all. My earlier announcement of support was for show. It means nothing in the grand scheme of things," he states coolly.

"And me?" I challenge. "What am I to you, Gage? What is my part in all this?"

"My redemption." Gage catches my gaze and holds it firmly. "You aren't mine, but I will protect you as if you were, while you restore balance. You have my word."

"And what happens when I do?" I study his face. "What happens to you when you finally get the revenge for Camilla that you so desperately want?"

"Peace. Fucking peace, so that maybe, just maybe, I won't feel numb."

"And Nassa?" I whisper. "I know she means more to you than you let on."

"She has no knowledge of any of this. Nor will she, for her own protection."

"Don't you think she deserves to know?" I ask. "It wouldn't hurt to let her in, Gage."

Gage's jaw clinches. "I've hidden my scars for so long they've become a part of me. I hate that my heart feels empty, but letting Nassa in isn't the answer right now."

"You can't go through this alone anymore," I plead. "She cares about you."

"In my world, I'm better off alone, and she's better off without me tainting her future."

"Nassa comes from your world, Gage. Let her into the pieces of the life you had before."

"I'm not ready for that, love."

I lift my eyes to the now bright blue sky, filled with the warmth of the sun. Exhausted.

Gage stands and extends his hand for me to take.

"I'm sure the dark prince is having a heart attack that you're not back by now."

I place my hand in his and allow him to assist me up.

"You're not alone. I'm here, and if you let them, so are Nassa and the London clan. Whatever you do, don't slip away from us."

Gage's brows pinch together at my statement. He nods once and interlaces our fingers.

Suddenly, the air becomes unnaturally still around us. My eyes lift to the rapidly darkening sky. My lips part in confusion. A second ago, the heavens were cobalt and bathed in the sun's rays. Now, darkness is blanketing the atmosphere in inky black.

An angry clap of thunder crashes overhead, and ominous clouds churn and dance over one another as danger lurks closer. I watch the chaos below us as people run to take cover.

The heavens produce a deep rumble, introducing thousands of dark silhouettes. Inhaling the putrid smell of sulfur, I choke back the bile rising in my throat. This scene is eerily similar to a recent vision. I drag my focus back to Gage, who meets my panicked expression.

"The dark army is descending. We need to get inside the cathedral, love," he orders.

Sensing a threat, energy begins to flood through my body, embracing me, threading itself through every part of me at the lure of the danger the dark army emanates. Gage closes the distance between us with a single stride and snakes his arms around my waist.

"We need to move. It's unsafe to be out here," he whispers in my ear.

My fingers twitch at my sides, as the need to release the light becomes more and more insistent. "There are innocent people down there, Gage. We can't just run and hide. We have to protect them," I insist, moving us toward the ledge.

Gage tightens his hands around my body, pulling me back to him. "Eve, you are my charge at the moment. The humans can't see the demons. All they see are darkening skies. They're taking cover, assuming the sky will open up, sending rain down on them. I promise, we'll help if they are in danger. Right now, *you* are the only one who is."

Surrendering, I nod my agreement to do as he asks. Just as we're about to transport, the heat from Gage's body disappears. Whipping around to see where he went, I come face-to-face with a demon.

I cast my gaze over the dark being's shoulder to see Gage entwined with two more of the dark army's minions, and immediately withdraw my daggers.

"Is there something I can do for you?" I snip out at the demonic creature.

The scaly, black-leather-fleshed demon snarls. "Daughter of Heaven, your time has come to an end." His chin dips, like a dog ready to attack, as his white irises focus on me.

Tightening my grip on my daggers, I summon the light within me, drawing it to the tips of my fingers. "You want me? Come and get me then," I taunt.

The serpent-like demon lunges forward, and a furious blast of energy funnels through me, slamming into the beast with enough force that it staggers backward.

Interestingly enough, it doesn't poof into blue flames. *Shit.*

Standing straighter, it shakes its smooth head, and two more identical demons appear by the first one's sides. My eyes slide to Gage, who continues to fight off at least ten of these things. *Crap.* I back up, trying to strategize, while pulling the power source to me again.

The light rushes through me, out of my palms and into my daggers, splitting like lightning bolts, hitting all three targets at once. The demons stand without movement, their forked tongues flicking out in displeasure. *What the hell?*

The scales must be repelling the force somehow. Hundreds, if not thousands, of dark creatures begin to fall from the sky, landing gracefully on the platform of Notre Dame. I meet the dread in Gage's gaze. There's no way the two of us will be able to handle the dark army alone. Gage disappears, and within seconds, he materializes in front of me, putting his body between the demon and me.

"Stay behind me," he orders.

"I think we're outnumbered."

"Excellent observation, love."

"Thank you."

"When I tell you to, grab onto me and don't let go," Gage instructs.

"Okay."

The dark army moves forward as one entity. Each silent movement is taken in unison. It's as if they're one being. My breath hitches at the sheer volume of them. My eyes lock onto Gage's gray flexed wings. The muscles in his broad back twitch under his cotton black shirt.

"Now, love," Gage barks, pulling my focus back to our situation.

I wrap and lock my arms around his waist, pressing my body to his back. Within seconds, we're airborne before Gage and I dematerialize, leaving the dark army behind.

A few seconds later, I land with a hard thud in cold water. With my legs scissoring, I push my body to the surface and gasp for air while my arms flail, as I try to get my bearings.

Gage's laughter floats over to me from the side of the pool, at the manor in England, where he is sitting on a lounge chair, completely dry. *Damn gargoyle.*

I narrow my eyes at him. "Every. Fucking. Time, Gage?"

His face relaxes as he leans his elbows on his knees. "I'm sorry. It's just that . . . getting you all wet and bothered brings such joy to my life."

I girlie growl at him and pull myself out of the pool. "I hate you."

"You don't." He easily falls into our usual banter.

Wringing out the water from my hair, I sigh, trying to hide my smirk. "I do too. A lot."

He holds my gaze with amusement clear on his face as he stands and takes a step toward me. Once he's close enough, I notice a small cut above his eye. I move slowly to inspect the wound, but Asher's pissed-off, deep voice stops me in my tracks.

"WHAT IN THE FUCKING HELL, GAGE!" Asher shouts as he and Nassa reach us.

I turn and place my hands on Asher's chest, attempting to calm him down.

"Easy, Ash. The dark army had us cornered at Notre Dame. Gage teleported us out."

Asher's eyes drop to mine before he yanks me by the hips and pulls me to him.

"Are you all right, siren?" he questions, scanning me for injuries.

"I'm fine, Asher," I reply, sliding my gaze to the sorceress.

Nassa is studying Gage, intently. Her expression is a mixture of pissed off and concerned. The sorceress moves toward Gage, and I watch his body become rigid at her approach.

Asher backs us up so Nassa has a clear path while she prowls toward the ashen protector. Gage works his jaw in agitation as she steps into his personal space, going toe-to-toe with him.

Nassa's petite arms fold over her chest, and she nods her head to his cut. "You're hurt?"

"Why do you even care, buttercup?" Gage lashes out unexpectedly in a harsh voice.

I watch as her shoulders visibly drop, the only sign his words affected her.

"You're right, Gallagher. I don't fucking care," Nassa bites back.

She turns to storm off, but not before Gage's voice cuts through the awkwardness.

"I'm not yours to worry about," he comments in a low, pointed voice.

I hear her sharp intake of breath before she stops and

turns back to Gage. "No shit."

Asher and I silently watch the uncomfortable standoff before Gage shifts awkwardly and lowers his voice.

"I can't offer you the world. Christ, I can't even offer you a tomorrow," Gage proclaims on a long breath before stepping around the sorceress and walking toward the manor. After a moment, he stops and looks at her over his shoulder. "I'm broken."

5 Evening Star

I shift my focus to Asher's and watch his eyes darken to a midnight blue, and I know I am in deep trouble. When he draws back, I take a step forward as if an invisible thread stretches between us, pulling me to him. However, the intensity and anger in his glare stops my progress.

"The dark fucking army, siren?" His heated voice cuts right through me.

Needing a moment to collect myself, my eyes float to Nassa and take in her rigid posture before returning to Asher's irate demeanor.

"What in the hell were you thinking, going to Paris, alone? Unprotected."

"I wasn't alone and I was protected. Gage was with me," I remind.

"Of course he was." Asher snorts, running his hands

over his face in frustration.

"I'm fine," I promise. "Although I could use a few moments to dry off."

Asher's tight expression cascades over my soaked figure before releasing a long breath.

"Please," I beg and shift my focus back to Nassa, hoping he will pick up on the hint.

His head tilts back, toward the sky, and his eyes slide shut before returning to watch me, watching him. "This discussion about your unprotected disappearance isn't over."

A small smile forms on my lips. "It never is. That's the beauty of forever. You can brood about my missteps until we are, like, a bazillion years old."

At my gentle tease, Asher's body relaxes, and he plants a gentle kiss on my forehead. "Using our bond to calm me? Well played, siren. I'll curb my need to cut off Gage's oxygen supply until he's an inch from death, for allowing the dark army within ten feet of you. I guess I'll go check on Galena and Fiona instead."

"Thank you," I whisper and brush my lips across his.

Asher steps back. I watch him make his way into the house before I turn toward Nassa, stepping to her side. With a sideways glance, I notice the blankness on her face.

"Gage was in Paris to clear his head," I offer as a lame attempt to smooth things over.

"Where Gallagher was, and why he was there, isn't my business," she answers evenly, not looking at me. Though her words are harsh, her body language tells me it does matter to her.

I turn toward her. "He's different with you, you know."

She shrugs. "It doesn't matter. Camilla is a ghost that will haunt his heart forever."

"I understand it's complicated, Nassa," I respond. "Love normally is."

"Love," she snorts. "Look, it's nice that you care for him. Gallagher should have people around who love him deeply. I'm just not one of those beings," she states in a detached tone.

"If you don't try, Nassa, you'll never know what you could be missing."

"Don't put your and Asher's lovey-dovey bullshit on us, Eve."

I inhale, ignoring her outburst. "You calm his storms. We all see it."

She toes her Converse on the ground. "You're wrong. There's nothing in his heart for me."

I can see the hurt in her eyes as she forces out each word, willing herself to believe them.

"If there was a small spark in his heart, would you want to give yours to him?"

Her lips part as she stares at me blankly before composing herself. "He doesn't have a heart to make room for me in. Just broken pieces from the destruction of a life before me."

"Maybe you are the glue he needs to mend the broken pieces?" I offer.

She laughs harshly. "Even if that was true, I have too much self-respect to wait around for some guy to never make me his priority."

"I've seen how he looks at you, Nassa," I begin, but she interjects.

"He likes fucking me, Eve," she snaps. "That's it. So no, I will not become a cliché and ask him to pick me. To choose me. To love me, because he won't," she says on a shaky breath.

"Isn't he worth fighting for?" I ask, disregarding her incorrect read of his feelings.

"I certainly am. Yet, he isn't wearing his battle gear. Is he?" she counters.

"I get that you're scared. I do—"

"I won't chase him, because once I do finally catch him, Gallagher is just going to pull me under, and I know I'm going to drown. There is no life preserver with a guy like Gage. I'm not prepared to jump in, knowing he won't save me," she explains.

"Then I guess you aren't worthy of him," I whisper sadly.

"I never said I was."

The normally bright and airy room is cool as I step into it. The silk curtains are drawn closed, keeping out the light. The darkness dulls the buttery yellow walls. Quietly, I close the door and step into the bedroom, careful not to disturb the peaceful bedside vigil being held.

I swallow my apprehension and focus on the heartbreaking expressions marring the faces surrounding the beautiful, petite werecat. Her short brown hair has lengthened slightly and her cheeks have hollowed during her coma. I can't help but feel somewhat responsible for the panther's state. Galena was on guard duty, protecting me, the night she was attacked.

My eyes skim the room in search of Asher, but he isn't here. A warm, welcoming limb wraps around my shoulders, pulling me to a hard chest. These arms always make me feel safe, and for a moment, I'm grateful not to witness this scene alone.

"Is this . . . a bad time?" I ask in a whisper.

"Of course not, cutie. She'll be glad you're here," Callan assures calmly.

"Asher mentioned coming to check on Fiona and Galena. Was he here?"

"Yeah. He's in the study with the rest of the clan now. Pay your respects and I'll take you to him," Callan offers.

I make my way toward the grey-haired, plump woman stroking her daughter's pale face. Once there, I place my hand on the caretaker's shoulder and squeeze lightly. A frail hand reaches up and covers mine, tapping an appreciative acknowledgment.

"Has there been any change, Fiona?"

Somber yellow cat eyes meet mine. My heart sinks as the clowder's alpha stares at me for a moment, with a lost expression, before speaking in a solemn voice. "No," she answers.

"I'm sorry, Fi," I say in a grave tone.

The panther sighs and pats my hand again. "Aye. Me too."

A few moments later, Callan ushers us out, allowing Fiona private time with her daughter.

"I can't believe Galena still isn't awake," I mumble offhanded.

"It's what we're meeting about now." Callan guides us into the study.

As soon as I step into the room, Asher prowls toward me and snatches me away from his younger brother, planting a gentle kiss on my forehead and tucking me into his side.

"Onix has agreed to the meeting," Nassa rasps. She's looking everywhere but at Gage.

"That's excellent news," Keegan replies. "Thank you for reaching out, Nassa."

I meet McKenna's narrowed sapphire eyes before she rolls them. *She's always so lovely.*

"Who, or what, should I say, is Onix?" I question.

"Onix is a dark mystic, a very powerful witch. They practice their mysticism through spell weaving," Asher interjects. "Because they only speak through telepathy, they're forced to use their hand gestures to create their enchantments. Hence the term spell weaver."

"And you think this dark mystic—," Gage starts.

"Onix," Nassa states flatly, cutting him off.

"Onix," he repeats with a slight annoyance to his tone, "can help Galena?"

Nassa shrugs, continuing to avoid Gage's eyes. "The mystic might know something about the dark magic surrounding the panther's aura," she explains. *Okay, this isn't awkward.*

"When do we leave?" I ask, trying to cut the tension.

Asher's callous laugh vibrates in my ear. "No, siren. Not this time."

"Excuse me?" I step away from his hold. *What the hell?*

"Dark mystics live in solitude and are aloof. They are highly evolved and intelligent and their messages can be . . . cryptic and confusing. The human mind is fragile. A mundane who goes before them could become mentally unstable," Asher points out.

"Are you saying if I look upon this *spell weaver,* I'll go mad?" I clarify.

Asher's expression tightens. "It's possible and it's not a risk I'm taking with you."

We hold one another's headstrong glares. "I can handle myself, Asher."

"Your light source is useless in a magical cavern. Fear and pain don't register with spell weavers. Do you understand?" he asks. "You will stay here."

I narrow my eyes at his dominance and turn to Nassa. "Who else is going?" I ask her, ignoring Asher as he mutters under his breath about how *stubborn* and *infuriating* I am.

"My candle magic is strong enough now to transport four," Nassa replies.

"Then Keegan, McKenna and I will join you, Nassa," Asher states.

"Actually, dark prince, I'll be joining you and Nassa," Gage interrupts. "Not negotiable."

Nassa's entire demeanor becomes crestfallen at his words. "Gallagher," she growls.

Gage leans on the wall behind him, bending one of his legs so his foot is resting on it.

"There's no way in hell you're going to a spell weaver without me, buttercup."

At his severe tone, the rest of us avert our gazes, knowing what's coming next. Never engage a sorceress. Never. Nassa snaps her angered attention to Gage, dramatically flicking her black and purple streaked hair over her petite shoulder.

"I don't need your protection."

"I'm not interested in protecting you."

"Then why the fuck do you want to come?" she challenges.

He shrugs and pulls out a cigarette, rolling it through his fingers. "I'd like to meet Onix."

"What?" she says on an aggravated breath.

Gage casually pushes off the wall. "Magical caverns and shit sound fun."

Nassa stands taller as Gage makes his way to her, looming over her tiny frame.

"Fun?" she repeats.

"Like we were supposed to have had last night." Gage taunts her in a seductive voice.

I inwardly cringe. If I was on the receiving end of Gage's panty-dropping looks and sexy tone, I think I would be a puddle of water by now. Point Nassa for holding her own.

"Fuck off, Gallagher." She spins to leave, but he gently grabs her arm.

"I'm coming with you. End of discussion," he states, staring deeply into her wide eyes.

"I don't want you to," Nassa counters.

"This isn't about what you want, buttercup. It's about what I need," he replies.

After a few moments of boring their heated gazes into one another, Nassa nods, giving in.

"Fine." She pulls her elbow out of his grasp angrily. "Come. Maybe I'll get lucky and you'll go mad."

"One can only hope," McKenna mumbles under her breath behind me.

Gage lifts his unlit cigarette, bringing it to his mouth. "I thought you liked it when I came, buttercup," he murmurs. "Besides, you've already turned me batshit crazy."

"I really despise you." Nassa releases a tight smile before turning on her heels.

Gage watches her retreating form before snapping his unlit cigarette in two and throwing it against the wall. "Goddamn stubborn-ass sorceress," he barks out.

Asher tilts his chin toward Gage. "You and Nassa? How's that working out for you?"

"Screw you, dark prince," Gage snaps and saunters out of the room leisurely.

"Guess that only leaves one more spot for me," I exclaim, victoriously.

"No," Asher replies.

I fold my arms over my chest and give him a pointed look. "I don't care how dark and broodingly sexy you are. The next time you say no to me, I will end your existence."

Asher arches an eyebrow. "Using your daggers?"

I cock my head in challenge. "Care to find out?"

A silent beat passes between us. "You win, siren," he concedes matter-of-factly.

"Holy shit! Did anyone else feel that?" Callan questions and we all look around, confused.

"Feel what, baby?" Abby asks her mate with an amused expression.

"The chill? I think hell just froze over," he responds with a shit-eating grin. "I do believe his highness, the great and menacing Asher St. Michael, just submitted to his *human* mate."

Keegan laughs. "I believe it's called being whipped."

Asher just shrugs. "Submission is underrated. Isn't that right, siren?" He looks me up and down with a sexy eye roam. "Not to mention, I'll be there to protect you."

I smile at his antics. "Now that you've submitted to me, perhaps I'll protect you."

"Good to know you both will be using protection during submission," Callan muses.

My eyes roll and slide to the adorable gargoyle. "Charming."

"In all seriousness, be careful. Dark mystics aren't to be taken lightly," Keegan warns.

"I always am, brother." Asher assures him with a pat on the back.

Abby takes my hand in hers. "Come on, Eves. I have the perfect outfit for a cavern trip."

I groan as she drags me out of the room. "I take it back, I don't want to go."

જીન્છ

The smell of musty, damp earth assaults me as we make our way down the darkened tunnel composed of rocks and soil. The stench is off-putting. It smells like the inside of a damaged soul. There are no plants, no animals, and no life. I shiver at the thought as we descend into the cool, stale air.

The knee-high, flat boots Abby chose for me sink into the dirt path with each step. I try to keep my breathing even in an attempt to not panic as we walk through the earthy passageway. An almost impossible feat since it feels like it's closing in on me with every movement.

I sigh and wipe the sweat and dirt from my hands onto my jeans. Thank goodness Abby forced me to wear the dark ones. After what feels like an eternity, Asher stops the group from moving any further.

My lips part when I see the opening in the cavern's mouth. Darkness extends for miles, lit only by the amber glow of a small, ancient city built within the grotto. I take in the sight with unease as my gaze floats between two castles, sitting atop a peak, looking down on the ancient city.

"Welcome to Xnuk Ek'," Asher says.

"Xnuk Ek'?" I repeat with trepidation.

"It's Mayan for evening star, love," Gage answers.

Why does that sound familiar?

"Evening star?" I play with the words. "Doesn't Lucifer's name mean the morning star?"

Gage slides his gaze to me. "This realm is named after Venus. It's the first star to shine in the evening and the last to fade at dawn. It's said that Lucifer was created at dawn. The mystic's statement is poetic when you think about it, love."

"How so?" I ask.

Gage places an unlit cigarette to his mouth before he speaks. "They will be the last to fade at the hands of the one born at dawn," he replies, flicking open his lighter, and at the same time, inhaling the nicotine from his habit.

I find myself in a trance, watching Gage's agitated movements with curiosity. His face is shadowed as he shakes his head and draws in another deep inhale. The glowing embers of his cigarette reflect briefly in his sea-green eyes. I'm curious as to what has him so worked up.

"The settlement is divided into separate compounds." Nassa's voice cuts through my stupor, pulling my focus back to the ancient city below us. "To the right, where you see the small mud huts with the straw roofs, that's where the less-powerful mystics live. On your left, the stone building is the Temple of Rituals. In the middle, you'll see the Pyramids of the Sun and Moon. They're laid out on a geometric pattern for sacrifices. The large fortress on the ledge, the one with the fireflies circling the drum tower, houses Aigle, the light mystic. The backlit monument in between the two castles is Ometeotl, the Lord of Duality. The palace on the right, surrounded by shadows, is where the dark mystic can be found," she points out.

"What's the alcove with all the lit candles?" I ask.

"Sacred ground. Where the dual mystics were supposedly created," Asher adds. "One of light and one of dark."

My eyes lift to the enclosed dome of the township, and a feeling of dread washes over me. I've come to the realization that there is only one way in and out. *Crap.*

"Let's get this over with, yeah?" Asher sighs and steps toward the dark castle.

Half an hour later, we reach the first gatehouse protecting the fortress' entrance. As we cross over the bridge, Nassa tugs on the back of my shirt, forcing me to face her.

I offer the sorceress a curious expression while she silently takes my hand, placing a smooth stone in it. Meeting my gaze, she folds her hand around mine so the mineral is secure.

"It's eye agate mixed in with beryl and mugglestone. It will protect you from dark magic. The mugglestone sends evil spells back to the sender, acting like a mirror, so hold it at all times, Eve. I mean it," Nassa instructs. "Don't fuck around with this. Do you understand?"

I nod and offer a small smile. "Yeah, okay. Thanks."

She tightens her grip on my hand and begins to quietly chant in Latin. Within seconds, I feel a warmth wrap around my head, like a blanket. Then suddenly, it's gone.

"What the hell was that?" I whisper.

"I placed a protective barrier around your mind. The dark mystics speak in circles. Like Asher explained, sometimes it's too much for humans to take in. You will be no use to anyone if you go mad," she adds. "Don't tell Asher or Gage I've spelled you, okay?"

I pull my brows together. "Why not?"

Her expression turns to surprise. "I thought you wanted to prove to them you could do this? No offense, but your chances of surviving a spell weaver without my magic are slim to none. You'd be in a padded cell faster than you can blink."

"You're helping me . . . to show Asher and Gage up?" I question with skepticism.

"Trust me, it's more for my enjoyment than yours," she offers me a secretive smile.

"Where is your Noir?" Her familiar is usually present.

"Crows hate mystics," she replies offhandedly.

"All right then," I mumble lamely to myself and we follow the group.

Every so often, Nassa says something that reminds me she is the niece of Sorceress Lunette. Both are unique and oddly quirky. *Must run in the family. Or is it a witch thing? Focus, Eve.*

"Any idea on how we get in?" Asher asks, staring at the wooden door we've approached.

Gage lifts the circular black wrought iron handle and pushes the door open with force.

Asher nods his head. "Logical."

"Good to know I'm useful for something," Gage states and we step in.

It takes a moment for my eyes to adjust to the inky inner ward. It's pitch black and frigid.

"We should probably make our way to the keep since it's the highest point. My guess is it's where we'll find Onix," Asher suggests, taking my hand in his and pulling me closer.

"What is a keep?" I inquire.

Asher looks at me as if I've asked him what chocolate was. "The strongest and most secure place in the middle of a castle," he responds. "Common knowledge, siren."

"Guess I missed Professor Davidson's lecture on castle structures," I banter.

"You should have paid less attention to the sexy, awesome gargoyle to your left and shown more interest in the incredibly dull and astute architecture professor," he reprimands.

"Lesson learned," I quip sarcastically as he drags me through the dark.

After navigating a few circular stone staircases and exiting the tower, we make our way down a long hall. At the end is an open arch exuding a faint blue light. On instinct, one of my hands tightens around the stone Nassa gave me while the other squeezes Asher's.

As we step into the cerulean glow, my lips part. Across from where we stand is a stone balcony, overlooking the ancient city below. It runs the length of a full wall and has floor-to-ceiling slim arched openings. It's framed on either side by unmoving, sheer burgundy curtains, hidden behind an oversized brown and gold marble spiral column.

Huge palm trees are sprinkled throughout the space. *Apparently dark mystics prefer island motif.* I snort-laugh at my own thought before my eyes land on an oversized brass birdcage. The cage is empty but it's emanating a golden glow. *Odd.*

"Guess that would explain Noir's mystic aversion," I whisper, nodding to the enclosure.

Nassa gives me a told-you-so glance and focuses her attention on a low glass table decorated with a crystal carafe and glasses. Both are filled with a red liquid secreting vapor.

"The cage contains a protected portal," she rasps.

A slight motion to the left has me shifting my focus to an . . . um . . . hermaphrodite? *What in the hell?* Though the androgynous figure's body is curvy and voluminous like a woman's, its face is angular and strong like a male's. The stranger's skin is pure white with gold tribal tattoos from its neck to its bare feet.

The genderless being is wearing a brass belt adorned with a slim, long piece of cloth covering a noticeable bulge under the fabric between its legs. Brass covers hide the nipples on its generous female breasts. The only additional piece of clothing is a sleeveless, floor-length robe made of red and gold silk. It has a high collar that sits straight like peacock's tail.

The being sits motionless. It doesn't even acknowledge our presence. A mass of long, thick, curly black hair is pushed off its face with a brass and ruby crown featuring the head of a snake. A chill runs through me and I try not to pee my pants when I take note of the chocolate boa constrictor rolling over the hermaphrodite's body, like some weird fashion accessory. *Holy crap this is insane.*

The unknown entity is relaxing casually on a red velvet chaise lounge, ignoring our mere existence. I study its snow-white face, blood-red lips and black-outlined white eyes, which are focused on the oddity in the middle of the room. Just when things can't get stranger . . .

A liquid female form floats over a circular pond of water, elegantly decorated with large jade lily pads and enormous white lotus flowers. Her naked figure is completely transparent. I can see right through her body and her skin is in constant motion, smooth like glass.

This live water statue is the female replica of the being on the chaise. Every detail of her body matches, except this one is undressed and her skin is clear, completely without matter. It's like I've stepped into one of Gustav Klimt's paintings.

"Mystics love erotic dualism, love." Gage's voice is at my ear in a low tone. "Even though the male has gender neutral parts, he is the dual form of the fluid female in the pond."

"This is a complete mindfuck," I exhale.

"You haven't seen anything yet, siren," Asher groans.

"Why have you come?" Neither being's lips move, but the sound escapes the female.

"Thought transference." Asher reminds me of how they communicate.

"I'm totally going to need therapy after this." I meet Asher's questioning expression. "I mean, more so than I already do."

"Noted." He smirks, amused.

Nassa pushes her shoulders back and begins to take a step toward the being on the chaise, but Gage grabs her hand before she can, refusing to release her.

The sorceress looks down at their connection with irritation. "Let go, Gallagher."

"I don't think I can, buttercup," he admits on a long breath.

6 Cruelty of Youth

A dark shadow passes over us and a flash of red catches my eye. I watch the creature on the sofa, whose pallid eyes have turned cherry, with apprehension. My jaw clenches as I push down the fear and compel myself not to run, but instead to stay where I am, next to Asher.

"Why have you come?" the water form asks again with unmoving lips.

Nassa squirms out of Gage's death grip, using a spell. *Clever.* She huffs out her annoyance and authoritatively approaches the floating liquid female, unafraid. *Girl has balls.*

"To seek truth in the endless days the shifter suffers from," Nassa answers.

"One who cannot be heard must be silenced," the

mystic replies cryptically.

"Are you implying someone hurt her on purpose, so she wouldn't talk?" the sorceress attempts to decipher. "Why? Galena is an innocent in all of this."

"Wounded conditions are consequences of betrayal," the male thought-transfers.

My vision slides to Asher, who has his brows knitted. He shifts on his feet in agitation.

"Betrayal?" Nassa repeats in a confused voice.

"Bring forth the children of light and dark, sorceress," the feminine form demands.

Nassa's steady gaze flicks to mine before lowering to my hand wrapped around the stone she gave to me. Her intense stare never drops from my closed fist, while Asher guides us toward the mystic. Once he and I approach the liquid figure, Nassa steps away, and in an instant, Gage is by her side.

I smirk to myself at the way he's slightly in front of her. *Not protecting her my ass.*

"So young and beautiful. Does he still love you, daughter of Heaven?" the measured female voice asks, and I'm hit with the strongest sense of déjà vu. "I smell your aching soul. You yearn for him. And he you," the voice trails off and my lips part in recognition.

I lift my gaze to the water figure. "It was you, in the field?" I half-question, half-state, recalling the vision I'd had when staying with Marcus and the Manhattan Clan, in New York.

"When you get to Heaven, do you think they'll let you bring your protector?" The male voice enters the conversation and I spin to face the genderless-looking creature on the chaise.

"Siren?" Asher says while watching me worriedly.

"D-do you hear them?"

"No," he answers, looking between the two beings. *Crap.*

"The prince, he's so full of darkness," the woman whispers flirtatiously from behind me.

Her words cause my heart rate to increase and my pulse to make itself present in my ears.

"You're one of flesh and spirit now. Your dark side radiates almost as much as the light. You're tainted."

"I don't understand," I say on a quiet exhale, as I did in the vision.

"Understand what, love?" Gage asks. *Clearly, I'm the only one who can hear them.*

"Your mistakes are great, innocent one. You chose to be tested. To prove yourself. Falsehoods have put you in harm's way. A narcissistically distracted bloodline trait, Eve." The male voice rises in anger as it floats through my mind again, bringing with it a haze.

The hand clutching Asher's begins to shake, along with the rest of my body, and my vision becomes fuzzy. My muscles ache, causing me to release a painful groan. I squeeze my eyes closed in an attempt to alleviate the strain on my brain, but it's not helping. Psychedelic, nonsensical images run through my mind, both confusing and scaring me simultaneously.

"Eve, remember you're protected," Nassa says from somewhere in the distance.

I let my mind recall the warm embrace her spell enfolded me in, and my body begins to relax, pushing out the bizarre images. Once I'm calm, I lift my challenging eyes to the mystic and stand straighter, resisting Asher's protective attempt to pull me closer.

"Wrong human to fuck with, psycho."

"Siren!" My nickname is a warning off Asher's lips.

At my lack of response to his admonishment, Asher steps between the mystic and myself.

I scowl. "Who did Galena betray and why was she hurt?"

"Stupid child," the female voice answers.

In response, I dip my chin, looking over my left shoulder at her.

"The shifter's soul suffers for pleasure and protection," she continues.

"We need to help Galena. How do we do that?" Asher asks.

"You must let what happens happen as it is meant to," she answers.

"Enough of your riddles, spell weaver. Who. Did. This?" Asher asks with a harsh tone.

Guess everyone can hear them now. I inhale a relieved breath.

"I did." A baritone intonation cascades over us, causing goosebumps to form on my skin.

With shocked expressions, the four of us turn at the same time.

Asmodeus saunters into the keep. The demon of lust's tall, long-limbed, muscular body is outfitted in his signature look, black leather pants, black boots, and a white button-down shirt, reminding me that he looks more like a rock star than the King of the Nine Hells.

"What are you doing here, my lord?" Nassa manages to question, slightly bowing.

As he approaches us, the hairs on the back of my neck stand at attention. Cool, black irises train themselves on Nassa before shifting to me, roaming over my body. The heat in his gaze, once again, makes my skin crawl.

"Eve," he drawls out the seductive greeting.

"Creepy uncle," I counter.

The demon of lust stops within a foot of us and slides his focus back to Nassa. "My dear niece, you're lovely. It's a shame your beauty is marred by the supernatural trash you've chosen to keep company with these days."

"What the fuck do you want, Asmodeus?" Asher asks briskly.

The demon lord's cold eyes bore into my protector. "It would seem you are not as astute as one would expect a gargoyle prince to be," he admonishes. "Do you think a dark entity as powerful as Onix would grant you an audience without my favor?"

Asher barks out a laugh. "I didn't realize mystics played on Team Lucifer."

"Your wit is infamous, dark prince." Asmodeus's lips lift disingenuously. "Onix is indebted to me. Hence why I am here today. To collect the balance due."

Asher's eyes flash with anger. "Why would a dark mystic indebt themselves to a demon?"

"In exchange for Onix's assistance with a . . . personal matter, I've agreed to protect this realm."

"And what exactly is the debt owed to you, Asmodeus?" Gage interjects.

"My mate was recently beheaded. I'm in the market

for a new one." He pins Asher with a cold, challenging stare. "Your kind responds to the eye-for-an-eye principle."

I stiffen at the demon's statement. Asher's raven wings violently snap out of his back and his posture takes on a rigid warrior's stance. A low, warning rumble releases from his chest, directed at the demon lord's insinuation as he steps slightly in front of me, shielding me.

"The fairy queen's death is on you, not us, Asmodeus," Gage reminds.

The black of the demon's eyes deepens. "Do not speak of my dead mate."

A sick horror makes its way into my gut. "How does Galena fit into this?"

"Galena is my—how shall I put this delicately? Favorite mistress." The demon watches our stunned expressions, delighting in our shock and disgust.

"You lie," Asher accuses.

"I do, dark prince. In fact, I do so often and as much as I can. However, I never tell untruths when it comes to a beautiful woman and sex. Especially about one that is as good on her knees as the panther-shifter is," he taunts.

"Galena would never consort with the likes of you," Asher says, stepping menacingly toward Asmodeus, and my heart pounds against my rib cage out of fear.

Gage grabs Asher's upper arms, holding him back. "Easy."

"When my kitten lover discovered I had taken Lady Finella as my mate, she was . . . upset. In her blind rage, Galena threatened to go to you, Asher, and warn you of what my queen and I were conspiring to do with regard to the Eternal Forest and Priestesses. That, I couldn't let happen."

"So you bartered with Onix to spell her?" Nassa deciphers.

"A dark mystic's spell weaving is impenetrable and undetectable. Onix placed Galena in a state of unconsciousness, essentially silencing her before she could reach Asher and tell him of my musings," the demon confirms. "In exchange for the hex, I offered the mystics protection from my boss and the dark army. Everybody wins, really."

"If Galena was such a nuisance, why not just kill her?" Gage asks, pointedly.

The demon smiles, holding a wicked secret. I swallow hard.

"Insurance. I know how much Fiona, and her daughter, mean to the dark prince and his clan. Therefore, I knew that when the time came, she would serve a purpose, alive."

At the release of Asmodeus's words, several of his guards enter the chamber, taking their stances around the room, including his Samoan bodyguard, Isaac.

"You've cursed her as a means of blackmailing me?" Asher snaps.

"I will allow Onix to return Galena to her healthy state, in exchange for Eve."

"You're out of your fucking mind, demon," Asher replies coldly.

Asmodeus cocks his head. "Surely, dark prince, you wouldn't allow the woman who raised you and your brothers as her own, to suffer the loss of a child? Imagine how devastated Fiona would be to discover the death of her only daughter happened at your selfish hands?"

My heart sinks and my stomach roils at the pointed

threat. He's right. Fiona would never survive losing Galena. I study Asher's erratic breathing pattern. He understands too.

"You will get your hands on Eve over my stone body," Asher bites out.

"I'd be happy to arrange that, Your Highness," the demon offers, motioning to his guards.

Gage scoffs. "You know what I think, demon? I think you're full of shit. I'm sure there is another way to save Galena without negotiating with the devil himself."

Nassa solemnly shakes her head. "There isn't, Gallagher." Her voice is defeated. "A mystic's spell can only be broken by the spell weavers themselves. Only Onix can heal Galena."

I slide my focus to Gage and observe the way he drags his top teeth over his bottom lip in a combination of frustration and contemplation. *Crap. This is going to end badly.*

"Clock's ticking, future king. What will it be? Eve or Galena's death?" Asmodeus prods.

I step around Asher, willing my voice not to crack. "Eve."

The demon's lips turn up gleefully.

"No fucking way, siren," Asher barks and tries yanking me to him.

I turn and level him with my glare. "Let me go."

"Over. My. Cold. Stone. Body." He bites out each word through a tight jaw.

"Asher—," I begin, but he cuts me off.

"Is that what you want? Me ceasing to exist?" Asher tries to sway me emotionally. "I will fight until my last breath, siren, before I allow you to go anywhere with this piece of shit."

"If something happens to Galena that we could have prevented, Fiona will be devastated. It's the only way, Ash. You have to let me go," I plead.

"Never," he growls. "You're mine."

"Let go," I whisper.

"No."

"This is the only way to save her. I've got this."

"Fiona would not want you to sacrifice yourself like this," Asher says.

"Don't do this, love," Gage adds. "We will find another way. I promise you."

"You don't even know Galena well enough to make this sacrifice on her behalf," Asher inserts desperately. "Giving yourself over is not the solution."

"Fiona is like a mother to you and your brothers, Asher. She raised you, which makes her and Galena family. I promised to protect your clan, as your mate and future queen," I remind him, taking a small step back, out of his grip, toward the demon king.

"Siren. Do. Not. Do. This," Asher implores, taking a step toward me.

"I'm sorry." I take another step so I'm out of his reach.

"You promised." Asher holds my watery eyes with an angry glare. "You said you wouldn't leave me of your own accord. This, what you are doing, is choosing to leave me."

I shake my head slowly. "I love you. This is simply my way of protecting our family."

"Siren." Asher's voice cracks.

"It's the only way." I ignore the desperation reflecting back at me in his eyes and turn to face the demon. "Tell Onix to release Galena before I go with you, or there is no deal."

Asmodeus smirks wickedly at me. "The cruelty of youth and innocence." His voice draws out as he nods his head to the two entities which make up the dark mystic.

After a long, tense pause, the male's voice breaks the silence. "It has been done, my lord."

With my back to Asher, I inhale. "Asher, text Keegan and make sure Galena is awake."

"Eve," he growls.

"Do it, or I'll have Gage do it," I reply.

"Fuck," he spits out. A few moments later, I hear him sigh. "She's awake."

I take a step toward Asmodeus, and Asher grabs me, spinning me to face him. When my eyes meet his, my heart stops in my chest. My resolve crumbles instantly. "Stop," I implore.

"I won't let you do this." Asher's voice is even and raw.

"It's already been done," I retort and drag myself out of his safe arms.

Immediately, I'm yanked into Isaac's large and rough hold. Asher whips out his Angelic Sword and Gage steps closer. "Get your fucking hands off her, asshole."

"Don't ever try to outsmart a demon lord. We win every time," Asmodeus mocks.

"I will come for you," Asher states firmly, holding my gaze.

"Trust in me, Asher," I release in a strong voice and his brows pull together.

"Checkmate," the demon king taunts my protector.

"Compel me," I whisper and all eyes swing my way.

"Pardon me, daughter of Heaven?" the demon lord inquires.

"Demand me to give up my free will and join you by your side," I suggest.

A small evil glint appears in the demon's eyes. "You want to play rough in front of your love? I underestimated you, Eve. I think I'll rather enjoy having you as my mate."

"Then demand it of me, or I won't go," I counter.

"My lord," the mystic interrupts with urgency, probably sensing what I'm about to do, but Asmodeus's ego is too large to not meet my challenge. His hand lifts, silencing Onix.

The demon lord steps to me with a snarl on his lips. "Something you'll come to learn about me, as the demon of lust, I don't mind taking what I want by force. Today, I curse you. I strip you of your free will. From this day forth, anyone who you've ever loved, shall suffer. You will fight for only me. Be loyal to only me. You will be by my side as my eternal slave while your heart feels nothing but anguish. Your soul belongs to the darkness now."

I lift my head in a show of defiance and Asmodeus steps in front of me, snatching my chin between his fingers harshly, forcing me to tip my head back and look him in the eyes.

"Welcome to the end of your existence, Eve Collins," he sneers.

I release a short, biting laugh into his face.

Asmodeus narrows his eyes. "Something funny, daughter of Heaven?"

"Checkmate," I say softly, and Isaac drops my arms as if they've burnt him.

A light is released from my hands, swirling around the demon king and singeing his skin.

"What is happening?" Asmodeus roars, looking around in confusion while dropping the hold he had on my face.

I inhale and step to Asher's side, lifting my hand slowly and revealing the stone. "Mugglestone. It deflects darkness, sending the curse back to its originator. By compelling me to be yours, you've just damned yourself, Asmodeus. Everything you've obliged from me is now your burden to contend with."

The King of the Nine Hells just stares with a perplexed look on his face.

A low growl vibrates from Asher's chest, expanding his wings and raising his sword.

"Seems my queen is much smarter than you will ever be, demon," he snaps.

"This isn't over," the demon spits out.

Asmodeus's skin singes and smokes, releasing the putrid smell of sulfur. I swallow the bile threatening to rise in my throat and take a small step back. One by one, I watch as the demon king's minions disappear, leaving blue flames in their wake, including Isaac.

Nassa steps in front of Asher's slightly lowered sword and stares down her uncle. "It is over. You see, I had the light mystic, Aigle, spell the mugglestone. As you are aware, dear uncle, a spell weaver's enchantment cannot be undone, except by the original weaver."

Cold, black eyes lift in anger. "You set me up?"

Nassa shrugs. "Look at it as more of a compliment. I've learned from the best. As soon as I assessed Galena's condition, I picked up on Onix's spell. Don't ever try to outsmart a sorceress. We win. Every. Single. Time." She throws his words back at him with disdain.

"I warned your father to destroy you at birth. You're a disgrace to the demon blood running through your veins," he snips.

Nassa bends at the waist while the demon falls to his knees in pain. "Since we're discussing the cruelty of my youth, you should know that I did this. To end you," she pushes out through gritted teeth. "I had the light mystic add a differing layer to the spell. Your hexes have been returned to you. Your free will—gone. You now belong to the divine." She smirks. "Your soul belongs to the light. Welcome to the end of *your* existence, uncle."

Asmodeus's eyes widen at her statement and she steps back triumphantly.

"Christ. Your manipulative side is hot, buttercup," Gage says.

"Keep it in your pants, Gallagher," Nassa replies.

"I'll offer you redemption, Asmodeus," I announce at a barely audible level.

"What?" Nassa and Gage bark out at the same time.

I step toward the suffering demon. "I'll release you of the reversal, allowing you to go back to serving the dark army, and your boss, conditionally."

"Siren?" Asher's voice flitters over me.

"He's not meant to serve the light," I explain. "Everyone deserves redemption."

"Meaning?" Asmodeus grits out of clenched teeth while trying to suck air into his lungs.

"Nassa will have Aigle release the reversal spell if you

promise never to come after my family or me again. That includes Nassa and the sorceresses, Fiona and the clowder, and the entire gargoyle race. No harm must come to any of them, ever, at the hands of you or your minions. In addition, you must also promise never to go after innocent souls."

"You do realize I guard the Nine Gates of Hell?" the demon challenges.

"I'm not saying you can't take deserving souls, just not innocent ones," I clarify.

"The dark army will continue to hunt you, regardless of my involvement," he adds.

"Understood."

Asmodeus's face pinches as another wave of pain from the light hits him. "You'll release me of the divine sentence if I promise not to harm you, the gargoyle race, the panthers, or the sorceresses?" he reiterates.

"It will be as if you never existed in my world. Your part in this . . . is over," I declare.

"Deal."

My eyes shift to Nassa. Her jaw is tight. After a stubborn pause, she nods her head.

"Gallagher, I need you to teleport us to the light castle, so I can make the request."

"At your service, buttercup." He smirks and wraps his arms around her waist.

Within seconds, they vanish, only to reappear moments later. The sorceress' shoulders rise and fall with a heavy and unhappy sigh. "Aigle has agreed."

I purse my lips, hoping I made the right decision. "Thank you."

Without warning, Asmodeus's skin stops charring and

his overall health improves. Slowly, he rises to his feet and a small smile plays on the sides of his lips. "You are a formidable adversary, daughter of Heaven."

"It was a team effort." I cut an appreciative side-glance to Nassa.

Asmodeus straightens himself before pushing his hair back with a steady hand. "It would seem then our time together is over—for now. Consider my end of the agreement fulfilled."

I dip my chin and Asmodeus disappears. I turn to face the group, cross my arms, and exhale a relieved breath. "One demon king down. That just leaves a half-demon and half-gargoyle, a gargoyle king, the dark army, and Lucifer himself," I point out.

Gage lifts his brows. "You're planning to take them out one by one, love?"

"Yes."

"Ambitious," Gage responds with a lightness to his tone.

"Or stupid," Nassa argues with a snort.

I take a deep, cleansing breath. Asher shifts and his irate gaze collides with mine. There's darkness behind his eyes, an intensity that both scares and enthralls me.

"What do you think? Ambitious or stupid?" I ask him.

"I think . . . my opinion didn't matter to you twenty minutes ago, siren, so why the hell does it matter to you now?" he spits out. "Let's get the fuck out of here. I'm done."

My stomach drops at the feeling Asher is done with more than just this realm.

7 Silence

My gaze roams over the room before landing on Asher. His eyes darken when they lift and lock onto mine. My skin tightens and burns under his scrutiny. It's amazing how he can destroy me with just a cool caress of his unreadable expression.

I study his hands as they clench and unclench in aggravation before an angry Fiona pops into my sightline. The plump woman has her small hands on her full hips and her pale mouth is pressed into a disappointed line. *Crap.* I brace myself for the inevitable lecture.

The alpha of the Pishyakan clowder pins me with her yellow-green cat eyes. "I don't know whether ta hug ye or swat yer behind, lass," she scolds, her brogue thick.

Asher's mouth turns up in a smug, agreeable smile. *Damn gargoyle.* I open my mouth to defend my actions but Fiona cuts me a harsh glance, which silences me immediately.

"Don't ye dare try en argue wit me," she warns. One of Fiona's hands comes off her hips and she wildly motions toward Keegan, Asher and Gage as they observe our interaction. "I raised dese here hoodlums, en I won't tolerate ye're mouthin' off ta me. Aye?"

"Yes, ma'am," I mutter.

She sighs in displeasure. "As much as I luv ye, lass, I am very disappointed in ye, Eve. Ta put ye'reself en danger, fer me daughter, 'twas brave, but very stupid," she reprimands. "Yer like one of me own now. Do ye really think me heart would survive dat type o' sacrifice? One child fer another?"

When I don't answer immediately, she begins to pace and mutter crossly under her breath in Gaelic. My heart plummets at her flustered state, knowing I caused it.

I frown. "I didn't think about it like that, Fi. All I was focused on was that I had a way to save Galena, so I took it," I explain. "It was never my intent to hurt you. I just couldn't face breaking your heart, knowing we could have saved her and did nothing."

The shifter's shoulders sag. "Yer age makes ye unwise. Me heart, 'tis broken. Galena's choices will not go unpunished. However, when Asher told me o' yer actions, lass, 'twas da final hammer dat smashed me heart inta pieces."

My lips part at her sternness and my demeanor becomes crestfallen.

"If something happened ta ye, I would have never forgiven meself. 'Tis time ye start thinking wit' yer head, instead o' yer heart, because if ye don't, 'tis not only me heart dat will be broken," she cautions, stepping around me furiously.

My gaze locks onto Asher's. "We're done," he snips before shifting his attention to Keegan. "Let's go help Fiona and the rest of the clan deal with Galena, yeah?"

Keegan averts his eyes and simply nods his agreement, following Asher out of the room.

"You all right, love?" Gage's voice breaks my contemplation.

"I won't apologize for what I did. It was the right thing to do, Gage."

He lifts his palms in surrender. "I never said it wasn't."

"It's too bad not everyone shares your sentiment."

Gage flashes me a devastating smile. "Asher likes to brood. The dark prince is just pissed that you put yourself in danger. I have no doubt he will grant you forgiveness, later."

I shrug, pretending disinterest. "Or not. Maybe I don't need his highness's pardon."

He stares me down with amusement. "Or not." He shrugs. "Fiona is right about one thing, you need to start thinking with both your head and heart. Using only one will get you killed."

"Meaning?" I inquire.

Stormy eyes slide their focus to the glass pane of the window, watching the sorceress standing near the pool. "Meaning, like it or not, you are one half of a mated pair. You now have two hearts and souls to consider when you make decisions. Not just one. In the future, it would be wise for you to take a reflective moment and consider the dark prince in your choices before you jump into action. I assume you'd want him to show you the same type of respect."

"What if I can't always do that?"

His gaze slides back to mine. "Then there is no need to be mated to him, is there?"

Silence is like a dark omen. It claws away at your psyche, gnawing on each and every one of your insecurities. Mutely, the stillness judges you until you can't sense potential danger because everything is so contrived you become unsure if it really exists outside of your consciousness.

Asher storms into the family room, slamming the double doors and locking them behind him. I swallow, questioning whether or not he's a mirage. Since returning hours ago from dealing with Fiona and Galena, he has yet to speak a word to me.

The depth of his silence is both unnerving and mystifying. At the moment, his presence darkens the room like a shadow. My eyes slide shut involuntarily as the intimidating gargoyle prowls toward me.

The intense level of his fury emanates off of him in dangerous currents, like a warning. When I regain courage, I open my lids and slide my gaze past his, ignoring the throbbing sound vibrating in my ears from my unease.

Once Asher approaches me, he cages me in with his body, placing his palms on either side of me, allowing them to rest on the pool table, which at the moment is the only thing keeping me upright. Heat radiates off his body, commanding my attention.

There is a pained, desperate ache in his expression. I go to speak but stop when Asher lets out a disapproving groan. "There is nothing you can say in this moment, siren, that will take away the panic and complete fucking terror you caused by offering yourself to Asmodeus. So don't speak."

I flinch at the statement. He just used a tone that I'm sure will haunt me for weeks to come. Cold, stormy eyes challenge me to try to say something in my own defense. I don't. Instead, I bite my tongue and permit Asher's cool stare to go straight through me.

I remind myself that this is what we do. Our relationship is a game of chess, built off strategy and power. We both hold our positions, awaiting the other's next move. His tongue darts out, lightly running over his perfect lips, and I watch with morbid fascination.

Sensing the shift in my emotions, Asher's body takes on a cool, confident sense of arrogance, knowing what his closeness is stirring inside of me. Damn him for always having the upper hand in this game. *Crap. I need to get my hormones under control.*

I shift, aware of every inch of his body and the minute space of air hanging between us. Each of my nerve endings is alive, and the mate mark on my lower back pulses with anticipation. I wish he'd stop looming over me and causing desire to run wildly through my veins.

"Don't," falls from my lips in an odd whispered plea.

"Don't what, siren?" His voice is ragged and thick as his hot breath caresses my lips.

Asher's brows lift in a dare for me to respond. Heat pools between my thighs and I have to press them together to stop the ache he's setting off. Awareness of my discomfort becomes evident in his expression, and with a wicked smirk, he lifts and skims a finger over my neck.

The calculated touch is done with a gentleness that doesn't match his hard expression. The ease of his finger's trace causes me to bite back a whimper while need pulses violently inside of me. My guard drops, allowing him to move. He steps between my legs and presses his lower body into mine. His indigo eyes are demanding as they study my face, nonverbally asking me to submit to him.

I won't.

My chest rises and falls with difficulty because he looks completely ticked off at my lack of surrender, which makes breathing strenuous. I stand firm. Defiantly not giving in to him. Asher's features harden and his eyes cloud over with resentment.

"I know you're pissed, but I made the right decision," I manage to whisper.

He doesn't answer. I clench my teeth at his silence, frustrated that even in his current emotional state, he gets to me. My gaze roams over his intimidating stance. With each passing second, his eyes darken and look even angrier. I keep my chin high, not allowing his intensity to scare me.

"You can let me protect you, of your own free will, or you can keep fighting me, forcing my hand. I couldn't give a fuck either way. You'd do well to remember—you. Are. Mine," he says with a harsh bite, and my eyes snap to his in annoyance at his cruelty.

He gives me no time to process his words. One moment I am thinking of a *screw you* retort, the next I am being seated none too gently on the pool table with Asher hovering over my wound-up body. Large hands rest on the wooden sides of the table, preventing any movement by me, yet allowing his upper body enough space so it doesn't touch mine.

Desire burns in his eyes, deepening the hue. My heart begins to race when he trains his focus on my lips. I feel him draw nearer, hyperaware of how close he is to me, and at the same time, frustrated that no portion of our bodies are touching.

After what feels like an eternity, Asher's forehead meets mine. I can feel his soft, intense breaths across my lips. Instinctively, I raise my chin to seek out his mouth. A second before our lips touch, he pulls back, gliding his nose along my cheek instead.

I tremble from the almost-contact. The tip of his nose slides to my neck, where he stops over my pulse and inhales a rough breath. I shudder, overcome with sensations.

Suddenly, he grips my thighs almost painfully, forcing my legs open so he can push further in between them. One of his large hands lifts and grips the back of my neck possessively, tightening while he coerces me down so I'm laying on the pool table.

I'm not sure who moves first, but our mouths crash into one another, and all the desire I've been feeling for him swirls and takes control of my traitorous body. I kiss Asher so hard that for a brief moment, I believe I might actually be able to take away all the pain and darkness in him. He returns the kiss. Hard. Molding my mouth against his, deepening the kiss.

Frustrated, I cling to him, digging my hands deeply into his back, trying to pull him to me because he refuses to move closer. His body just lingers above mine, without contact. After a few moments, Asher takes control again, forcing his tongue inside my mouth, without reprieve. My lips fight to keep up with his pace and punishment.

The hand clutching my thigh shifts, gliding with ease across my throat before pressing lightly. The gentle squeeze causes me to withdraw my lips from his and draw in a sharp gasp. I'm overwhelmed by the smell and the taste of him.

The need to feel his touch on my skin causes me to release a throaty, deep, uncontrollably needy sound. In response, Asher's lower body pushes heavily into mine, pressing so tightly that I can't decipher where he begins and I end.

My head falls back, hitting the felt with pleasure, and my eyes slide closed. I'm exhaling with such ragged force I can't make out what is a pant and what is a moan.

Asher's breath is coming harder when he releases his hold on my throat, grabbing my wrists with one hand and pinning them above my head. His other hand drops out of sight, and suddenly, his expression shifts from desire-filled to smug and triumphant. *What in the—*

The sound of metal clanking breaks through my lust-induced state, and I drag my eyes to the set of handcuffs he's securing my wrists together with. *Where the hell did he get those?* Shifting my now-attached arms, he latches the cuffs to something on the table.

I level him with a glare and try to wiggle free. "What the hell are you doing?"

Wordlessly, Asher bends over me, dropping the lightest kiss on my lips before gently sucking on my bottom lip. With the softest touch, his hands find their way under my tank top and trace a path over my breasts before lowering.

My eyelids flutter at the contact.

A few moments later, I feel his fingers slip into my cotton shorts, circling the slick skin before pressing into me. My stare meets his. All I can do is absorb the passion in his eyes as he watches my breathless reaction. "I love you, siren, but I won't continue to be disregarded."

With each intense movement he makes, my body rises and falls into the sensations. Asher's gaze slides over every inch of my glistening body. I'm just about to fall over the edge when he removes his presence from inside of me, leaving me empty and aching for him.

I exhale an aggravated breath in protest. "Asher?" His name is a curious question on my lips while he straightens his stance.

Asher's expression becomes withdrawn, and his eyes meet mine with nothing but a serious glare. "It's fucking frustrating, isn't it? To be right there, on the edge emotionally, needing something from someone you love, yet they won't give it to you. It's no fun when you beg for something from a person who is supposed to love you with their entire soul. I want you to remember this the next time you exclude me from your brilliant plans and ignore my pleas," he states cruelly.

My breathing is rough as I study his face, angry at the way he's decided to teach me a lesson. "So you're just going to leave me here? Chained to the table? Exposed?"

Asher rights himself as if nothing happened. He smiles warmly, and I suddenly feel very stupid as I take deep breaths to calm my body. "Now you know what it's liked to be exposed, siren. Completely. Fucking. Exposed. Left for everyone to witness you bleeding out while the person you love turns their back on you. Welcome to my hell," he replies calmly.

"You have to be fucking kidding me?" I mumble.

"When you're ready to be truly mated, come find me," he adds before leaving the room.

"I'll find you all right, Asher St. Michael, and when I do, you better run," I shout after him.

Once my body has calmed down, I try to wiggle my arms free. Unfortunately, whatever Asher attached me to isn't budging. Seething, I continue to attempt to free myself for what feels like an eternity before I hear the doors of the family room open again.

I prepare myself, waiting for the asshole to approach and apologize so I can kick him in the balls. Only the gargoyle that comes into view isn't Asher. *Crap.* My heart sinks, almost painfully, and I internally cringe at the set of blue eyes staring at me in entertained curiosity.

"Eve," he greets in a formal tone.

"Keegan," I blow out in annoyance.

He clears his throat awkwardly. "Asher stopped me in the hallway and mentioned something about you needing assistance."

I wiggle my handcuffed arms to make a point. "He and I aren't seeing eye to eye."

Keegan dips his chin. "That much is obvious."

The stony protector walks around the table and lifts my arms off the hook they were placed on. I sit up as he produces a key, unlocking and removing the metal shackles. In a rare show of kindness, Keegan rubs my wrists, then he refastens the metal together and sticks the set into his back pocket. *I wouldn't have pegged Keegan and McKenna as the type.*

I eye him, still guarded. "You conveniently had a key . . . to handcuffs?"

Keegan leans next to me, against the pool table. He crosses his large arms and fixates on a spot on the wall in front of us. "I've had to restrain Kenna a few times." He shrugs. "Nothing major. A wall. Some furniture here and there," he trails off.

My eyebrows lift. "Wow. That's . . .weird."

His brow arches. "Says the girl handcuffed to the pool table by her mate."

My head falls forward. "Touché."

"I normally make it a point to not get involved in my brother's love life, however, it would seem that Asher's pretty ticked off this time around. Want to discuss it?"

I rub the fading red on my wrists and right myself. "Oh, you know, I offered myself to a demon lord in exchange for healing a shape-shifting panther, without first discussing the plan, of course, with my supernatural gargoyle protector and mate. Just another day in my world."

Keegan makes an odd sound in the back of his throat. It almost sounds like a chuckle.

"Eve, part of being mated to an alpha gargoyle is that he needs to be in control of the protector bond. I know you're still young, but normal relationships consist of two people who are open and honest with one another. You've got to keep him in the loop, and when applicable, allow him to lead. Otherwise, he's going to chain you to more than just the pool table," he points out.

"Yeah? How's that strategy working for you and McKenna?" I counter.

Keegan stands and turns to face me. "Say what you

will about Kenna and me, but we respect one another, as friends and mates, because we have open communication and are honest with each other. We have one another's backs. We're a team. A *real* team."

I raise an eyebrow. "Says the gargoyle who carries an extra key to handcuffs."

Keegan's lips pull. "Touché."

I meet his steely gaze. "I get why he's pissed, Keegan. What I don't appreciate is the way he expressed his emotion. Don't restrain me, use words."

"Do you know why Kenna and I work, Eve? We respect the protector and blood bonds, and what they mean to each of us. Asher is not human. He is a protector. A gargoyle. One who has a dark side, and if you continue to treat him like you would a human mate, then you are bound to be disappointed when the darkness takes over. Consider the truth in my words before you retaliate," he says, placing a hand on my shoulder and squeezing.

I study the floor, allowing my anger to dissolve as Keegan moves toward the door.

"Where is he?" I ask over my shoulder.

Keegan leans against the doorframe. "In the kitchen, planning our next steps with regard to our father and moving the clan back to Massachusetts."

I bite the inside of my cheek. "Thanks."

"Everyone loves darkness, until it consumes them." Keegan adds, taking his leave.

And once again, I'm met with silence.

8 Into the Night

My heart is thumping wildly in my chest as the private jet dips in and out of the turbulence. Threatening dark clouds blanket the circular windows, making visibility impossible. I frown when I see Abby rushing toward the ladies' room, again, with Callan on her heels. Poor girl, this is like the fifth time she's gotten sick in the hour we've been airborne.

The weather from London to Boston is horrid tonight. I sigh and curse the ominous sky on her behalf. Then I shift my annoyance to Asher. As soon as he received word from Tadhg that Garrick was on the move from Egypt to England, the clan sent Fiona and Galena to the clowder for safekeeping. Not long after, we were packed and in flight, heading for the U.S.

I glance over my shoulder at the closed door. After a

brief contemplation, I unfasten my seatbelt and unsteadily make my way to it. Across from me, Gage arches a brow in a judgmental way, but says nothing. Ever since Nassa announced she would be visiting her aunt, Sorceress Lunette, instead joining us in Massachusetts, he's been bad-tempered.

My hand lifts to knock, but then I think better of it. Changing my mind, I simply push it open, stepping into the darkness and quietly closing the door behind me. A small glow emits from the overhead lighting located above the bed, allowing me to see the gargoyle.

Asher's back and head are resting against the cushioned headboard. His bare feet are crossed at the ankles. A novel sits in both hands with his focus on it. The corded muscles of his stomach draw my gaze upward, past the black cotton pajama bottoms he's wearing, to his chest. I soak in the expanse of his shoulders.

My eyes land on the protector mark before his voice yanks me out of my gawking.

"Like what you see, siren?" he questions without looking at me.

I decide not to dignify his question with a response. Clearly I do. *Who wouldn't?*

"Abby isn't feeling well. Maybe you should offer her the bedroom," I suggest.

Asher closes his book and lays it across his lap. The very same lap I want to crawl onto and glue myself to. *Crap. Focus, Eve. He left you on a pool table. In handcuffs!*

"This is a Boeing 757 business jet. There are two other bedrooms," he replies haughtily.

The plane dips again, causing me to stumble forward. Asher flinches to come to my rescue, but stops himself as soon as I even out my stance. His jaw ticks with apprehension.

"I see," I mutter, feeling stupid. "I'm sorry then for interrupting you, Your Highness. I just wanted Abby to be more comfortable since the turbulence is making her queasy."

Asher flashes me his signature sexy smirk. "I'm sure Callan will see to it that Abby is well taken care of, siren. It's what mates do—protect and look after one another." *Was that a dig?*

I narrow my eyes. "Do they also use sex as a weapon to teach their loved one a lesson?"

He shrugs. Actually shrugs. "From time to time. When needed." *No he did not.*

My patience lost, I decide to give him a taste of his own medicine. "Good to know."

A playful gleam lights up his eyes. "Is there anything else you need?"

"Actually, Asher, there is something I need." I drop my tone to a husky one right before I awkwardly tumble forward, thanks to another quick descend. *Super sexy, Eve. Fucking plane.*

Asher bites his lip, hiding a laugh, and I roll my eyes at my lack of seductive smoothness.

I manage to pull myself together and crawl across the bed on my hands and knees next to him. The gargoyle's expression turns curious, but his stare is guarded.

I rake my teeth over my bottom lip and watch Asher watching the movement. Instantly, his eyes darken and a light blue hue emits from them. That's when I know I have him.

Slowly, I take the novel off his lap. My face pinches when I see it's *Prince Lestat* by Anne Rice. "What can we do but reach for the embrace that must now contain both heaven and hell: our doom again and again and again," I quote Lestat's words from *The Vampire Chronicles*.

Asher's eyes dip to the book, then lift and lock onto mine. "I know what you're doing, siren, and it's not going to work," he warns.

Silently, I lick my lips. His focused gaze follows the movement. I strategically lean over him, placing the hardback on the table next to the bed, and smirk to myself when I feel him inhale the scent of my hair. *Gotcha, protector.*

Moving back over him, my chest brushes his. At the connection, he swallows audibly.

I present Asher my best bedroom eyes. "I have no idea what you're referring to, gargoyle," I whisper across his lips while straddling his lap.

I gather, from the large hard-on he's sporting, my lame attempt is working. His hands twitch, itching to touch me, but he keeps them securely on the bed.

From under his sooty lashes, he stares at me intently in that all-consuming way that makes me feel like he can see directly into my soul. I take in a slow breath and remind myself to stay in control. It's the only way I'll win this round.

Holding his gaze, I grab the hem of my shirt and tug it up, over my shoulders and head, exposing my bra, then toss it behind me onto the mattress. The plane hits another air pocket and my body bolts forward clumsily burying Asher's face into my cleavage. *Oh. My. God. How unsexy is this?*

Asher chuckles into my skin, his hot breath causing a

rush of warmth to flow through my veins. "Is your plan to suffocate me with your absolutely fucking perfect breasts? If so, I'm not going to lie, siren, that would be one hell of a way to die."

The tip of Asher's tongue peeks out and slowly makes its way up my chest and neck. I release a contented sigh. At the sound, Asher captures my mouth in a searing kiss. His touch is hungry, traveling along my trembling body, which is compliantly melting into his, as it memorizes every inch of me.

My lips become urgent as he deepens the kiss. His hands squeeze my waist before sliding to my lower back, flattening and pushing on the mate mark. It hums in pleasure, though the sensation is dulling slightly. *Odd.* Oh God. What if it's disappearing?

Asher slowly ends the kiss, pulling away and angling his head. "What's wrong?"

I ignore my unease and whisper across his swollen lips. "I'm supposed to be doing this to teach you a lesson."

His brows arch. "And what lesson is that?" Lust lines his voice.

"If you ever use sex against me again, I'll cut off your piercing." I hold his eyes.

Fighting a grin, he recoils slightly. "There is no need to threaten the piercing. Lesson learned. I'm sorry," he says sincerely in a gruff voice and nips at my bottom lip.

I moan. "Do you promise to never do it to me again?" I ask, brushing my mouth over his.

"I was wrong and pissed off. It was misguided. I apologize for my behavior. The handcuffs, though, we will be exploring again." He wiggles his brows, sucking on my lip.

I pull my bottom lip away from him and into my mouth, mashing my top one over it.

"I was wrong too. We're mated now. I should have told you what I was planning to do so you didn't panic. I'm sorry." My voice is full of need.

His hands on my lower back push me forward as he lowers his head, brushing his lips along the curve of my jaw before moving upward.

"I want you," he growls into my ear.

Asher's hands slide to my waist and his grip tightens, jerking me roughly along the length of his lap so I can feel how much he wants me.

"I couldn't tell," I tease breathily, rolling my hips over him again.

At the friction, Asher exhales noisily. "Always, siren. I'll always fucking want you."

My chest rises, grazing his, and Asher's lips find mine again while his hands skim up over my arms, capturing my face so he can deepen our connection. I shiver, and after a few languid moments, pull back, a little dazed. *Game over. He wins. Again.*

"I'm done," I exhale.

"That was quick," he murmurs against my lips. "I have to admit, even I'm impressed with my own awesomeness this time."

On a grin, I bark-laugh and place my fingers over the protector tattoo, tracing the lines.

"No. I meant that I'm done with the game I was trying to win."

Asher plants a light kiss on my bruised lips. "You

weren't really winning."

I pout. "Was too."

Asher brings my face forward, trailing a path of sexy, open-mouthed kisses over my face before his lips are at my ear again. "I fucking love you," he murmurs.

"I love you too," I exhale, tightening my arms around him. "I'm scared that someday, I'll have to let go."

"You don't ever have to let go," he assures quietly before sucking on the spot under my ear in a bruising way. "I'm yours, always."

All of a sudden, Asher's body becomes rigid. All humor and desire leaks out of his expression, which is now hard and focused. "Don't make a sound," he warns, his voice low.

He releases his hold on my cheeks, and I follow his roaming eyes around the room. Abruptly, he leans us backward, grabbing my shirt and helping me to get it on quickly. Once redressed, my gaze darts to his in question.

Asher brings his index finger to his lips, instructing me to stay quiet while he gingerly moves me off his lap, onto the bed. He stands and tilts his head, listening.

Worried eyes meet mine before his wings angrily snap out of his back, startling me. Swiftly, he throws the pillows off the bed and takes hold of his sword, which was hiding under them. At the same time, he clutches my wrists and yanks me to him, protectively.

I recognize the fury in his expression, though he's trying to mask it. "What's happening?"

Asher's gaze meets mine, and something in the depths of them causes me to shudder.

"The—," he begins but gets cut off when the plane

jolts hard.

My gaze flicks to the door in shock when a loud explosion comes out of nowhere, rattling the jet. Seconds later, a loud rumble permeates the air. Asher swings opens the door and looks back and forth, taking in the destroyed cabin.

"Fuck," Asher growls and tugs me toward the grouping clan.

"The dark army is attacking. No sign of Garrick," Gage says.

"The explosion?" Asher asks Keegan.

"They blew out the cockpit," he replies calmly. "The crew is gone."

The plane drops quickly, jerking us all forward. Asher's grip on me tightens as we attempt to keep our balance. My heartbeat thumps heavily in my chest while the aircraft swerves and dips. The metal rattles and groans like it's twisting and snapping as we descend rapidly.

The hairs on the back of my neck tingle when the lights flicker. We begin to spiral and tumble through the air at a faster rate and Asher pulls me into the air so we're hovering over the wreckage. The furniture shifts and slides underneath us violently.

The force of the plunging aircraft causes pieces of the metal to peel off the plane. A large hole rips into the ceiling above us. The harsh wind and frigid night air burst into the cabin, making it hard to hold onto anything. Tiny flickers of electricity begin to spark throughout the now darkened cabin. I gasp and my stomach roils.

Callan stares at the opening, eyes wide. "We need to get out of here," he bellows.

Asher nods in agreement and leans into my ear, yelling over the noise. "Hold on, siren."

Each gargoyle releases their wings, and seconds later, we're all hovering in the inky sky, watching the large airplane fall hundreds of feet in the air before it shudders and hits the ground with a hard bang. Smoke fills the atmosphere below us before the mangled carnage erupts in flames and explodes.

"Holy shit," I exhale and study the tiny fireball below while clutching Asher, because we are really high up, and to be honest, I am petrified.

"It's a good thing we have insurance," Callan jests.

Everyone's shaken expressions shift focus to the adorable gargoyle.

He shrugs. "Please. You know you all were thinking the same thing."

"Is everyone all right?" Asher asks, surprisingly calm.

A chorus of "We're fine" erupts before a low thrumming pulses through my entire body.

"I think we have company," Abby points out just as hundreds of demons surround us.

The night's shadows conceal their scaly, black-leather flesh, but the red glow of their eyes gives away their presence. There are so many of them. If their eyes weren't crimson, from this height, someone could almost mistake their presence in the sky for stars.

Keegan's nostrils flare. "Looks like the vermin have arrived."

"Fucking demons," Asher grits out of a tight jaw, tightening his hold on me.

"How can we help you fine beings this evening?"

Callan banters. *Fucking Callan.*

A demon with white eyes moves forward. *He must be the leader.* "The girl," he demands.

Callan folds his arms. "Which one? Not counting Asher, there are three of them."

The demon's jaw tightens and his nostrils flare. "The daughter of Heaven."

"Let's see." Callan flaps his wings and spins, facing Asher and me before winking and twisting back to the fiend. "No one here by that name. Sorry to disappoint you."

"Eligos, she's here. I sense her," another demon states in a slithery cool tone.

Asher's grip on me constricts and Eligos senses my presence, straightening and turning his gaze our way. The edges of Asher's vision tinge and his body stiffens. The tension radiating off him alerts me that he's ready to shoot across the sky and strike if need be.

Callan soars in front of us, so we're not in the general's sightline. "Listen, dude, we're in a bit of a pickle here." He snickers at his own joke. After a few seconds, he recomposes himself. "You wouldn't know this, Eligos, but given my new hobby, that statement was pretty ingenious. Unintentional, but clever nonetheless. Right, babe?" His head twists to Abby.

She smiles but it's forced. "Very shrewd of you, baby." Her voice is tight.

Unnoticed by Eligos, Gage moves closer. Asher transfers me into the safety of his arms without much effort or protest, given our elevation. Once Gage has a firm grip on me, he edges us back a bit from the demon army leader.

Asher does his best to control the pissed off glare

Restoration

wanting to take over his stunning features as he and Keegan shoot forward and take their places on either side of Callan.

My protector's lips turn into a cold twist of a smirk. "What my brother is trying to say is that you fuckheads have to be a special kind of stupid to destroy a one-hundred-million-dollar private jet. Then again, demons aren't known for their high levels of intelligence."

Eligos's gaze moves over Asher's shoulder, toward me. "We came for the girl."

Rage whirls through Asher, and he shifts his body, blocking me from Eligos's sightline. "If you look in her direction again, or breathe her air, I will kill you," he threatens.

"Listen, dude, if you're having trouble getting a girl, maybe brush up on your cooking skills," Callan quips casually. "Also, the creepy eyes probably aren't helping your case."

Eligos advances and is suddenly pushed back by a heavy gust, courtesy of Abby.

Angered, the demon moves smoothly through the air. "Enough of this foolish behavior."

He nods to one of his minions. At the command, the demon soldier rushes forward just as Keegan's fist crashes into his ribcage, doubling him over. In one swift move, Keegan lifts the demon's upper body and pushes his fist into the demon's face, knocking him out, before running a knife through his heart, causing him to vanish into a blue flame.

Asher tightens his grip on his sword. "You and I both know that no matter how hard you or this army try, you will not succeed. She is protected by this clan. You. Will. Get. Nothing."

I can feel Gage's heart rate increase as Eligos narrows his eyes and screws his mouth up at Asher. Gage's arms tighten around my waist and he pulls me against him in a firm grip. "Easy, love," he coaxes while the energy source pulsates through me, sensing danger.

"GIVE ME THE GIRL!" Eligos hisses through his bellow.

The Angelic Sword twists in Asher's hand before he cocks his head. "If you don't want to know what it feels like to have your limbs ripped from you one by one, I suggest you leave."

"You don't scare me, protector," the general snarls.

"Take her to the safe house," Asher states, using an even tone.

It takes a moment for it to register that he's talking about me. "No," I shout.

"That was fucking brilliant, blood of Eden," McKenna says offhandedly.

At my outburst, the entire demon legion locks their focus onto Gage and me. *Guess Asher was vague on whom for a reason.* Moving as one unit, the army begins to advance.

"Fuck," Asher spits out, turning and facing us. "Get her out of here, Gallagher!"

I struggle in Gage's arms. "No," I screech again. "You need my light source."

Asher's expression hardens. "I need you safe, siren."

"I can help fight!" I reply, panicked.

"You don't have wings. I can't keep you airborne and fight at the same time," Asher counters.

I shake my head adamantly. "I won't go without you,

Asher," I cry.

Asher's callous gaze meets mine. "It's not your decision."

"Don't do this," I shriek and plead. "Don't let me go."

At my words, Asher's expression becomes wrecked before he looks away.

"NOW, GAGE!" he orders coolly.

Eligos lunging for Asher is the last thing I see before we disappear into the night.

9 Slip Away

In the blink of an eye, Gage and I slip away and are safely relocated into a dark, warm room. I spin, slamming my hands into Gage's stomach, pushing him back and tearing myself free of his grasp. I wheeze, trying to draw in a breath. *Crap. I'm having a panic attack.*

The walls begin to close in on me, and my chest squeezes tightly. I struggle through my breathing, and on shaky legs, fight through reality. My gaze slowly lifts to his guarded one.

"You need to calm down, love," Gage says in an attempt to pacify me.

Is he serious? I cock my arm back and smash my fist into his perfect jaw. A sick satisfaction wraps itself around my insides while I watch him lift his hand to his shocked face, rubbing the red spot where I pathetically sucker punched him.

"Take. Me. Back," I bark through a tight jaw.

Gage snaps forward, his face contorted in frustration. "No."

I match his stance. "I need to help them. They need my light source."

He grunts and lowers his hand. "Because the light source worked so well against the dark army at Notre Dame. Right?"

"Fuck you," I seethe. "Fuck YOU. FUCK YOU. FUCK YOU!"

"There's the eighteen-year-old. Nice to see her again." Gage steps around me.

I jerk back at the insult. "You can't just expect me to sit around and wait here for them."

"That is exactly what you will do, Eve." He moves around the room, flicking on switches.

One by one, the lights pop on, revealing our location. As I take in my surroundings, everything around me slows. A raw pain runs through my heart and I suck in a breath.

"Why are we here?" I whisper in a defeated voice.

Gage's expression softens. "This is the safe house. Garrick and the dark army can't find you here because Michael has it well protected. We're to stay here until the clan arrives."

I meet his stare and pinch my lips. "I can't stay here, Gage."

He sighs. "You will. It's a direct order from your mate and future king."

My expression turns violent. "I'm human. I don't take

orders from Asher. Or *you*."

"If you're to be our future queen, love, then I suggest you brush up on how our world works." He throws me a sharp look. "I need a smoke. Feel free to come find me when you're finished with your temper tantrum," he murmurs, storming toward the front door.

"If anything happens to him, I will never forgive you," I throw over my shoulder.

Gage doesn't respond. He steps onto the front porch, slamming the door behind him. The house rattles from the force, and my shoulders sag. Reluctantly, I turn and take in the warmth of my comfortable childhood home. Memories flood me, and tears begin to sting my eyes.

With apprehension, I approach the antique chest housing the snapshots of my life. Each one is a sorrowful reminder that my mother, Elizabeth, is dead. Being here without her feels wrong somehow, like I'm an intruder.

A painful lump grows in my throat as I pick up the framed photo from last Christmas. We're all in front of the tree, and everyone looks happy. Forcing away a sob, I place it back.

My steps are light on the hardwood floors as I make my way into the eggshell-blue kitchen. With a light touch, I brush my fingertips over the modern bronze handles and smile at the recollection of when my mother and I found them in the hardware store.

I take two more steps into the petite kitchen and gaze out the windows, over the sink, onto the now unkempt garden. At the sight of something she put so much love and time into, being in such disarray, my heart splits, and I'm suddenly filled with irrational anger.

I don't recall how I got outside. One minute I'm staring out the window, and the next, I'm kneeling in between the overgrown plant life, pulling and yanking at the weeds. I choke and clench my teeth irritably, trying to steady my breathing. I struggle to keep the tears from stinging my eyes. I push away the anger that everyone I love has been taken away from me.

My eyes slide shut and I tighten them. *Please. Please bring Asher back to me. I need him.* I beg anyone who will listen to the plea before reopening them. Out of nowhere, my gaze lands on a lone perfect pink rose presenting itself in the decaying garden. I tilt my head in curiosity and cup it gently with my palm, reminded of Aria. Another person I love, gone.

Sadness sweeps through me like a current and, without thought, I crush the flower between my fingers, releasing a raw, painful bellow. I cover my face with my hands and rock on my knees, trying to make all the hurt just stop.

In an instant, Gage is there. Protective arms wrap around my body. "I'm here, love. I'm here," he whispers into my hair and tightens his hold on me.

"It's too hard," I snivel.

Gage sits on the dirt floor and pulls me into his lap. "I know." His voice cracks.

Clutching onto his shirt, I weep uncontrollably into his chest.

His fingers tangle in my hair as he sways. "Let it out."

At his words, my sobs become deeper and more painful. He holds me tighter, engulfing me in the mixed scents of cigarettes and spice. After a while, my hiccups slow and I pull back, wiping my tear-stained cheeks with the backs of my hands. My eyes drift downward in embarrassment that I've unleashed so much emotion on him.

Reaching for my chin, Gage lifts my face. "Asher will come back to you."

"I know," I whisper and sniff in. "I'm just overwhelmed by being here."

Gage helps me to a standing position. With his right hand, he brushes the lingering drops of water off my cheek. "Let's get you cleaned up." He smiles sadly.

I nod and let him lead me back into the house on Martha's Vineyard. Once in the kitchen, he motions to the countertop and I slide myself onto it, dangling my feet like a child. He tears off some paper towels and runs them under the faucet before gently wiping under my eyes.

I still, watching him, unsure of how to react to how nurturing he's being.

"You know, the first time I reentered the loft after Camilla's death, I destroyed everything that was hers. Or reminded me of her." He flips my palms over and begins to wipe the dirt from them. "It's my one regret. I wish I'd kept one thing. Just one. Something. Anything, to remind me that she was real," he admits.

My watery eyes meet his and his jaw ticks. Angrily, he balls up the wet towel and throws it in the trash before running his hands over his face and through his golden blond hair.

"I'm sorry I punched you earlier. I may have overreacted just a bit." I wince.

Gage nods once. "I can't say I didn't have it coming, love. Let's just call it payback for all the times I've dropped you in a pool of water after teleporting."

An awkward snort bursts out of me and I sniff again. "Deal."

Gage folds his arms and cocks his hip, leaning on the counter next to me. "Sometimes we have to sacrifice our own wants and needs to help others fulfill theirs. Asher couldn't protect you while fighting tonight. As you so elegantly pointed out a few moments ago, you're human. There are limits to your capabilities. Fighting in flight is a limit. That's why he sent you away. Not because he doesn't trust your ability to help."

I release a slow exhale. "I know."

"Why don't you go shower, so when he gets here, you don't look like . . ." he pauses, looking me over, and frowns. "Well, like this." He motions at me. "I'd rather not be on the receiving end of another *I told you to take care of Eve lecture* from your overprotective mate."

I slide off the counter with a small smirk. "Understood." Before I make my way out of the kitchen, I stop in the doorway, throwing him a quick glance over my shoulder.

"Thank you, Gage, for being here for me tonight—and protecting me."

His lips press into a flat line, and his face becomes ashen. He dips his chin in acknowledgment of what I said, but I swear he looks as if he is about to be sick.

☙❧

I clasp the last button to my flannel pajama top and put the hair dryer back under the sink. Since our belongings burned along with the plane, I had to rummage through my dresser and pull out a pair of my old pajamas. I'd forgotten how comfy my Victoria's Secret sets are.

My bare feet grace the last step of the staircase just as the aroma of greasy cheese and tomato sauce hits me. Before I can seek out the pizza, I'm grabbed by a large set of familiar arms. The well-built owner smashes my face against his chest, making breathing difficult.

"Welcome home, princess," the archangel Uriel's rich, masculine voice greets.

Using all of my strength, I push at his chest. "C-can't breathe."

He releases his hold with a grimace. "Sorry, angel, I forget that you're human."

I take a step back and inhale slowly. "What's with the princess and angel?"

Uriel gives me a sheepish look. "I've been told it's normal practice for uncles and nieces to have terms of endearment. I'm trying out different ones to see which one sticks."

I arch a brow, suddenly aware of how tired I am. "How about, just Eve?"

Uriel's expression contorts. "If that's what you want, just Eve."

I roll my eyes. Clearly, he misinterpreted my request. I turn to the other divine being watching us curiously with his deep jade eyes. "Hello, Michael."

"Eve." He dips his head formally.

As I study the warrior of Heaven's straight-faced expression and flawless skin, I'm instantly transported back to our first meeting. I note the angel's dark-blond, neck-length hair is still pushed back with effortless style. Once again, he's wearing black dress pants and a white button-down shirt. Michael's powerful presence is meant to intimidate. And it does.

Inhaling, I elevate my chin and fold my arms over my chest protectively before sliding my gaze to Uriel. Unlike Michael, his larger-than-life gold wings are on full display.

In contrast to the warrior of Heaven, this archangel's blond hair is flowing down the warrior's neck and casually lying across his broad shoulders. I laugh internally, noticing he's still wearing his gold armor. The chest plate is decorated with a scroll, and his forearms are adorned with metal shields, one on each arm. Red silk fabric drapes on his lower body.

"Still refusing to wear pants?" I smirk and point to Uriel's muscular bare legs.

Warm, good-natured amber eyes dance with amusement at the jab. "As I have mentioned before, daughter of Heaven, if you had these calf muscles, you wouldn't wear pants either. It's really too bad you got your tiny little chicken legs from your dad."

At the reminder that Michael is my biological father, the room falls silent.

I clear my throat and meet Gage's unreadable expression. "Any word from Asher?"

"No, love. Sorry."

"Wait, *he* gets to use a nickname?" Uriel throws Gage an exasperated look.

I shrug. "He's one of my protectors."

"I'm blood," the archangel counters.

"Technically, Uriel, you are not," Michael interjects.

A second awkward pause of silence beats between the

four of us.

Uriel's voice rumbles through the quiet room. "So, Mikey, how does this work?"

"How does what work, Uriel?" Michael inquires formally.

"Do we tip the babysitter? Or do I just offer him some pizza and a ride home?" he asks.

Gage narrows his eyes at the archangel in some weird form of challenge.

"Sorry, protector," Uriel apologizes. "I'm new at this whole *uncle* thing."

Gage's expression turns sour. "Christ, I need another cigarette."

I toe the floor, tongue-tied, and watch him escape drama for the second time tonight.

Uriel puts his brawny arm around my shoulder and heaves me to his side. "There, there, just Eve. Daddy and Uncle Urie are here now. There is no need to be gloomy."

My gaze slides to Michael's displeased look. "Uriel," he warns sharply.

"What are you both doing here?" I ask dejectedly.

Michael takes a cautious step toward me with a concerned expression on his face.

"Mr. Gallagher said you had an emotional breakdown earlier. Is that true?"

I avert my gaze. "This is the first time I've been home since my mother died."

"This is your home, Eve. Libby would want you to be happy here. Not despondent."

"Yeah. I'll work on that . . . Dad." My voice drips with sarcasm.

Michael lifts an arched brow at my statement. "I forget how young you are, Eve, until you use tonal inflections like the one you just used on me," the archangel reprimands.

"Mikey, I believe the word you are in search of is *sass*. She sassed you. You know, often a teen's behavior cannot be explained, justified or understood. It just is," Uriel offers.

I sigh and change topics. "How is she?"

Michael's expression brightens. "Libby is well. She's gardening and spending quite a bit of time correcting what she perceives as inappropriate human behaviors and divine habits."

Uriel releases a boisterous laugh. "Basically, she's retraining him."

I nod. "She deserves to be happy. You both do . . ." I trail off.

My self-appointed uncle drops a kiss to my head. "Sorry it's taken so long for us to come, but I had one very unhappy goddess to placate." He shivers as if the memory terrifies him.

A small grin crosses over my lips at the memory of our recent visit to the Ice Catacombs to meet with Zyla, the demigoddess of protection. Apparently, the goddess granted me the gift of protection, in the form of my light source, a deity favor to express her love for Uriel.

It would seem the archangel and demigoddess have, an on-again, off-again relationship. Which he spat on when he slept with her sister, hence the need to calm her anger. I snort, thinking how perfect Callan's shirt saying is. *Family drama: the gift that keeps on giving.*

"So she's forgiven you then?" I ask with a guarded tone.

"I believe I've managed to tame her rage for the time being. A deity as powerful as Zyla is not a goddess who easily forgives, just Eve," he explains. "Given the opportunity, I do believe she'd freeze my gentlemanhood, until they are blue, to make a point."

I release a slow breath. "Stop calling me *just Eve*."

Uriel's brows pinch. "I thought that was what you wanted me to call you?"

"No. I meant, just. Call. Me. Eve," I clarify. "No nicknames."

"Tell you what, I will stop calling you 'just Eve.' However, we are going to work out this pet-name situation, lollipop," he retorts. "Speaking of sweets, where is Callan? I've been craving his cookies like a mad angel." He unceremoniously rubs his stomach.

My gaze shifts between the two divine beings. "He's with the rest of the clan. Fighting the dark army. We were attacked mid-flight on our way here."

Uriel frowns. "Well, in the meantime, little one, I brought pizza."

"I'm not hungry," I declare at the same time my stomach growls loudly.

The archangel rolls his eyes. "There is nothing I despise more than when someone says they're not hungry, and then their stomach growls like a bear. It's not cute. It's annoying." He sighs and points to the stools at the counter. "Sit. Eat. We'll visit."

I begrudgingly follow his orders, taking a seat and picking up a slice of the cheesy goodness.

Michael drops his tone to a whisper as he addresses Uriel. "Really, brother? There is nothing that you despise more than a human's growling stomach?" he challenges.

Uriel inhales two wedges. "Well, evil sucks. Other than that, nothing comes to mind."

My gaze lifts to Michael's. "Isn't there anything you can do to help Asher and the clan?"

Michael's face falls. "Eve, you know—"

I cut him off. "We don't get involved in matters of supernatural disputes." Irritated, I mimic his words.

"If you know this, why do you ask again and again?" he questions.

"I don't ask *all* the time," I argue like a petulant child.

"You do have a habit of repetition, DOH. When we first met, after your ascension, you repeated a lot of what I said back to me," Uriel points out. "It was adorbs." He grins widely.

"D-O-H?" I replicate.

"Daughter of Heaven."

I put my half-eaten piece down. "No."

Uriel waves his hand dramatically. "I wasn't married to it either."

Michael takes a seat next to me and thoughtfully watches me.

"So you both came down from your divine duties to what? Babysit me?" I ask.

"Nope. That's his job," Uriel replies, pointing to Gage as he makes his way over to us.

"I need a shot of brandy. Do you have any in this house, love?" Gage mumbles.

I wipe the grease off my fingers onto a napkin. "Under the sink."

"Libby allowed you alcohol?" Michael asks

paternally.

"Allowed? No. Snuck? Yes," I admit.

"Quite inappropriate for a daughter of Heaven," he scolds. "Or her protector."

"This protector drinks. You can credit your ball of sunshine over there for tonight's necessity," Gage retorts, nodding to me before he swallows a full shot of the liquid.

"SUNSHINE!" Uriel booms. "Of course. You'd think the angel of wisdom, in charge of the Orb of the Sun, would have thought of that on his own," he says quietly to himself.

"You're in charge of the sun?" I ask, with disbelief lining my tone.

"Wait, weren't you the angel that guided Lucifer to Earth?" Gage counters.

"An error I've spent lifetimes attempting to rectify," Uriel replies guiltily.

Michael exhales slowly. "Mr. Gallagher, I do believe we are all capable of missteps. It is the manner in which we become accountable and rectify them that permits redemption."

My lips part in surprise. "Pretty big mistake there, Uncle Urie," I jab.

Uriel winks and smirks with intent. "Makes for an interesting human existence, though."

"In your divine opinion. Not in my human one," I oppose.

He waves me off. "Listen, sunshine, whine to the 'rent about it later. For now, why don't you give Mikey and me the deets of what happened with the dark army earlier tonight."

"First, you seriously need to stop using pop-culture

slang. It's weird. Second, please, I beg of you, stop with the nicknames," I demand. "I'm eighteen. Not ten."

Uriel straightens his stance. "I know how old you are, Generation Z."

I smirk around a mouthful of pizza. "Newer than Millennials."

"That's a clever tag line," Michael interjects with a proud tone that makes me stop and study him. A weird feeling curls in my stomach at the paternal way he is beaming at me. "I like that you have Libby's witticism. And her hair." His expression softens.

"Thanks." I swallow hard and avert my gaze just as the front door slams open.

We snap our focus to the bruised and battered gargoyles as they walk in with solemn expressions. I stand and all but run over to them. One by one, they greet me and step aside, finally revealing Keegan, carrying my protector's lifeless body in his arms.

My breath hitches and my world tilts.

The silence of the room engulfs me.

And my connection to my protector slips away.

10 Letting Go

My abdominal muscles clench like I've been punched in the stomach. I can't move or breathe. Numbly, I just stand there, unmoving and gaping at the sight before me. Everything around me stirs in slow motion. It's as if time has stopped.

Through the pulsing in my eardrums, I faintly hear an echo of Callan's voice. I watch his lips move, but the words aren't registering. Instead, my conversation with Gage at Notre Dame floats through my mind.

"My body felt empty and my heart hollow. It was as if my soul left me. And I knew. I knew she was gone. Even still, my mind wouldn't believe it to be truth," he said.

The poignant meaning of his statement seeps in, and I

exhale the feeling of complete dread that I'm experiencing, because in this moment, my soul is bleeding dry, and the fullness in my heart is fading away. I can feel the link Asher and I share slipping away, diminishing with each passing second.

My matching mark refuses to pulse. Our connection is letting go.

I watch with parted lips and dull fascination while Keegan steps around me, taking the stairs two at a time to the second floor. My gaze stays locked onto his retreating back, and my feet remain planted, unable to move forward. The darkness is descending again.

"Eves." Callan uses a firm voice that cuts through my haze.

"What happened?" My voice quivers on the question.

Abby averts her eyes and McKenna lifts her chin before following after her mate.

"He was pierced in the heart," Callan explains in a gentle tone. "From behind."

"Eve." Keegan's intonation makes its way down the staircase. "A moment, if you will."

I look around the room, taking in the sober expressions on the gargoyles and angels before making my way to the second floor. My steps are slow and measured as I walk into the master suite toward the bed. I drag my gaze up to meet Keegan's. The pressure clamps down on my chest when I see the worry behind his eyes. *Oh shit. This is bad.*

I turn my attention to Asher's still form. My hands tremble as my gaze travels over his unmoving body. His chest is rising and falling with shallow breaths and his skin has a sickly washed-out gray tint to it. The color ignites recognition within me that our bond was the only thing preventing him from turning into stone this evening.

My breath hitches in panic. If our connection fades, then Asher will be in danger in more ways than one. By not finishing the bond, I've left him unprotected. *Shit. Dumb, Eve.* I look around my mother's master suite, awkwardly.

"He should heal in stone state. He can't do that here," I blurt out the obvious.

Keegan closes his tired eyes and runs his hands over his face. "We can't bring him to any of the manors. It's unsafe. My father has access to the chambers."

My shoulders sag. "How the hell is he supposed to get better then, Keegan?"

"You're bonded to Asher. You two share healing energies. I would think what my mate is saying is pretty straightforward, blood of Eden," McKenna retorts.

"You want me to heal him *here*?" I ask, looking around.

"It'll take longer, but if you push the energies into him, it will work," Keegan answers.

Crap. I don't want the clan, especially Keegan and McKenna, to know the bond has begun to grow fainter. Abby warned me that if I didn't infuse the mate mark with Asher's blood, our connection would disappear gradually. She was right. It's begun to fade, and now, I may never have the chance to truly become his. My stomach roils at the thought.

"I'm not su—," I start, but Keegan cuts me off with a sharp glance.

"I understand it looks bad, Eve, but he'll be okay. With your help," he encourages.

My help. After an uncomfortable pause, I clear my

throat. "I'll do whatever I can."

Keegan watches me suspiciously before granting me a curt nod. "I need a first aid kit."

My eyes roam over Asher's body, landing on the spot where his protector tattoo is, and my hands curl inwardly, clenching tightly in anger. He sent me away, and I wasn't there to protect him.

Damn gargoyle.

"EVE!" McKenna barks. "FIRST. AID. KIT," she repeats each word, loudly.

I startle and drag my attention to Keegan. "Under the sink . . . in the hallway bathroom."

"Thanks," he mumbles and hurriedly stalks out.

McKenna narrows her sapphire stare at me. "What the fuck is wrong with you?"

I exhale slowly. "What?"

She steps into my personal space. "My blood runs through your veins now," she states snottily. "I can sense your emotions. I expected buckets of tears. I expected you to fall to your knees at the sight of him. I expected you to go on and on about how you can't survive without him. Instead, you look like you're planning to run in the other direction. Why?"

"You think because I'm not hysterically falling apart that I don't care that the love of my life is unconscious and covered in blood?" I huff. "Shared emotional link or not, you have no idea what I'm feeling, McKenna, so don't act like you do."

"Everything all right in here, ladies?" Callan asks from the doorway.

I turn my attention to him and Abby as they step into

the room. "What the hell happened tonight? That gash is not a small wound, Callan. Who was protecting him?" I rant wildly.

Abby's face visibly pales, and Asher's brother has the good sense to look guilty.

"I'll tell you who *wasn't* protecting him," McKenna scoffs.

I spin so fast toward her that her eyes widen slightly. "He sent me away!"

"I found the kit," Keegan announces, walking into the shit storm.

"EXACTLY!" McKenna bellows.

"What the hell is that supposed to mean?" I yell back.

McKenna's shoulders roll back and her chin lifts. "You will always hurt him. It doesn't matter whether it's intentional or not, or if you're present or not. The feelings he has for you blind his ability to protect himself and this clan. You. Make. Him. Weak."

"STOP!" Abby shrieks, storming over to us. "Just. Fucking. Stop it. Both of you!"

McKenna's and my expressions turn to ones of startlement at Abby's furious demeanor. Abby's angry gaze shifts between McKenna and me. Her expression enraged, I notice the red hue of her cheeks matches her hair. *Shit. A mad Abby is not a good thing.*

"Asher is hurt because of me. Not Eve," she admits, dropping her voice.

"Baby," Callan says in order to silence her.

Abby throws him her *be quiet* look and steps in between McKenna and myself.

"It's true. I'm the reason Asher is lying on that bed,

probably bleeding out because you two are bickering like children instead of allowing Keegan to help him," she scolds. "Callan, help Keegan to clean and attend to your brother's wounds please," she orders.

I inhale sharply at her reprimand. McKenna's rigid stance softens. Our juvenile power struggle ends and I slide my gaze to Asher. *Abby's right. He's probably bleeding out. Crap.*

Keegan and Callan storm around the three of us and begin to remove Asher's blood-soaked shirt before nursing and washing the wound on his back where he was slashed.

My nostrils flare at the sight. "I don't understand," I breathe out. "Why would you be the reason he's so badly injured, Abby?"

Her crystal blue gaze falls to the floor as she swallows. "I was focused on protecting Callan. His back was turned, and a demon was about to attack him, so I swung around and sliced the demon's throat in order to protect my mate," she explains in a soft whisper.

McKenna smirks evilly. "A gargoyle protecting one's mate, what a revelation."

"Fuck you," I snip.

"By the grace, you two. Would you please, please, just stop," Abby begs, and suddenly I become aware of how exhausted she looks. "I was so focused on Callan that I didn't see the second demon coming straight at me until it was too late. I panicked and froze. Asher immediately leaped in front of me, taking the strike instead, protecting us."

I frown. "Us? You mean, you and Callan?"

Her head moves from side to side, slowly, and her hands splay across her stomach.

"No. By us, I mean, the baby and me. I'm pregnant."

The entire room falls silent. I just watch Abby with parted lips, stunned at her admission. I'm not sure why I feel the need to stare at her. Maybe it's because I'm eighteen and haven't really ever known anyone pregnant before. I think I'm waiting for her to vomit, or ask me for ice cream. I should say something encouraging. Luckily for me, McKenna speaks first.

McKenna's face falls. "You're pregnant? And . . . you told Asher before me?" she barely releases in a quiet tone.

My brows lift. I think this is the first time I've ever seen McKenna hurt. Or have an emotion other than hate. *Holy shit*. Sadness is not a pretty look on her. It's actually freaky.

Abby's eyes dance with unhappiness. "Nooo," she draws out a little too high-pitched, taking McKenna's hands in hers. "You are not just my cousin, you're my sister, which makes you one of the first members of this clan I wanted to tell. I swear, Kenna."

"Really?" McKenna asks in disbelief.

"I promise," Abby assures.

Callan comes over and places his arms around Abby's waist, pulling her back into his chest. "After we got settled here, we were going to have a family dinner and make the announcement. You know, in a peaceful, chocolate-cake-filled environment. The kind we'd like our child to be raised in," Callan teases solemnly.

"Asher knows—he stepped in to save you and the baby?" Kenna clarifies.

My eyes fall onto my resting mate while Keegan repositions him on the bed comfortably.

"Please," Abby rolls her eyes. "Everyone knows that Callan is a gossip queen. Asking him to keep a secret is like asking a rabbit to resist a carrot. It's unheard of."

"Hey! I can keep a secret," Callan sulks.

"Clearly, you can't, babe," she counters. "I'm sorry he told Asher first." Abby looks apologetically between McKenna and me.

"And me," Keegan interjects, cleaning up the unused bandages.

Abby's mouth falls open in surprise, and then her eyes narrow as she spins to face her mate. "Loose lips sink ships, Callan Thomas St. Michael."

Callan releases a light chuckle. "There are no secrets in this clan, babe. In my defense, you've flat out refused to stop protecting Eves, which places you, and my child, in danger. Asher and Keegan needed to know for security and safety reasons," he points out.

I frown. "Abby, you can't continue to protect me if you're pregnant."

She turns crossly in Callan's arms. "The hell I can't, human. I am pregnant, not dead."

"By the grace, Abigail. It isn't safe," McKenna adds. "Don't be stupid."

Abby stares at her cousin, then flips her annoyed gaze my way before stepping out of Callan's arms. "Listen here, you two, there is nothing I would love to see more than my child's aunts getting along. Nothing. That said, don't you two team up on this. I am a protector. It is what I do. My assignment is to help with Eve's protection, and I will do so without argument or being treated like glass. Are we clear?"

McKenna's face pinches before her frustrated

expression meets my matching one.

"Is this why you always smell like pickles now?" I ask, changing topics.

Abby makes a face. "No. That's all Callan. Pickles give me heartburn."

My eyes lift to Callan, seeking an explanation.

"What?" he asks innocently. "I can have sympathy cravings."

"Then have them for chocolate cake," Abby pouts.

"I hate to say this, but there will be plenty of time to celebrate our new family member later. Right now, Asher is resting comfortably. Why don't we give Eve time alone with him so she can help him heal," Keegan suggests. "The rest of us should get cleaned up. Callan and I will speak with Michael and Uriel regarding protection surrounding the house and update them on what occurred with the dark army. I'm guessing Gage could use a break."

Everyone agrees and leaves me alone in the room with Asher. He's stretched out in the center of the bed, on his stomach, with his head facing me. I watch each shallow breath that passes through his lips. *What if I can't heal him anymore? Shit! Pull it together, Eve. Of course you can help heal him. Just breathe.* I huff at my own dramatics.

All of a sudden, Callan is standing silently next to me. I twist to face him, drawing my brows together to question his presence. I'd thought he left with everyone else. He offers a small smile, and without words, opens his warm arms. I drop my chin and step into them gratefully. He pulls me tighter into a bear hug before dropping a kiss to the top of my head.

"Asher saved my son tonight, cutie," he whispers into

the top of my hair.

I bury my face into his chest. "How do you know you're having a boy?"

Callan chuckles lightly. "Oh, I know. I'm never wrong about these things. Trust me."

I bask in the warmth and comfort of his arms for a moment longer before stepping away.

"All good?" he asks.

"All good."

Callan nods, planting one last kiss on my temple before he leaves the room. I turn back to the bed nervously. I sit beside Asher with my gaze locked on his peaceful expression. His skin is so pale. My heart pounds in scattered beats while my eyes crawl across his body.

I slide my eyes shut. "I'm tired, Ash. So fucking tired." Tired of fighting. Tired of worrying. Tired of being sad and losing people I love. "I have no more fight left in me."

With great care not to disturb his injured body, I lie down next to him and curl into his side, wrapping both of my arms around one of his and placing my forehead under his chin. I inhale his scent and relax in the warmth he's emitting before falling into a slumber.

Confusion swirls inside of me as my lids blink open and I take in my surroundings. Small slits of light are peering through the sheer fabric covering the modest windows. I lay still for several moments, taking in the cream walls of my childhood home. Taking in a deep breath, I blink my eyes fully open and twist to look at the beautiful sleeping gargoyle next to me.

My heart rate picks up as I remember he's hurt and can't stone sleep, which also means we can't dream walk with one another. *Damn.* I lift my hand and allow my fingers to drift over his jaw, his constant five o'clock shadow scratching the tips.

Languidly, I trace the lines and brush my fingers over the curve of his soft lips. His skin is still ashen but the dark shadows under his eyes are gone. Asher's thick lashes are unmoving. Without realizing what I'm doing, I slide forward and kiss his parted lips.

With everything I have in me, I force my healing energies into his body, but I feel nothing except the static of a small push. An odd sound falls from my lips, half-pained and half-disappointed as I pull my lips away.

I drop my gaze to the small space between us to discover there are no dark tendrils of electricity. My heart sinks. I swallow down the panic that claws its way up my throat. I tell myself that it isn't too late, even though that dark whisper in my mind says differently.

"What's wrong?" Abby's concerned voice filters into the room.

I sit up and draw my legs to my chest, resting my chin on my knees. She brightly smiles and perches herself at the foot of the bed, red strands of silky long hair falling dramatically over her slender shoulder as she studies me with a concerned expression.

I stare at her, unblinking.

My silence causes one perfectly shaped eyebrow to lift. "Eves?"

Unease shifts through me, and I pull my bottom lip into my mouth. "I can't heal him." I force the words out past the dryness in my throat.

She blinks slowly and her lips fall into an O shape. Her

lashes lower while she pinches her angelic features.

"My mate mark is fading, and the bond is lessening. I can't push healing energy into him, Abby. You warned me that if we waited too long to infuse the mark, this would happen. It's happening. I can feel our bond slipping," I explain. "Our souls are losing connection."

"Oh, sweetie," she exhales before waving me off. "We'll fix it, I promise." With an exuberant amount of energy, she hops off the bed and bounces around the room.

My gaze follows her while she searches around like a crazy person. A few seconds later, she claps giddily and grabs the first aid kit off the floor. Placing it on the dresser, she opens the lid and begins to wildly rummage through it, evidently on a mission.

"What's going on, Abs?" I ask with curiosity at the swing in her behavior.

"Got it!" she exclaims, pulling out a syringe and stalking toward the bed.

I jump up quickly and step in front of her path with my palms out. "What are you doing?"

Abby rolls her eyes. "I'm going to extract Asher's blood and infuse the mark. What does it look like I'm doing? Don't get mad, but Kenna is right, you do ask a lot of obvious questions."

Dumfounded by her statement, I just stand and stare at her before coming to my senses.

"Um, Abby, you can't do this."

"Why not?" she huffs, removing the plastic covering from the needle.

My brows shoot up to my forehead at the insanity. "Why not?" I repeat and look over my shoulder at Asher's comatose state. "He isn't even conscious to give his consent, Abby!"

"By the grace, sweetie." She takes a step in my direction, needle facing upward in the air. "Clearly, he wants to be mated to you. Now, please move."

"NO!" I shout. "I'm not going to permanently mate with Asher under duress."

"You do realize you and he are starting to sound alike?" she remarks.

I exhale and drop my hands to my hips. "You don't just take someone's choice of life-partner away from them while they're dead to the world," I state. "Christ, Abby. How would I even explain that to him when he wakes up? Surprise, we're official! Forget that you were passed out for the ceremony, but hey honey, I'm yours forever," I shriek in a mocking way.

She pauses, wrinkling her nose. "I thought you wanted to be his forever?"

I stare at her. "I do. But not like this." I motion to his limp form.

Abby watches me, pondering the conversation before she inhales, dropping her arm with the syringe. "Oh. My. God. It's because you want a ceremony." Her eyes light up. "In a forest, with candles . . . and flowers . . . and a pretty dress. Aw, Eves, you want it to be official."

"What?" I whisper. *The gargoyle has lost her damn mind.*

"I get it. All right, we'll wait for Sleeping Beauty to wake up," she squeals perkily, before throwing a stern look my way. "Then we are having this mating ritual so this doesn't happen again," she adds. "I could feel the panic flowing through you. Was that what it was about? Not being his anymore?"

"Is this crazy, extreme swing in conversation a pregnancy thing?" I ask.

She tilts her head to the side. "Are you saying I'm acting like a wild pregnant person?"

I tense and my eyes fall to her hand, which is still clutching the needle. "How about you put the syringe down and then I'll answer your question."

She releases a light and airy laugh and returns the needle to the first aid kit. I sag back onto the side of the bed in relief. A few moments later, she joins me, and we both watch Asher sleep.

"Well, at least in this state, he isn't brooding," she mumbles.

The right side of my lips quirk and I cup his cheek. "Do you really think he'll heal on his own from a wound this severe . . . without my help or stone state?"

"Absolutely. It will take a bit longer, but Ash is tough. He'll pull through, Eves."

I nod and face her again. "Don't tell the others about the bond fading, okay?"

"Well," she exhales. "It's obvious Callan can't keep a secret, so yeah, let's keep this little gem to ourselves."

After a few moments of silence my gaze falls to her stomach.

"I'm sorry McKenna had to be the one to save you after you hit your head. If we used my blood, we risked the possibility of you becoming bonded to the baby," she explains.

My gaze meets hers. "I get it now, Abby. It's fine.

You're going to make an amazing mother. I didn't have the chance to say this last night, but I'm so happy for you."

Her eyes dance with happiness. "He or she is lucky to have you for their aunt."

A twinge of pain pierces my heart at the title. "What if the fading bond is a sign?"

Her brows pull together. "A sign of what?"

"Maybe it's time to . . .let go."

11 Compromise of Truth

As the skies grow darker, the air becomes colder. The shoreline embraces the constant battering of the waves as they toss and turn before violently crashing onto the sand. I wrap my sweater tightly around my body and stare into the clear blue-gray water, watching the tides roll in before the currents sweep them back out again.

Asher's image flickers in my mind, haunting me like a ghost. He's been in his healing sleep for five days. Every hour that goes by, I feel as though I'm losing my grip on reality. My sanity is hanging on by a thread, as is the mate mark and our connection.

It feels like all we do is wait. Wait for the dark army to attack. Wait for Garrick to resurface. Wait for Deacon to be captured. And for every moment I wait, I'm reminded of my sacrifices, because the pain they've left in their wake beats away at my heart, like the constant battering of the ocean's waves.

Michael takes a seat on the cool sand next to me, taking in the beauty of the ocean for a few moments before he speaks. "It is not safe for you to be here without a protector," he points out with his old-world-divine accent.

My gaze slides to the archangel's admonishing expression before I tilt my head over my shoulder, in the direction of Keegan. The gargoyle is perched a few feet away on a rock wall.

Michael nods his acknowledgment at Asher's older brother and turns back to the water.

"You are sad," he states quietly.

I don't answer him. It's becoming harder to recall a time when I truly felt anything but.

"Your protector will awaken," he states, as if he's demanding it of the world.

I exhale and keep my focus trained on the water, admiring its constant motion. I'm unsure how much time passes as we sit without a word between us. I notice the skies darken further.

"I feel like I'm slowly fading away," I whisper the admission.

"We all get lost in the rain from time to time, Eve. It is part of what makes you human."

"The old version of myself seems like a distant memory. This person I've become—I struggle with accepting her." My eyes briefly flick to the angel, taking in his thoughtful facial features before returning back to the churning water. "Before, I would have fallen apart at the sight of Asher's injured form. This Eve—she's numb to the cruelty, violence and pain."

"The moment one's innocence is lost, it is never truly regained." He sits back casually with his palms in the sand. "Once you've seen the darkness, it can never be unseen."

My brows pull together. "There's something you don't see every day, an archangel paraphrasing John Milton's *Paradise Lost*."

A ghost of a smile plays at his lips. "Seemed a fitting parallel to your journey."

I lift my gaze and meet Michael's. "Everything I love seems to disappear, except the pain. There is always the pain. I miss being in the dark, unaware and naïve."

Michael remains quiet for a moment, pondering my words. "Free will can often lead to a division of one's sense of duty. A sentiment I am not unfamiliar with, Eve. It takes a great deal of courage and determination to step out of the darkness, into the consciousness of the light."

"What if I'm not courageous? What if I'm just a girl who wants to be free from all this?"

"Your freedom comes with recognition of your place on this journey. If you reject your destiny, there will be disastrous consequences," he states. "Justice lies behind actions."

"If my freedom comes with a contingency, then I need you to help me understand how my fate plays into the balance of power, and what I need to sacrifice in order to end this."

"What exactly are you asking of me, daughter of Heaven?" he asks with caution.

"Why am I the key to all of this?" I wave my hand

around the beach, ocean, and sky.

Michael's expression becomes tight as he sits up and lets his arms hang over his knees. The vein in his neck begins to pulse while he slides his gaze to Keegan, then back to the ocean in front of us. The silence lingers between us before he sighs heavily and dips his chin.

"You are to sacrifice love," he states, using a divine tone.

"Love?" I repeat. "I don't understand. How does love end the war?"

Michael's face pinches. "It doesn't. Lucifer wants one thing, to regain control over Heaven. The only way he can do that *is* with war. Your sacrifices will not *end* anything."

I stare at the archangel for a moment in shock, and a sinking feeling buries its way into my stomach. Suddenly, my conversation with Asmodeus at the Midnight Temple resurfaces.

"Somehow you've been misled to believe that you are more significant to our kind than your mundane life actually is."

"If that's true, then why is the dark army hunting me so persistently?" I question.

The demon shifts in his chair and shrugs. "Don't be fooled, daughter of Heaven. Your existence is of no consequence to my boss. Your creation is simply one more hypercritical stab in the back. Obtaining you, and ending your life, is a statement. A show of declaration."

"What does Lucifer want then?" Gage asks from my left.

"War," Asmodeus replies harshly.

My eyes shift to Gage and then back to the demon.

"Attaining me is an end to the war."

"Wrong," the demon barks. "Securing you is a strategy."

My nostrils flare as I attempt to pull air into my lungs in order to calm my anger. "You have got to be kidding me. When I first met Asher, he told me the Angelic Council, in an attempt to save Heaven in the event of a war with Hell, allowed a redeemer, me. The council believes this *liberator* will save mankind, allowing Heaven to prevail in the war."

Understanding crosses his expression. "Yes, that is the truth that was presented to you."

"The truth tha—" I stop, forcing myself not to strangle the angel.

"Are you saying that Asher lied to me? That *you* lied to me?"

"As part of your protection, I do believe we are all guilty of compromising the truth, Eve."

"Un. Fucking. Real," I exhale.

Michael throws me a sharp glance. "Information is provided to you, at my direction, which I feel is important to impart to you at certain times. This is done for your protection. Mr. St. Michael was given that information by me to, in turn, provide to you."

I just stare at the divine being with parted lips. "Is my life some sort of game to you?"

Michael sits straighter, as if insulted. "I do not understand your question."

"Do you feel anything for me that resembles a father's love for his child? Or am I just some human pawn whose life you enjoy toying with?" I seethe in hurt.

As each of my words sinks in, his jade gaze fills with

regret. "Do not misinterpret what I am saying to you. You were created out of my love for Libby. I am a divine warrior. My capacity to bond with you on an emotional human level is limited. I understand that may seem hypocritical to you since my love for your mother is abundant, however, my protection is what I can offer you as a fatherly duty and show of affection. The rest will have to come with time. I will learn to connect with your human sentiments. I ask that you be patient."

Crap. What do you say to that? "If I'm not meant to end the war, then why am I the key?" I change the subject as an attempt to push off my conflicting feelings of rejection and love.

"After your creation, your security was designed as a protective measure for Heaven. Not a means to *end* our long-standing war, but to *stop* it," he replies. "You and Asher, together."

At the sound of Asher's name, my irritation recedes. "You'll have to do better than that."

"When we discovered Libby was with child, our first thought was of your protection. You are the only one of your kind, born of a non-fallen angel and human. If you were discovered, the divine would see you as a betrayal of my service," he explains. "I knew Lucifer would destroy you no matter what. The divine, though—if I positioned you as a weapon to tip the balance in the war, then I knew they would protect you with all of the offerings of Heaven."

"This is all information you've already imparted," I point out.

The right side of his lips lift in a half-smile. "Consider it a brief reminder then."

"How did you convince the council that I would tip the scales? By doing what?" I ask.

"By creating the divination of redemption and preordaining the souls of the daughter of light and the prince of dark to join together. I vowed that united, as one, you two will bring redemption to creation until the end of days." He repositions himself so he's facing me.

"Thanks for the arranged marriage—*Dad*," I say sarcastically.

"I sought Asher out because I was aware of his protector bloodline. I knew, with his gargoyle lineage, he would guard you with his life once the divine ceased their security."

I shift on the sand. "I know all of this. What I don't know is how we are the key?"

"Through his connection to the dragon spirit," he replies.

"Why?" I whisper. "What significance does his dragon lineage have?"

"In the first war between Heaven and Hell, the dark army used a legion of dragons to attack Heaven's gates. Lucifer himself took on the dragon form. After that, the creatures were demonized and represented darkness to the divine," he says quietly. "I am not proud of this, however, I played off the council's fear and assured them that the weapon I created, you, would not only carry Heaven's pure bloodline, but that lineage would have an eternal bonded link to the dragon spirit. A connection designed as a reassurance that a dragon would never again, under the dark army's control, attack our gates. The bond you have with Asher, as his mate, ties your bloodline to the dragon spirit, effectively securing your existence as a weapon of protection against the dark army. The divine would never destroy you, because in their eyes, you tip the scale by protecting the gates from darkness. Do you understand?"

"Holy shit," I exhale.

My eyes scan the inky black of night settling over the ocean. My mind reels while I recall pieces of the story Asher and Keegan told me about their ancestry at our first dinner together.

"It's been said that during the seventh century, there was a legendary dragon that lived on the River Seine in France named La Gargouille. Apparently, he was so grotesque to look at people said he would ward off evil spirits. According to history, the dragon terrorized the town and people. The archbishop of Rouen, St. Romanus, attacked and killed it. During the battle, Romanus slaughtered the dragon, but not before it bit him on the left shoulder, almost piercing his heart. The bite was significant and bled badly. Unbeknownst to both during the fight, Romanus's and the dragon's blood mixed, causing the soul of the dragon spirit and the soul of the man who served Heaven to become bound together for eternity."

"Wow, that's remarkable. But how does that relate to your family?" I ask.

Keegan's authoritative voice pierces through me. *"Unfortunately, Romanus didn't view being bonded to the dragon's spirit as a blessing. During this time in history, archbishops were permitted to take a wife and have children. Romanus did this, but with each child he created, the bloodline continued and was connected to the dragon's spirit. Each generation produced from the archbishop's lineage was tied to the dragon eternally. Our father's ancestors carry the bloodline of Archbishop Romanus. Hence, our family connection to La Gargouille."*

"Romanus killed La Gargouille," I murmur, "tying Asher's family to the dragon spirit."

"The dragon Romanus slaughtered was a demon sent by Lucifer. By attacking an archbishop, a man who served God, he hoped to start another war. However, darkness always underestimates light. In the end, the divine were able to tie the two spirits together, and the gargoyle race was created in order to protect mankind against evil."

I just sit in silence, pondering the knowledge Michael is granting me. All this time, I thought that Asher needed me to survive, to keep his soul alive so he wouldn't cease to exist from stone petrifaction. I was so wrong. It's me who needs our bond in order to stay alive.

I turn to Michael. "Am I to understand that you've tethered our souls, our very existence, together? Are you saying that neither Asher nor I can survive without the other? Ever?"

"Each of your continued existences is reliant on the other's, yes."

I scoff. "Does Asher know this?"

The angel doesn't flinch. "Mr. St. Michael is operating under the assumption that he is your protector, at my request, fulfilling a divine assignment. His understanding of the divination of redemption is clear, but only as it relates to his existence."

"So if I break our bond, for any reason, not only will the dark army hunt me, but—" I begin.

"The divine will as well," he finishes. "A consequence

that even I can't protect you from."

"Well, that is just fucking peachy," I retort.

"The Angelic Council permits your existence because of your promised bond to Asher through the divination of redemption," he says slowly. "Your love for him is the purest form of sacrifice. If you are connected to Asher, then you will honor that love by helping him control the darkness and protect Heaven. It takes a dragon to fight a dragon."

"And in return for sacrificing my love to a bond, I have divine protection," I add.

"Yes."

"Keegan and Callan both stem from the same bloodline. Why'd you pick Asher?"

"The council has a long standing relationship with the London clan. We've partnered with their family for centuries on divine protection assignments. After speaking with Garrick on numerous occasions, and observing the connections each had with the McIntyre and Donovan girls, I assumed that Asher would be the one unmated when you turned eighteen."

"I see." I nod once. "And our bloodlines?"

"At my order, both your and Asher's bloodlines were altered by Everley, the cherub angel of ancestry. Yours at birth, to derive from Eve, Adam's second wife, and a light of Heaven, and Asher's was altered right before your protector link. His was to include the bloodline of Lilith, Adam's first wife, and a demon of darkness. Lilith's ancestral tie enhanced his dark gifts, making Asher the stronger male and next in line for the throne. The additional demon lineage also allowed Asher to accept your pure blood when he became your main protector through a blood connection."

"Wow, you've really thought of everything, warrior of Heaven," I snap.

Without warning, Uriel appears in front of us. His soft golden glow lights up the dark evening sky. The sound of water sloshing over the earth pulls me back to reality and I stand, brushing the sand off my pants. Michael follows the movements but remains seated.

I stare at Michael in disbelief. "Sooo, Dad," I draw out. "My takeaway from this bedtime story is that you knocked up my human mother, and then needed to protect your secret. So you created a predestined blood tie to an unknowing gargoyle prince, who I happened to meet at college and fell in love with through a nonconsensual blood bond, all to protect Heaven's gates. Your boss must be thrilled. Hope you're up for a raise."

"Is this true, Mikey?" Uriel questions as if he was unaware of the full plan.

"It was posed a bit angrily, but yes, I suppose that synopsis is accurate."

Uriel releases a loud laugh. "That is the most fantastic plan I've heard. We're good."

Michael frowns. "*We* are good?"

"The plan was clearly a joint effort, strategized through my intellectual portion of our shared DNA," Uriel suggests. "I am the archangel of knowledge and wisdom."

I stretch my neck from side to side. "What about the earth realm and the humans? If I protect Heaven, then who protects mankind from the demonic legion? I was under the assumption the divination of redemption has Asher and I redeeming mankind."

"That is why there are protectors. Without the darkness, there is no need to protect the innocent, and the gargoyle race would cease to exist," Uriel points out before sighing dramatically. "It's a vicious cycle really."

"As bonded mates, your and Asher's moral choices will decide fate. Mankind has free will. They have the ability to rebel against the darkness or embrace the light. Together, you and Asher will lead the next generation of protectors, keeping this realm safe," Michael adds.

"No pressure," Uriel jests.

"Why didn't you just tell us from the start?" I ask.

Michael's expression softens. "Regardless of my limited dealings with human emotions, you are still my daughter. It was Libby's and my wish for you to find true love. In spite of the bond and altered bloodlines, you have chosen to love one another of your own free will."

"Also in spite of the fact that he's foul-mouthed, tattooed, and a gargoyle," Uriel interjects with a shiver. "I guess this really does mean a power angel is out."

Michael and I both turn our attention to the quirky angel before returning it to one another. "I guess this explains why you allowed the blood connection in the first place, knowing only death could break it. And I suppose this is why you approved Asher's and my visit to the Eternal Forest, to see Priestess Arabella, knowing we'd have to stone state to get there, and what that meant for our bond. All those times you pretended to be upset, you weren't. You wanted Asher and me to fall in love."

"Love is your sacrifice, daughter of Heaven," he replies.

"A sacrifice that won't end the war between Heaven

and Hell," I add.

"It doesn't end. The balance cannot shift." He sighs heavily. "It never could. One side will never rise to power, just as one side will never fall to fate," he explains. "Everything in life must have lightness and darkness within it to survive."

"So what is the point of war then?" I ask.

"We must always keep the balance, Eve," Uriel states.

"I guess the real question is, will I risk it all for love?" I counter. "And if I do, who will pick me up and put the pieces of my heart back together when they finally shatter?"

"I will," Asher's deep, masculine voice floats to me.

12 No Regrets

My heart stops at the sound of Asher's voice. I inhale with relief and turn to face the beautiful gargoyle. The moment my gaze collides with his, the darkness inside me fades. A rush of shivers crawls over my skin at the sight of my protector watching me with a raw, painful expression.

I allow my gaze to roam over him, taking in every piece. My lower lip trembles as I shift my weight from one foot to the other, sinking into the sand. I soak him up with my eyes. A collection of memories plays in my mind—our eyes meeting for the first time in architecture class, his declaration of love in the rain when he returned to me, his promise of forever as he made me his. Despite what Michael contrived, every cell in my body knows I'm Asher's.

I love him.

I *would* risk it all for him.

The End.

Tears burn my throat as our gazes hold one another's. He grants me his signature sexy smirk and I become light-headed. My intense feelings for him swell in my chest. Within seconds, my veins flood with love and warmth, and I step toward him on shaky legs.

Each step I take becomes faster and faster as I cross the distance on the beach. Without realizing it, I've broken into a full run before jumping into his open and waiting arms. Asher firmly catches me, not allowing me to fall. Ever. He'll always catch me.

With shaky hands, I wrap myself around his body, burying my face into his neck so I can breathe him in. Our contact sears through my clothing, branding my skin. Asher pulls me to him tightly before releasing me and setting me down gently.

Once I'm steady, he clasps my cheeks with his warm palms, lowering his head until our mouths are a breath apart, sharing the same air. He doesn't move. Instead, his indigo gaze travels over my face, committing every inch of it into his memory.

"You heard," I say, my voice cracking.

"Every word," he whispers. "It changes nothing, siren. You are mine, forever."

A little spark of hope infiltrates the confusion I was plagued with after my conversation with Michael. For the briefest of moments, I thought this wasn't real. Seeing Asher, here, awake and in front of me, I know it is, with every fiber of my being. We belong together.

"I'm sorry. I'm so sorry all this was manufactured,

Ash." My voice cracks again.

One of his hands slides off my cheek and curls into my hair at the back of my head. His other hand trails down the length of me, settling on the curve of my waist, tugging me against him. My hands clench as they fold into the cotton material of his T-shirt, clinging to him, afraid he'll disappear. I'm so scared all this will be too much for him and he'll walk away.

Sensing my distress, Asher's arm circles around me in a tighter embrace. The fingers on his other hand spread across the back of my head, pressing my cheek against his heart. I squeeze my eyes shut, basking in the sound of his heartbeat and his scent.

"It's okay," he whispers against the top of my head before pressing his lips to the crown. "I understand. You saw me and couldn't resist my good looks and charming personality. I get it, siren. Because of my gargoyle awesomeness, you assumed I was way out of your league, and you didn't trust it to happen on its own. Totally explains why you had your archangel dad scheme and plot so I would fall in love with you."

A faint smile crosses my lips. "Seemed like a good idea at the time," I play along.

"It was. I've seen me," he teases.

I choke out a half-sob, half-laugh. "I'm so afraid that someday you'll see us as one big lie and walk away, leaving my heart in thousands of pieces."

Asher tightens his hold. "I've broken every protector rule and gone against my kind to be with you. I mated with you, killed demons for you, and would light the entire world on fire to keep you safe. Nothing in this world, or any other world, will ever change or diminish my absolute fucking love for you."

"I was so scared when that door opened and Keegan carried you in," I trail off, swallowing several times as the emotion clogs my throat. "When he said it wasn't safe to get you into a stone state healing sleep, I nearly lost it."

"I will always come back to you, don't ever doubt that," he vows.

I nod and inhale. After a few moments, I let go and take a step back.

Asher's eyes flick to the two archangels behind me. "Excuse me for a moment."

I watch as he steps around me over to Michael and Uriel. Keegan stands and comes to my side, also watching with confusion.

Asher dips his chin in respect before looking Michael in the eyes. "Divination or not, I love Eve. It's that simple. She's mine and will always be. I would give it all up for her." Asher's gaze slides back to me then returns to the archangel.

Michael's expression softens as his focus slides between Asher and me. "I'm glad to hear that, Mr. St. Michael. You have not only my divine blessing, but my paternal one as well."

Asher tips his head and returns to stand in front of me with a wicked smile before placing a light kiss on the corner of my lips, eliciting a shiver from me. A long moment stretches between us before Asher takes one of my hands and places it over his heart.

"All of these lies lingering in the air don't matter. *WE* matter. Whatever the reason that you were brought into my life, I'm grateful. You've ended the darkening skies in my world. *YOU* are all I want. *YOU* are all I need." He swallows, flicking his gaze behind me before meeting mine again. "I've never dreamed that I could love someone the way I love you, siren. The fragmented pieces of my life only come together when I'm with you."

Tears sting my eyes, and I fight to catch my breath with each of his words. *I love him.*

"You live in fear that no one will hear your cries—I hear them. I'll catch you when you fall, always. All of your broken dreams—I will make them fade away. When you're lost, I will find you and bring you home. I will pick you up when your world shatters."

A deep ache settles into my chest as his love rattles through me, touching my soul. Asher's focus shifts to Keegan, and one of his hands releases mine, reaching toward his brother. A moment later, the glint of a granite sword catches the moonlight bouncing off the water.

Asher releases my other hand, holding his sword in both of his as he takes a knee in front of me. Softly glowing eyes lift and watch me through dark lashes as he places his sword at my feet.

"Here in the darkness of the night and in the light of the moon and stars, I vow this to you. There is nothing I will fight harder for than to love, shelter, and revere you, forever, with every fiber of my being. Nothing stronger exists than my love for you, Eve Marie Collins. I will protect you, always." He bows his head to me and falls silent.

I sniff as the tears flow freely down my cheeks. My words are lost for a moment while I study the sword at my feet and the striking protector on his knees in front of me. My hands shake as I grip the soft material of his shirt at the shoulders, forcing him to stand.

I bend down and lift his sword, laying it back in his open palms so we're both holding it.

"You are truly, in every sense of the word, my soul's mate. There is no one else I want with me on this journey, Asher. I love you. We do this, together. Mated. Bonded. Forever."

"No regrets." He steps closer.

"No regrets." My voice cracks.

Asher's mouth presses against mine, parting my lips while he kisses me like he's starving. The sword falls to the sand and a rush of sensations tremble through me, causing my legs to become unsteady.

There is nothing soft or tentative about this kiss. It's hard and demanding. It's one hundred percent Asher St. Michael. He's showing me that what he feels for me is real and not insincere.

He's claiming me, forever.

❦

I swallow the bile threatening to crawl up my throat at the sickening sight. *Oh. My. God.* I try to avert my eyes to no avail. In a strange way, it's mesmerizing to watch. I guess it's similar to seeing a zoo animal eat its own poop. Gross, yet, you're fascinated.

"I'm not sure how much longer I can stomach this." I still stare.

Asher sighs. "Unfortunately, we have another six or so months of this."

"Don't either of you dare speak to me," Abby scolds around her chocolate-covered pickle.

I narrow my eyes from across the kitchen. "I thought pickles gave you heartburn?"

Abby releases the hold her ravenous mouth had on the condiment. "Do not change the subject, Eve Marie Collins. I can't believe Asher got on his knees, *TWICE* now to ask you to be his mate, and I was not present for either proposal," she sulks.

"Uh oh. My girl is using middle names. Better run, cutie," Callan suggests.

I pfft. "She doesn't scare me," I reply and give a pointed look to Abby. "You don't sca—" I stop because the look she's giving me scares the shit out of me. I step closer to Asher.

Angrily, she rips another bite off the poor pickle and crunches loudly like a wild animal. "I mean," she continues with a full mouth. "Keegan was there. Of all the clan members to be at the poignant moment, he's the one who gets to see it." She huffs and takes another large bite.

I watch her, with a tiny bit of disgust, gnaw on the thing like a horse with a carrot.

"It was really heartwarming," Keegan adds sincerely and Abby shoots him a harsh glare.

Callan gives us his megawatt toothy grin. "I hear you did the whole sword thing. Nice."

"Abs, want us to reenact it for you?" Asher asks, moving his lips toward mine.

"No!" Abby bellows but it's muffled because her mouth is full.

I scrunch my nose. "Why do you have to dip them in chocolate?"

Angry crystal blue eyes narrow at me.

"Never mind," I mumble and cower back into Asher's side.

Abby sighs and places the fake cucumber down. "All I crave is chocolate so it's the only way I can eat them. Plus it takes away the heartburn."

Callan steps next to her and puts his arm around her shoulder before dropping a kiss to her head. "That's not all you are craving, baby."

"Settle down, brother, isn't that how you got into this predicament," Asher jests.

Gross. "I thought we've discussed boundaries?" I bark out.

McKenna strolls into the small space we've all managed to cramp ourselves into. My beach home isn't that large, but for some reason, we always end up in the tiny kitchen.

She looks around the limited counter space and rolls her eyes. "By the grace," she huffs. "How much more of this shit are you planning to pickle? This house is bursting with the damn things," she balks, looking around at the jars.

I have to give it to her, it is kind of ridiculous. "It does seem like you have some obsessive-compulsive issues to work out." My eyes skate around the room.

"I've said this before, ladies, pickling is a fine art. One that is highly underappreciated," Callan says.

I give him a pointed glare and smirk. "I thought role playing was a fine art?"

Callan's eyes twinkle. "They both are. In different ways, or the same, depending." *Ew.*

"Well, I appreciate it, baby." Abby beams and dips another whole kosher dill into a bowl of dark chocolate before meeting my grossed-out expression. "Don't judge me, human."

"It's kinda hard not to, Abs," I counter.

"It's also pretty difficult not to watch," Keegan points out.

Abby rolls her eyes and continues chomping away.

Callan's hands drop to his hips. "Listen, all the ladies in this clan suddenly don't want my badass cookies. '*They're too sweet,*'" he mimics in his version of a girlie voice. "So, I started with the chili. '*It's too hot,*'" he mocks, using the same voice. "So now, it's pickles."

"It would be great if you would actually make something useful, like, beer for instance," Asher replies and the room falls silent.

"There is no pleasing this clan," Callan grumbles.

"I hate pickles," McKenna throws out.

Callan's head tilts toward her. "Those who hate pickles can't be trusted."

"What?" I laugh. "That's ridiculous. If she doesn't like them, she doesn't like them."

McKenna throws an appreciative look my way. Our first. *Holy shit.* The rest of the clan just stares at the two of us with shocked expressions before averting their eyes.

"Give us a few reasons why we should come to the dark side," Asher poses.

"For starters, pickles are too awesome to hate," Callan states.

"Technically, not a reason," Keegan points out.

"Cleopatra attributed her beauty to eating a lot of pickles," Abby interjects.

"It's also a scientific fact pickles make you happier,"

Callan continues.

My eyes slide to Asher's impressed ones. "Show me that data," I mutter.

"If it weren't for pickles, Columbus wouldn't have found America," Keegan states.

"I thought that was spices?" McKenna argues.

Abby holds her iPhone up. "November fourteenth is National Pickle Day."

Keegan nods. "Napoleon was a huge fan of pickles."

Callan steps out of the room for a moment before returning. "Abs got me a new apron," he points to the words. "It says *pickle smoocher* on it." He smirks adorably.

Abby drops her gaze, fascinated with the bowl of chocolate as my mouth falls open.

Asher's face pulls. "Dude, you do realize what a pickle *smoocher* is?"

Confusion floats over Callan's happy-go-lucky expression. "Enlighten me, smartass."

Abby's eyes widen as she studies Asher's cocky smirk. "Ash, don't," she pleads.

"It's a euphemism for someone who likes to give head," Asher states with a grin.

Keegan begins an uncontrollable coughing fit. My guess is it's to hide his laughing.

"By the grace," McKenna exhales, clearly annoyed.

Callan slides his glance from Asher to Abby. "That true, baby?"

Abby sighs and drops her head in her hands. "Yes," she answers in a small voice.

"Holy shit, that's brilliant." He laughs.

"It was supposed to be a private thing," Abby points

out.

"Nothing in this clan is private." My lips twitch into a small smile.

Her gaze locks on mine. "Speaking of private, have you and Ash discussed the timing for the mating ceremony? Since your mark is fading, we should probably do this quickly."

The entire room falls silent. *Crap. Crap. Craaaappp.* Asher turns to face me, nostrils flaring. His fists clench as he stalks toward me, backing me into the counter before caging me in with his arms and body. His eyes narrow to a thick slit of blue.

"The mark is fading?" he all but growls.

My heart begins to hammer wildly in my chest, and I throw an annoyed look at Abby.

"Thank you for this." I motion toward Asher. *Damn gargoyles.*

She points a pickle at me. "Hey, you started it by judging me."

His head lowers so we're at eye level. "What the fuck, siren. When did this start?"

I blink slowly. "I noticed it when we were on the plane coming back here."

He doesn't move. "Turn the fuck around," he demands.

"Asher," I exhale.

"Do. It. Now, siren." He holds my gaze.

After a few seconds of suffering his intimidation, I twist and he lifts up my shirt.

I squeeze my eyes shut at his sharp intake of breath. "Fuck," he draws out. "It's lighter."

"It's also why I couldn't push healing energy into you," I admit.

Asher releases the hem of my shirt, allowing it to fall back in place before he steps into me, pressing his chest to my back tightly. My hands curl around the kitchen counter as a breath shudders through me, caused by the way our bodies fit together. I bite back a moan.

Asher leans into my ear and drops his voice to a husky tone. "Tonight."

"Slow your roll there, gargoyle." Abby stands and forces her way in between us.

I exhale slowly, grateful for the space before I twist to face Asher. Although, to be honest, after seeing his intense expression, I'm regretting turning around at all.

"I can't just throw together an entire ceremony in ten minutes," she balks.

"A production is not needed," Asher counters.

"Oh *hell* no, Asher St. Michael. After all these months, after all you two have been through, and whatever it is we're about to fight—" She inhales, calming herself. "Let me be clear. There will be a dress. And candles. And romance." Abby stomps her foot. "Do not take this away from me." Her gaze slides and meets mine. "I mean, Eve. Of course I meant you."

I arch a brow at her. "Clearly."

"Keegan, have Gage reach out to Sora since he's in Paris," Asher requests.

"Will do."

"Who is—" I begin but McKenna cuts me off.

"What about the council?" she asks.

"In light of recent events, they have no authority over

gargoyle law anymore. Agreed?"

My shoulders sag, and a chorus of agreements glide through the clan.

"We'll need extra security tomorrow," Kenna adds. "The last thing we need is the blood of Eden being murdered on her mating day."

"Aw, cupcake, you do care," I taunt.

"Not an issue." Abby beams.

"We should also reach out to Michael," Keegan adds and Asher nods.

My breath hitches. I hadn't even thought about the archangel's presence. My gaze drifts around the house, and suddenly, I'm hit with a pang of sadness, knowing my mother won't be there. The moment is cut short when Abby's face appears in front of me.

"I was hoping that we would visit the House of McQueen. Like a sisterly bonding moment, where you try on dresses and McKenna and I cry, and oooh, and ahh," she says.

McKenna snorts. "Because that sounds like us."

Abby throws her an annoyed glance. "Instead," she goes on, "I'll make a few calls and see what I can do to get the dress to come to us," she chirps brightly.

"Okay," I reply, feeling overwhelmed.

Abby claps excitedly before spinning around and taking on her warrior stance. "Gage will get Sora. Keegan, you reach out to Michael and handle the guest list. Kenna and I will handle the wardrobe and décor," she ticks off.

"Can't wait," McKenna feigns excitement.

Abby turns to her mate, ignoring her cousin. "We need to discuss a menu."

"Anything you want, babe." He plants a light kiss to her lips before turning his attention to Asher. "You see that, Ash. Happy wife, happy life. Lesson number one." He winks.

Wife? Oh shit. My head starts spinning from all the commotion.

"You okay, siren? You're white as a ghost." Asher's gentle tone is at my ear.

I need some air. "I just need a . . . um . . . moment," I push out through erratic breaths.

Asher's hand is in mine and, within seconds, we're outside in the arid gardens. Asher's hands cup my cheeks, and he forces me to lift my head and meet his intense stare. I study the depths of each layer and everything else fades away.

"It's you and me, siren." He breathes across my lips.

"You and me," I repeat.

"We're all in. Forever."

"Forever."

"No regrets?" He waits.

"Only one," I whisper.

Asher shifts his weight nervously. "Which is?"

"Agreeing to let Abby pick out the dress," I reply.

A beautiful smile crosses his kissable lips. "I fucking love you."

I sigh happily as his lips meet mine and push all thoughts of tomorrow away.

A ceremony.

As if we have the luxury of time for such things.

13 This Love

Wisps of amber-lit fog twist through the dark fields of white lilacs and cream-colored wildflowers, cocooning us. I release a nervous breath and place a hand over my heart, willing the erratic beating to slow down.

My eyes slide closed while I focus on the hum of thousands of monarch butterflies. The constant motion of their wings lulls, and for a brief moment, everything around me becomes peaceful. When my lids flutter open, I take in the lightning bugs that sparkle and dance in the inky night sky, like my very own tiny stars.

The warm evening breeze brushes over my hypersensitive skin, causing a small shudder to run through my body. *Be brave, Eve. Be brave.* The haze presses in. My focus glides over the candle-lit fields of Sorceress Lunette's cottage, in the magic dimension. It's breathtaking.

I inhale when I'm unexpectedly bathed in a soft golden glow, which is diverting my attention.

Michael smiles at me with warmth overflowing from him. "You look lovely, Eve."

"Thank you," I reply shyly.

Sadness clouds his gaze before he blinks it away. "I am sorry Libby was not permitted to traverse planes for this, but rest assured, she will be watching with love and pride."

I nod my understanding and push away the darkness threatening to coil around me.

"Are you sure you don't want one of us to escort you, kiddo?" Uriel asks.

I attempt a small smile. "I'd prefer to take this walk on my own."

Abby reenters the cottage and her eyes widen when she sees the two archangels. Long red strands of her hair fall over her exposed shoulders as she shakes her head in disapproval. The understated champagne gown she's wearing glistens in the golden glow emanating off the angels, enhancing her ethereal look.

"By the grace, you would think divine entities would adhere to and respect rules a little better." She steps behind them, shooing the larger-than-life archangels toward the open door.

Uriel stops and looks down at her. "I don't want to go out there."

Abby tilts her head. "Why not?"

He fidgets uncomfortably. "Sorceress Lunette keeps hitting on me."

Abby looks over her shoulder at me and we both break

into a fit of giggles.

Michael's brows pull together. "I was under the impression that Professor Davidson accompanied the sorceress this evening."

Uriel's lips press into a flat line. "Exactly. Also worth noting, Zyla is not an understanding demigoddess. I'm afraid if the sorceress pinches my backside once more, my lady will literally bring the wrath of the Gods down on this realm."

"Well, that's just a chance we'll have to take. Out you go," Abby orders.

I smile at the scene before Abby turns back and catches my eyes, rolling hers. "In the future, Eves, be more careful what you wish for."

"What do you mean?"

"You wanted a family. It doesn't get much more typical than an eccentric cougar sexually assaulting a hot, yet quirky, uncle at a family gathering," she elucidates, her eyes lit with amusement. "Who knows, maybe we'll get lucky and Keegan will get drunk and fall into the cake," she adds sarcastically.

"There's cake?" I counter, causing her to sigh and fiddle with my hair.

I ponder her words for a moment. Taken aback at my reaction to them. They're true. All my life, all I've ever wanted was a family. I take a step toward the open door and study the seated guests. My eyes land on Marcus and Stephan, then Nassa, Gage, and Fiona, and I laugh at the weirdness of it all. I guess supernatural creatures are my new normal. My family.

I face Abby again. "Thank you for doing this."

Her glistening eyes take me in. "You look amazing."

My gaze drops to the sleeveless cream dress, picking at the heavy tulle netted bottom. It's simple and elegant. Abby steps over to me and readjusts the sage sash at my waist.

"This was Elizabeth's. It was a piece of the baby blanket she wrapped you in when you were born," she explains. "It was her wish that I use it today, per Michael."

My heart stops. "Really?"

Abby nods. "Elizabeth wanted you to carry something meaningful that you shared."

A large lump makes itself known in my throat and I fight back tears.

"You okay?" she whispers.

"Yeah. I'm good."

"Ready?" She squeezes my hand.

"Lead the way."

I watch Abby's retreating form as she makes her way down the narrow trail, lit stylishly with white hanging twinkle lights and ivory candles.

Exposed twigs coil around one another above her, providing a canopy of gothic archways, laced with pure white flowers intricately woven throughout the bare branches. Intertwined at each portico's center, the Celtic symbol of protection watches over us.

Abby's form becomes less clear as she maneuvers through the draped wisteria dramatically swaying, like fabric dancing through the fields. Almost as if in slow motion, her steps become unhurried.

She turns her head and looks over her shoulder at me, offering me an encouraging smile. I inhale and study her features, bathed in candlelight. The warmth and happiness radiating off the beautiful gargoyle helps to calm my frail nerves.

Reminding myself of what awaits me, I take a small step onto the curved pathway leading to my destiny. I thank the style gods that Abby let me wear my flat, brown lace-up boots as I follow the glow of hundreds of candles, guiding my journey through the darkness. Everything twinkles and sparkles like the stars in heaven.

Every so often, I stop to admire the exquisiteness surrounding me. When I reach the last archway, I lift my eyes and become breathless. My body freezes when I see Asher.

He's in tailored black dress pants and shoes. A crisp white button-down shirt adorns his chest. My eyes fall to his steady hands and I notice his sleeves are casually rolled to his elbows, showing off the Celtic tattoo and his leather bracelets. *Good Lord.* He's magnificent.

I take notice of an unfamiliar older woman standing in front of Asher before quickly shifting my focus to McKenna and Abby, seated in the front row next to their mates. Keegan dips his chin and Callan smirks proudly in acknowledgment.

I slide my gaze back to Asher and release a shaky breath when his indigo eyes meet mine. The depths of love and appreciation are evident in his gaze. I hold his beautifully luminous stare, and a long moment stretches out between us.

Suddenly, I'm overcome by emotion at the way he's watching me. Like I'm his everything. I stand completely still, unable to move. Asher's gaze drops, taking me in slowly, bit by bit. His lips part and a long exhale seeps out of him. With every caress of his look, he etches himself into my heart, imprinting further onto my soul.

I steady my breath and take a small step toward him. His eyes deepen to a vibrant cobalt, causing a wry smile to form on my lips and my nervousness to disappear. A faint smile crosses his lips as I approach.

Surprising me, Asher doesn't reach his hand out for mine. Instead, his hands brush my bare shoulders and trail down the length of my arms, resting on the curve of my waist. He tugs me against him, fitting our bodies together before sweeping my hair over one shoulder. Painfully slow, he lowers his lips and presses a light kiss to my neck above my rapid pulse. I relax against him, breathing for the first time today.

"God, you are so fucking beautiful, siren," he whisper-growls in my ear.

"I'm terrified," I admit softly on a trembling breath.

Asher's gaze intensifies. "I promise to keep the pieces of your heart safe. You are mine to protect, always."

A small, warm fluttering makes its way through my veins as I look him in the eyes.

"Then let's finish what we started, pretty boy." My voice is barely audible.

He produces a wicked smirk before dropping his voice to a velvety seductive one. "Rest assured, siren, I always finish. Right after you do. It's my *ladies first* policy."

A throat being cleared interrupts our moment, yet neither of us releases our stare.

"May I begin, Your Highness?" the stranger asks kindly.

"Eve, this is Sora. She is a dear friend and an elder gargoyle. She's also the leader of the Spiritual Assembly of

Protectors," Asher introduces.

My irises relinquish the hold they have on his and meet the welcoming cornflower ones of Sora. "It's nice to meet you. Thank you for being here."

A bright smile crosses her lips, causing the delicate fine lines that run throughout her face to lift. She tilts her head and her shoulder-length toffee strands shift slightly.

"The honor is mine, daughter of Heaven," she says in an elegant French accent.

"Sora is here to oversee the binding ceremony, then bear witness and formally accept your pledge of loyalty to the clan and the Spiritual Assembly of Protectors," Asher explains, his focus trained solely on my face.

"Okay," I reply and the butterflies in my stomach rage to life.

"If you are both ready, Your Highness, I'd like to begin," Sora states.

Asher tightens his hold on me. "We are." His voice is firm as he looks down into my eyes.

In my peripheral vision, I notice Keegan hand Sora a small dagger made of Asher's healing stone. She places the glossy black weapon on top of an ancient book with intricate Gaelic designs etched into the leather. Sora closes her eyes and chants words in Garish.

"The dagger is carved and spelled from the same onyx used on my stone state bed. It's meant only to be used for my binding ceremony," Asher murmurs, squeezing my waist.

I exhale breathlessly.

Asher rests his forehead against mine. "I need you to unbutton my shirt, siren."

My eyes widen in horror at what he's asking me to do—in front of everyone. "W-what?"

"Sora needs access to the protector mark." Asher grins, amused by my confused state.

"Right. Of course." I lift my shaky fingers to his top button. *Crap, get a grip, Eve.*

As if reading my mind, he pulls back and then leans toward my ear. "Just the top three. Let's not go giving away the cow for free, yeah?"

I roll my eyes at his antics. After a painfully awkward, drawn-out moment, I manage to get the buttons undone. Once I unfasten the last button, I hold on to it for dear life. Asher uncurls my fingers from the small white closure, placing a kiss to each of my knuckles before taking a small step back. His thumb strokes my pulse, beating against my wrist.

Sora finishes with her blessing, lifts her head, and opens her eyes. "If you would both be so kind as to hold out your left palms," she instructs.

My brows pinch together in question.

"It contains the *vena amoris*, or vein of love." She smiles kindly and places her frail hand under mine. "Please keep still, Eve. This will smart only for a moment."

I watch as she takes the sharp tip of the dagger and pricks my ring finger four times, while chanting "in-zen, mání, vas-wís, ew ter-ort," between each puncture. The blade is so sharp I barely register the tiny stabs.

"Each represents your mating vows: heart, mind, body, and soul," she whispers.

Sora leans toward Asher, repeating her steps. I watch as the tiny holes ooze with the smallest amount of blood. The elder gargoyle turns to me and hands me the blade.

"Eve, you must bring the dagger to Asher's protector mark. In the middle, please make a small incision so that the wound can open, releasing his blood," Sora coaches.

My heart turns over heavily, almost painfully. I swallow hard and my horror-filled expression catches Asher's understanding one. Memories flicker through my mind of when I pierced Asher in the heart with my own dagger. I swore I would never hurt him again.

A heartbeat of silence passes before warm fingers wrap themselves around my wrists. Asher's grip is firm as he moves my hand and the weapon toward his heart and the mark.

"You won't hurt me, siren." His voice is silky, coaxing.

For a moment, I stop breathing as I watch the tip of the knife caress the scar that sits in the middle of his protector mark, reopening the wound. Asher doesn't flinch when the blood begins to seep out. Instead, his lips tilt in a trusting smile before he gently pulls my wrist away. With ease, he releases the dagger from my hand and places a chaste kiss on my palm.

Stepping closer, he tips his head and brushes his cheek across mine before his breath crosses my ear. "Turn around," he demands.

Slowly, I spin, revealing the deep cut in the dress, exposing my mark to him. At the sight, Asher releases a low, rumbling sound before his fingers lightly brush over it. Seductively, he raises the dagger, and with the lightest of touches, runs the tip down my spine, causing my body to tremble. Once the dagger is on the mark, he steps closer.

My eyes slide closed and I feel the slightest pressure before the blade disappears.

"Open your eyes, siren," Asher implores in a low voice, turning me back to face him.

At the familiar command, my lids flutter open. My insides twist at the depth of love, and the intensity of desire, floating in his eyes. He pulls me closer, pressing every part of my body against his so that not an inch of space exists between us.

My heart races at the sensation of his finger pressing into the open wound on my lower back. The warmth that floats through me when his blood mixes with mine, binding us forever, is intoxicating.

"I give to thee forever, Eve Marie Collins," he vows softly into the night.

Lifting my finger to his cut, I run it down the length of the wound, infusing his protector tattoo with my blood, again. This time, of my own free will. After a moment, Asher releases his grip on my waist and places his hand over mine, pressing it firmly against the mark.

My throat tightens as I repeat quietly, "I give to thee forever, Asher St. Michael."

Instantly, my heartbeat syncs with his, and my mind fills with emotions and images that aren't my own. My soul feels brighter and complete. My heart feels whole. The mark comes to life on my lower back again, pulsing and throbbing with want and desire.

"The Spiritual Assembly of Protectors and the gargoyle elders have accepted and blessed your binding on this day. You may heal the wounds," Sora announces.

Asher rests his forehead against mine. We push our

healing energies into one another. I watch with relief as the dark tendrils close the wounds. Sealing the binding. Making us one.

After a moment, his hand grips the back of my neck, forcing me to cling to him, my fists clenching his shirt. Asher's mouth meets mine in a deep, searing manner. I'm overpowered by emotions. His. Mine. Ours.

His hand tightens around my neck and he groans into my mouth. The vibration surges through my body, fueling my desire. The mark pulses in bliss.

"You are mine." His lips caress mine as he speaks. "Forever."

"I am yours, forever." I smile through his long, drugging kiss.

Realization filters through that we're not alone when I hear Callan's chuckle from somewhere far away. We pull away slowly, never releasing one another's gaze.

"Eve, the next step in the ceremony is to accept Asher's clan as your own family. Are you prepared to pledge your devotion to the St. Michaels? To declare unwavering loyalty to each member, to love, and embrace them as your own kin?" Sora questions.

Taking in a deep breath, I promise to. "I am."

"London clan, do you embrace your new kin and future queen?" Sora asks.

"We do," Asher's family says in unison and my heart soars.

Asher interlaces our fingers and leads me to stand in front of a seated Keegan. His gaze slides between his eldest brother and me. "You must complete the oath via blood ties."

Keegan and I lift our left palms at the same time,

holding one another's glance. Asher punctures each and guides Keegan's over mine. He covers our clasped hands between his.

"Zhen pri," Asher calls out.

"Zhen pri," Keegan and I repeat, together.

"It is a privilege to welcome you, Eve." Keegan lowers his forehead to my fingers.

Asher guides me to stand in front of McKenna. I lift my hand and wait. McKenna's sapphire eyes slide from my face to my hand. A silent pause beats between us before she snaps her palm out to Asher. With a quick piercing, she slaps her hand onto mine, forcefully.

"Zhen pri," Asher repeats.

"Zhen pri," we reply.

McKenna drops her forehead to my fingers. "It is an honor, blood of Eden."

She lifts her head and we hold one another's stare.

"It is I who am honored, McKenna, to be your family," I push out.

Her eyes widen slightly at my declaration before she dips her chin and sits back.

"It's my turn," a tearful Abby exclaims, grabbing my arms and pulling me to stand in front of her. She already has her hand out, waiting.

Asher releases a soft laugh and shakes his head at her enthusiasm, repeating the process.

"Zhen pri," Asher states, amused.

"Zhen pri," Abby exclaims in a cheerful tone and lays her forehead on my fingers. "We love you so much, Eves. I'm thrilled you are officially family now."

Leaning in, I pull her into a quick hug. "Me too."

Restoration

I step in front of Callan and he abruptly stands, picks me up, twirls me, and then returns my feet to solid ground. "Let's do this." He winks and holds his hand out to his brother.

Asher bites back another laugh then stabs Callan and places our hands together.

"Zhen pri," Asher says.

"ZHEN EFFING PRI!" Callan shouts in excitement.

He places his forehead on my fingers. "I have no idea what you see in my brooding, ugly brother, but it's official, cutie. You're one of us. Sucks to be you." He chuckles and lifts his head, planting a kiss on my forehead. "Family dinners will never be the same, Eves."

"There is just one last vow," Sora interjects, looking a bit frightened at Callan's proclamation. "Your oath to the Spiritual Assembly," she continues, taking the dagger from Asher. "Eve, present your right wrist to me, please."

I hold out my arm and watch as she makes a small incision across it, doing the same to hers before allowing a few drops of her blood to fall onto my wound. At Sora's nod, Asher immediately steps forward and heals the cuts on my palm and wrist.

"Do you come here today, of your own free will, to pledge your allegiance to The Spiritual Assembly of Protectors?"

"I do."

"Above you are the stars, below you are the stones. Like the stars, you offer light when faced with darkness. Like the stones, you offer darkness the ability to ground itself. It is a great gift that your heart and soul embrace both darkness and light. This balance will be an asset in showing resilience to your kin, both human and gargoyle. In taking this oath of protection, you will be expected to uphold, in the highest regard, human and supernatural life. Your binding to our council will make you an aegis against any and all evil. Divine assignments and defense of allies, clan, your mate, and king, will be called upon. As our future queen, you must promise to serve, honor, and protect your new race. On this day, Eve Marie Collins St. Michael, do you stand with us and recognize all that we ask of you?"

At the addition of Asher's last name to mine, I stumble and pause, taken off guard.

"Eve?" Asher encourages.

"Sorry, I do."

Sora places her hand over my wrist, which feels as though it's burning. Her thumb gently rubs over the skin, soothing it. "Through the darkness, you will be blind no more. Your soul shall not falter. You have the acceptance of the guardians of spiritual protection. May your daggers and shield keep you safe, always, Your Highness."

Sora releases my hand and I stare at the small Celtic cross that has suddenly appeared on my wrist. It matches Abby and McKenna's perfectly.

"You bear the mark of the Spiritual Assembly of Protectors. It is a great honor," Sora says and dips her head respectfully.

"Thank you," I reply in a quiet tone.

Asher steps in front of me, holding a few Shamballa bracelets, like the ones Abby and McKenna wear, only these are black onyx.

Gently, he takes my hand and slides the bracelets onto my wrist, hiding the mark. As soon as the cool stones hit my skin, the most magnificent energy runs through me.

"Why four?" I question, staring into the depths of his eyes.

Asher's stare bores into mine with palpable love and desire. "Heart, mind, body, and soul. They symbolize our mating vows."

"I do believe there is a final proclamation that needs to be made," Sora interjects.

Asher's eyes rake over my body in a tactile manner, a promise of things to come. Interlacing our fingers, he spins me so I'm facing the small group of guests witnessing our bonding. My eyes meet Gage's for a brief moment, and he offers me a small, sad smile.

Keegan steps forward and hands Asher his sword with an approving nod. A loud, happy sob releases from Abby and Callan wraps his arm around her shoulder while McKenna rolls her eyes at the dramatics of it all. I internally smile. It's nice to have family.

Asher takes a knee in front of me, his sword lying across both uplifted palms. I shiver as Asher looks up at me through sooty eyelashes, with a noble gaze. "Your creation was the first step toward the destiny we share. Know this, when the skies darken and this love is tested, we shall not run. When death becomes silence and the battle lines are drawn, we shall fight. On this day, we fall to fate, as one. Your light breathes life into the darkness. It is with duty, honor, and protection I lay my sword at your feet and declare my love, devotion, and loyalty to you in the presence of the supernatural monarchies." Asher bows his head and places his sword at my feet. "You are mine. My soul is yours. This love . . . is unbreakable."

14 Displaced

Strong hands curve along my cheeks and gentle fingertips run along my jawline. The touch is so powerful my skin glows and warms in response. I slide my eyelids shut when warm lips connect with my forehead. My heart clings to this moment, because it's one I want to last forever. A brief glimpse at perfection before it all gets swept away and displaced in the morning's light.

Asher sways us as one with the music in front of the blazing fireplace while staring into my eyes. "Do I own your soul, siren?" he whispers, his minty breath caressing my lips.

"Always," I reply breathlessly.

He angles his head, his eyes penetrating through each

of my layers, seeking out my soul. My cheeks redden under his desire-filled gaze. The back of his knuckles lift and glide over the pink while a cocky smirk appears across his lips.

"I fucking love that I'm the only one you blush for." His voice is a mere growl.

Hooded eyes flick to my parted lips, and before I can take in a breath, Asher's mouth brushes across mine. Heat spreads throughout my body. This kiss is delicate, tender, and loving as he cups my face and his thumbs softly stroke my cheeks. He stares at me for the longest time before speaking.

"Do you know how unbelievably sexy it is you're mine in every way possible?"

My arms wrap around his neck, pulling him closer. His mouth descends again without hesitation. God, this man is everything. Asher's kiss grows harder, more demanding, as he steals my breath with each stroke.

After a while, my legs become unsteady. Sensing this, and without breaking contact, his arm finds its way under my knees, and Asher scoops me into his arms.

He breaks the kiss, pulling back only an inch to gaze into my eyes. The amber flickers of the massive amount of lit candles bounce across the azure specs.

"Where is everyone?" I whisper in a needy voice.

Asher's sooty lashes lower over his eyes as they darken. "The clan returned to the Vineyard. Lunette offered us her guest suite and cottage for the evening. The charms are up and the dimension is locked out. It's just you, me, and my piercing, siren."

My lips tip up on the side as I rake my top teeth over my bottom lip, biting back a laugh. Asher's head dips back to my mouth, and he nips at my lower lip before running the tip of his tongue over it and dragging it into his mouth.

I moan in pleasure as he tightens his grip on me. Hurriedly swinging us toward the stairs, he takes them two at a time, rushing into the guest room.

"Always in such a hurry," I whisper.

Placing me on my feet, he arches a brow. "I can promise you, Eve, nothing about what I do to please you this evening will be hurried."

⁂

My eyelids flutter, trying desperately to open. The darkness is too powerful. It swallows me whole, pulling me into its deep, vast emptiness. Fear sits at the edge of my subconscious as the air engulfs me in cold and decay. The weight of doom and dread push heavily on my chest while I take shallow breaths.

I swallow. My throat is painfully raw from screaming and lack of water. With my eyes closed, I roll onto my back and realize my ribs are still broken. *Fuck.* I drop my head back in frustration, bumping the stinging spot on my scalp. It is raw from being yanked when I kicked and struggled before my body went numb and the darkness took over.

Another tremble rocks through me, and I float to the safety of my mind, where I'm with Asher and he's the cause of my uncontrollable shaking. Briefly, I allow myself to indulge in the memory of our last night together.

I remember, in vivid detail, the way Sorceress Lunette's cottage was lit with candles, bathing the entire chalet in warm light. I pretend to be surrounded by the scent of lavender from the fields around the magical dimension.

Warmth floats over me when I remind myself of what it felt like to be carried by Asher as we laughed and kissed endlessly.

A sick, odd laugh bubbles out of me. My sanity is slipping again. I picture Asher's intense gaze as he slid in and out of me, leaving me breathless. A tear slides down my cheek as my body recalls our connection when his skin slid across mine. Just for a moment, I pretend his mouth is at my ear, vowing his love as he devours every inch of my body.

I move slightly and my body protests from the agonizing pain I'm in. My eyes roll to the back of my head, behind the closed lids, threatening a black out. I try to fight off the ache in my skull, no doubt a side effect of being medicated over and over again.

The sound of metal sliding causes my heart rate to kick up a notch. My nerves jump and my muscles tighten. The thick steel door opens with a heavy groan, and I press myself into the dirt floor. Adrenaline courses through me, and my eyes fly open when the door slams. Steeling myself, I lie still, waiting, as the silence lingers in the air.

"Get up!" The command tumbles around the quiet cell.

After a few attempts, I manage to push myself up and drag my body across the dirt, ignoring the excruciating pain. For support, I prop myself against the stone wall. The coldness drifts over me as the being bends so he's eye level with me.

"So much for *epic* love, Miss Collins," Lord Falk, leader of the Royal Gargoyle Council of Protectors, spits in my face. Literally. *Asshole.*

My head lolls back from weighing heavily on my neck, forcing my chin to lift. I narrow my softly glowing gaze and seethe with anger and frustration.

"Fuck you," I reply, disregarding the dryness in my throat.

The sting of his backhand is quick and lingering. My entire head falls onto my left shoulder from the force. I inhale slowly through the pain and lift my head, not giving him the satisfaction of tears because it will show weakness.

Though inside, all I want to do is bury my face in my hands and cry for days.

The gargoyle sighs and stands, pacing in front of me. "You will show me some respect."

I bark a laugh. "I will show you nothing."

I cower back into the wall as the gargoyle pushes into my face, spitting foam from his mouth. "Listen here, human. *You* are nothing but a disgrace to our kind."

"Funny, that's what I've heard about you," I retort and suffer a harsh kick to the ribs.

I release an ear-splitting cry, because my ribs have already been broken several times over and I can't heal myself. My eyes water from the pain as I croak and wheeze, trying to suck air into my burning lungs, while at the same time forcing myself not to puke.

"I told you to watch your mouth," he roars.

The cell door opens again, allowing a sliver of light to enter the darkness. I immediately recognize the inky black neck-length hair and slate-colored eyes of the guard dressed in all black. His dark brown wings are extended.

"Everyone has gathered," Rulf states, pulling his brows together at the sight of me.

"Excellent," Lord Falk replies, grabbing a handful of my hair, forcing me to stand.

I squeeze my eyes shut and try not to pass out. The dizziness and pain are endless.

"Let's go," he barks, dragging me out of the stone prison and into a passageway, up several flights of stairs and through a few more passages.

"Why hasn't she healed?" Rulf questions, his tone tinged with annoyance.

"I had the cell spelled, a trick I learned from an old friend, Deacon," Lord Falk states.

While being yanked around, I notice Domus Gurgulio is not as pristine as it once was. Some of the stonework and statues in the alcoves appear damaged. There are burn marks marring the elegant rugs. I guess my light energy did some destruction during my last visit.

Through my displacement, I recognize the smashed carved wooden doors, hanging off their hinges in front of us. I'm unceremoniously pushed through and violently thrown down the aisle, only to collapse on my bound hands and knees in front of the stage.

Lifting my gaze, I take in the gargoyle council, looking confused at the commotion.

"What is the meaning of this?" Jarin, an elder member, questions, staring down from his throne at my battered body.

Now that I'm out of the charmed dungeon, a little of my strength returns, and I can begin to slowly heal from some of my minor injuries. The rest will take a healing sleep—and Asher's help. My heart skips a beat as his face flashes through my mind.

Knowing our bond has opened up deeper connections, I attempt to reach out to him but am immediately stopped by another vicious kick to the ribs. This time, the pain is too much, and I vomit all over the stone underneath me.

Out of the corner of my eye, I see Rulf flinch, but he stays put. *Smart.*

Lord Falk steps onto the raised stage. "Our king has requested Miss Collins's presence."

"Our king?" Jarin repeats, sounding perplexed as his focus drops to me again.

Lord Falk's face morphs into anger. "Help her stand," he orders Rulf.

My eyes lift and study Rulf's tight features as he bends down and gently places his arms under mine, assisting me upright. His stare meets mine in a sympathetic warning before turning back to the council, where the leader has taken a seat amongst his assembly.

"Where is her protector?" Lief, a younger male member, asks.

Lord Falk smirks, tenting his fingers under his chin. "His Highness was detained."

Panic crawls through me as my memories slowly come back. I'd woken in the middle of the night, needing water. I was standing in the cottage's kitchen. There was a quick pain on my neck, almost like a bee sting. My hand automatically goes to the spot. At the motion, the right side of Lord Falk's lips tilt upward. The next thing I remember is waking up in the cell. My pissed-off focus flicks to Lord Falk's knowing one.

He inhales with pleasure, sitting back into his throne. "It would seem Mr. St. Michael's love for you leaves him blind in matters of your protection, Miss Collins. Given the spells and dimensional lockdown, I'm sure you're curious as to which of your invited guests assisted in your abduction," he taunts, amused. "I understand the very private ceremony was beautiful. It is a sad day for love." His smile is cruel before it falls. "Consider for a moment, if you will, that while you slept quietly in the afterglow of your intimate evening, the love of your life was taken from right under your nose. Imagine the panic our young prince felt when he woke up to find you gone." He sighs as if he actually feels sadness. "What a shame that his clan wasn't there to help. It was such a gracious gesture for them to allow you and the dark prince an evening alone, with a false sense of security in the magic dimension."

Feeling stronger, I stop leaning on Rulf and take a step toward the stage. "The only shame here, Lord Falk, is that I didn't end your existence the last time we saw one another. Asher will come for me. He will burn down every realm in existence until he finds me, and when he does, I look forward to watching him tear you apart. Limb from fucking limb."

"You stupid girl," Lord Falk shouts, rushing at me from his seat. He pushes Rulf away and stands in front of me, closing an angry hand around my throat, tightening his iron grip.

My hands automatically reach for my daggers but, of course, they aren't there. *Crap.* Strong fingers press cruelly against my skin, leaving bruises. My vision becomes blurred, and just as I'm about to lose consciousness, he releases me, and I fall heavily to the ground. I cough and drag air into my lungs while a council of *supposed* human protectors watches in shock and horror.

"You're pathetic. Certainly not worthy of the title of queen," the leader seethes at me, storming back toward his throne. "Cassius, join me a moment," he barks out.

A sinking feeling crawls into my gut. I collect myself, stand, lift my chin, and stare into Lord Falk's eyes in challenge. Cassius approaches the leader, and just as he bows his head in a respectful greeting, Lord Falk runs a sword through his heart in a cruel and violent manner.

An odd gurgle comes from the young protector's throat before he turns to stone. Within seconds, he's gone. The chamber falls silent as terror and shock pass over each council member's face, and my own.

"What are you doing?" I demand, taking a step toward the throne.

"Teaching you a lesson," he answers in a bored manner.

Rulf wraps his hands around my upper arms, preventing me from lashing out. Even in my weakened state, I writhe, trying to fight him off.

"Let go of me," I shout.

"Easy, Eve," Rulf soothes. "You'll make whatever this is worse," he whispers in my ear.

"You can't do that," I cry out, pointing at the pile of dust at Lord Falk's feet.

"Miss Collins," the elder gargoyle chides. "I can do whatever I want," he continues in a sickly sweet tone. Without warning, he jumps up and is in my face, shouting at me aggressively. "Do not forget, I AM THE COUNCIL LEADER!"

After a moment, Rulf pulls us back, allowing for a small sliver of space between us.

Jarin stands. "Your title gives you no right to take another protector's life, Lord Falk."

The council leader spins so quickly I barely register

the movement. His sword finds Jarin's chest immediately, ending the other elder's existence. Again, my anger rises.

"STOP!" I yell while Rulf tightens his grip on my arms.

Lord Falk twists and catches my eyes with a wild and evil look. The disdain emanating off of him causes me to stop fighting Rulf. Realization sets in that he's planning to end the existence of the council, regardless of my actions.

I hold his stare. "As the future queen of this race, I order you to discontinue your efforts to dismantle this assembly. You are not within your rights to hurt these protectors."

Lord Falk stares down at me with an arrogant resolve, dropping his tone to a menacing level. "There is no future for you, only death. Return her to the cell until Garrick arrives."

Rulf tugs at my resistant body, forcing me out of the chamber and into the stone passageway. Not a difficult feat considering my current injured state. Once he's thrown me around a few hallways, he roughly releases his hold on me, causing me to stumble a bit before my hands meet a wall. I inhale, twist, and rest my back against the cool stones.

While both of us catch our breath, my guard runs his hands over his face and through his dark hair in frustration. I take that moment to start running. He easily catches me and yanks me against his chest, causing me to grunt in pain from my broken ribs.

"Holy shit, would you just calm the fuck down, Eve," he barks at me. "I'm not going to hurt you, or bring you back to the cell. So just . . . fucking relax," he exhales.

At his words, I stop my escape efforts, and he releases

me once more.

"Christ, you're feisty," he blows out on a winded breath.

I huff. "You would be too if you were kidnapped, beaten, and held captive for who knows how long by a council who claims they are supposed to protect humans."

Slate eyes roam over me. "Point taken." He nods, with his hands on his hips. "Look," his gaze snaps down the hallway we just came from before coming back to me, "we don't have much time. I had no idea this was going to go down the way it did. Since Falk is offing council members one by one, without cause, I think it's best if we get out of here."

I arch a brow challengingly. "No shit."

Rulf rolls his eyes. "If you can trust me, I will take you somewhere safe. Once we are out of harm's way, I'll reach out to Asher. I'm sure he's having a shit fit."

I fold my arms protectively over my ribs. "Why should I trust you?"

His eyes roam around the castle before landing on mine. "You seem to be out of options."

I sigh out my resolve. "Fine. But so help me, Rulf, if you touch me, the minute I get a hold of my daggers, I will cut your heart out after I stab you to death."

A small smile forms on his lips. "Believe it or not, those are the same words my last date used to accept my dinner invitation."

I narrow my eyes. "Are you joking with me? NOW!"

He lifts a shoulder. "Thought some humor might be appreciated, given the situation."

"Please, just get me out of here," I beg in a resigned

tone.

Rulf opens his arms, motioning with his eyes for me to step into them. I hold my ribs, unmoving.

"I can teleport. However, you need to hold on to me if you want to come," he points out.

I stare at him for a moment. *Fuck.* He's right. I am out of options. With no other choice, I have to trust him. *Crap. If he crosses me*—my thought is cut off by his amused voice.

"For the record, I'm also telepathic. So . . ." he trails off.

In my mind, I conjure up an image of myself giving him the finger. *Read that, asshole.*

He rolls his neck. "Clever. Do you want to get out of here, future queen, or continue our witty banter through a telepathic conversation?"

"Out of here."

"Good choice."

I step into his embrace, and within seconds, we're gone.

15 Silent Screams

My eyelids flutter in a desperate attempt to fall back asleep. The effort is unsuccessful. I force myself to sit up, ignoring the twinges of pain in my ribs. The rest of my muscles and joints crack and groan in protest at my movements, while I assess my body.

I'm still pretty badly injured, though some of the smaller wounds and bruises have healed. Sitting up, I swing my legs over the side of the soft bed and force myself into a standing position. My eyes squeeze shut as dizziness takes over. After a moment, it passes and I exhale.

My gaze floats around the ancient stone room accented in polished, dark woods and crimson silks. A large fireplace roars, and I ignore the nip of the cold floor as I move my bare feet toward the warmth. I pace anxiously in front of the hearth, soaking in the fire's heat.

Where the hell am I? And where is Rulf? I sigh into the silence, frustrated and agitated. I saunter toward two large picture windows, which span the length of one of the walls. My vision travels over the green shelved slopes the castle is nestled on.

One windowpane frames steep cliffs that drop to the sea surrounding two sides of the castle. The second glass panel highlights a narrow strip of land attached to a bluff. A gatehouse comes into view after my eyes stray to a steep path, headed straight to its doors. Various stone buildings and towers emerge across the rolling moss hills, spreading across its length.

I silently scream into the emptiness of the room's isolation. The cold stone walls are a reminder of my neglect and confinement. *All I want is Asher.* Memories of the previous day's captivity haunt me. The images cause me to tremble in both fear and anger.

"Yer awake." A cheerful, Scottish female brogue fills the silence of the room.

At the unexpected sound, my heart leaps, and I carefully spin as not to irritate my ribs, coming face-to-face with a very pretty young woman. Her long golden strands are intricately braided and pinned on the top of her head. Deep cerulean eyes twinkle warmly at me.

My gaze falls to the tray of fruits, breads, and cheeses she's holding. Oddly, she doesn't move. We stand silent for a moment before my questioning glance meets hers.

"Apologies. 'Tis just, ye'r th' prince's mate 'n I am not sure how tae address ye," she says, sheepishly. "Should I bow, or call ye yer highness?"

"No to the *bowing* thing." I smile awkwardly. "You can just call me Eve."

"Eve 'tis then." She dips her chin in resolve before crossing the room at a fast pace.

I watch her place the tray on a small circular table in front of the fire and busy herself pouring amber liquid from the delicate teapot into a china cup. Every so often, her gaze slides to mine in amusement before she lifts the fragile cup and saucer, offering it to me.

Grateful for the hot liquid, I take a sip, only to choke and swallow hard. My eyes water as I hand the cup back to her. "What the hell is that?" I ask through the burning in my throat.

"Whiskey. I thought ye could use some," she replies.

"Whiskey? In a tea cup?" I question, declining her second offering with a wave.

The petite girl simply shrugs and returns the china mug to the tray.

"I don't mean to be rude, but who are you? Where am I?" I ask, finally composing myself.

The woman's petite form spins, and she offers her small hand for me to shake, which I do.

"I'm Helena. Sean's mate 'n' Rulf's sister. 'N' yer on th' northeast coast o' Scotland about three kilometers south o' Stonehaven."

"Scotland?" I inquire in surprise. "You're Rulf's sister?"

"Aye. Yer under da protection o' da Scottish clan."

"Sean. He's the second in command under Griffin. McKenna's kin?"

"Aye." Helena takes in my confused state, worry

evident in her expression.

"I guess the supernatural world is very incestuous," I mumble.

She shrugs, not understanding my offhanded comment.

"Rulf doesn't have a Scottish brogue," I point out.

"Aye. He grew up wit' our mum en da States," she replies.

"Where is he?"

"He 'n' Sean left tae retrieve yer prince."

"They're getting Asher," I confirm and exhale in relief.

Helena nods and smiles before moving toward the bed. I watch as she pulls the sheets and blankets, putting them back in place. When they are to her liking, she turns back to me.

"Ye are badly hurt, Eve, so Rulf left ye here tae heal. In my care," Helena explains.

"I see. Well, thank you for taking care of me. I appreciate it."

Helena's expression falls. "It's me honor," she replies.

"Why did Rulf bring me here?" I inquire.

"I think he feels guilty fur yer troubles. He was th' one who brought ye tae Laird Falk."

It takes me a moment to process what she's saying because her accent is so heavy. When I finally do, my lips part in both astonishment and annoyance before I chew the inside of my cheek.

"Wait, are you saying Rulf was the one who kidnapped me and handed me over?"

Helena winces at my high-pitched tone. "Aye. He

meant ye no harm, Eve. 'Twas Rulf's understanding Laird Falk just wanted tae confirm th' mating bond. If Rulf had known what Laird Falk had planned, I assure ye me brother wouldn't have helped."

My hands hide my ribs, protectively. "I didn't even know Rulf was at the ceremony."

"Professor Davidson had tae leave early. Rulf took his place, escorting Lunette. Th' sorceress had na idea about th' kidnapping," she adds, as if reading my mind. "Can I ask ye a favor, I beg o' ye nae tae tell th' prince. He'll murder Rulf fur sure."

My eyes study Helena's pleading expression before rushing around the room. She's right. If Asher finds out Rulf was the one who took me from him, he'll kill him, slowly. I ponder letting Asher do it for a bit before I remind myself that Rulf did save me and brought me to McKenna's family for safekeeping.

I lift my gaze and am hit in the gut with guilt when I meet Helena's pleading one. She is taking care of me. *Crap.* Having trouble finding my voice, I simply nod my agreement not to tell Asher about Rulf's participation.

"Thank ye. Yer safe 'ere, Eve," she assures before her eyes roam over me with concern. "Yer badly bruised 'n' battered. 'Tis there anythin' I can git ye tae mak' ye more comfy?"

I drop my gaze and take myself in. She's right. *God, I look horrid. Asher will freak if he sees me like this.* "Maybe some fresh clothes?" I suggest. "And a place I can take a shower?"

"Aye." She smiles and bids me to follow her to a closed door on the other side of the room. She opens it to reveal a beautiful, grand bathroom. In the center is a large claw foot tub. "I can run ye a bath 'n' while yer soaking, I will fetch some clothes. I think we are about th' same size."

"Clean clothing would be amazing. Thank you, again, for your kindness," I reply.

Helena waves me off as if it's nothing that she's caring for a complete stranger and twists the tub's knobs. She tests the water, and once the temperature is to her liking, she merrily floats around the room.

She pulls out a jar of bath salts from under the sink and pours them into the bath. I watch as the tiny pink salts fizz and dissolve in the welcoming water. My body sags at the thought of relaxing. All my energy is drained, and I suddenly just feel very, very tired.

Helena turns to me. "Take yer time, Eve. If ye need anythin' just let me know. Leave yer clothes by th' door 'n' I will have them cleaned," she says, closing the door behind her.

I'm unsure how much time passes. It might be hours that I've hidden myself in the lavender-scented bubbles, allowing my muscles to relax in the warmth of the water. A few more of my injuries have healed, but my body is still more black and purple than cream.

Sadly, the water has turned from tepid and inviting to cool and uncomfortable. I pull the drain, carefully step out of the tub, and gently wrap myself in a fluffy towel. A set of fresh clothes, hair products, and makeup lay on the counter. I smile gratefully, though I don't recall Helena coming back in to place the items down. *Damn gargoyles.*

I take the tags off the new bra and panty set, throw on the black yoga pants, and cocoon myself in the warmth of the long cowl-neck sweater and matching socks. I pull on my black knee-high boots and address my hair before lightly applying some mascara and lipgloss to my battered face.

Once I deem myself presentable, I open the door to find an older woman standing by the fireplace, throwing more logs onto the flames. At my presence, she turns and smiles warmly.

"Hello, Eve. I'm Tabatha, Griffin's wife and mate." Her waist-length, straight gray hair sways as she dips her head regally at me. "Our clan is honored to have you in our home."

I return her welcome with a small smile of my own. It never occurred to me that the other clan leaders, like Griff, have mates. "It's nice to meet you too. Thank you for having me."

"I trust Helena has been taking care of your needs?"

I nod once. "She has been extremely gracious."

"Wonderful." Tabatha motions for me to come to her, then points at the tray of food Helena left. "You should eat something," she suggests. Her eyes roam over my face, taking in the purple bruises from Lord Falk's backhand. "I know you're human, however, nourishment will help you to regain your strength and heal faster," she points out, handing me some grapes.

"Thanks." I shake the bunch. "You aren't Scottish?"

Tabatha releases a light laugh. "Nope. American, like you. Hence the lack of an accent."

She waves to two leather chairs positioned in front of the stone hearth and we both take a seat. I wince as my ribs protest. "Griffin doesn't seem the type to marry an American," I tease, remembering his long beard and Viking-like appearance.

"Griff is rough around the edges, but soft and sweet inside. Like those grapes." She points to the wine-colored fruit before holding up a roll of gauze. I eyeball her curiously. "By the way you're grimacing as you move, I'm guessing your ribs are broken. Unfortunately, it is going to take your mate's healing energy to fix them. I'd be happy to wrap them for you, if you'd allow me to, so they don't hurt as much while you wait for Asher to come."

I swallow the juice from the fruit and nod. "Sure. Thanks."

Tabatha cocks her head. "We're technically clan, Eve. You must stop thanking me for doing what we naturally do for our own."

Family. "Of course. I'm sorry."

Her hand wraps itself around mine before she squeezes. "I'm very glad Asher has found someone to love in you. That unto itself makes you very special."

After what feels like an eternity of pain, Tabatha gently releases the hem of my sweater and runs a long hand over the back of my hair in a soothing and maternal gesture.

"Well done. I know that was painful," she encourages.

My mouth opens to thank her but loud shouting and commotion outside the room pulls each of our focuses toward the door. It bursts open, revealing one very pissed off gargoyle. My very pissed off gargoyle. I exhale and curb the need to sob like a baby at the sight of him.

Asher pauses in the doorway, his deep blue eyes flashing with emotion as he inspects me. His eyes fixate on the purple mark decorating my right cheek. After a drawn out moment, he lifts both his hands, running them over his face and through his hair, before linking them behind his head. A number of expletives fall out of his mouth in rapid succession.

Rulf visibly pales at Asher's reaction, standing behind him with Gage and Sean flanking him. My gaze meets Gage's. He's wearing an unreadable expression. Sean and Rulf begin whispering in harsh tones and my focus shifts back to my protector.

Asher just stares at me, holding my gaze to his. He looks worried and relieved at the same time. I know he needs a moment to compose his anger, but all I want to do is run into his arms. My body is too exhausted from the pain Lord Falk imparted. I can barely stand.

Asher's eyes flash again, this time with fury as he shouts. "EVERYONE OUT!"

At the order, silence falls across the group. Everyone seems to be unsure of what to do.

"Your Highness." Tabatha steps toward Asher, placing her palms up. "As you can see, Eve is fine and well cared for. She has eaten, had a warm bath, and was just about to rest."

Her words seem to penetrate whatever caused Asher to snap. I watch as his shoulders release some of their tension. My mate's focus swings to her, and his expression takes on an appreciative look. "Thank you, Tabatha." He swallows with difficulty.

"Family first, always." She dips her head respectfully before stepping around Asher. Spreading her arms, she ushers the others out of the room.

At the clicking of the door, I drag my gaze up and meet Asher's from across the room. The gravity of the past few days finally hits me, and unexpectedly, I no longer have control over my emotions. Tears sting my eyes and begin to fall down my cheeks as a loud sob releases from my throat. In four strides, Asher is standing in front of me, cupping my cheeks.

"I'm sorry, siren," he whispers. "I'm so fucking sorry." His voice is a hoarse whisper.

My body trembles, overcome with emotion, and all I can do is continue to weep. Asher wipes away the endless tears with his thumbs before his arms circle around me, crushing me to him and causing me to discharge a painful scream.

Startled at my reaction, he releases me. I inhale roughly, still holding my ribs. After watching me for a second, Asher's palms land on my damp cheeks, compelling my focus back to his.

"What the fuck, siren?" His voice cracks.

I release a slow breath, trying to gain control of the tenderness. Noticing my ache, Asher's gaze is everywhere on my body. No doubt taking in the purple marks on my face, hands, neck—his eyes hone in on my ribs before snapping back to mine.

"Show me," he implores softly while his hands snake into my hair, holding me in place.

Transfixed by his stare, I stand unmoving. I soak him in, telling myself this is real and he's really here with me. Pain flashes across his striking features, knowing what I'm doing.

My hands shake as my fingers move to the hem of my sweater, but he shakes his head.

"We're mated now. *Show*. Me."

I frown at what he's asking. During our visit to the Eternal Forest, Callan explained that gargoyles only allow their mates access to the private connection of their mind and memories, because once it's opened, it can't be closed.

Asher's grip tightens in my hair and his forehead meets mine. "Show me," he whispers.

I pull in an unsteady breath and am hit with the reality of our bond. I place the tips of my fingers along his stubble-covered jawline and focus all of my energy on my psyche, listening to Asher's heartbeat and syncing my pace with his.

My mental focus drifts into his mind. He opens the invisible door, and instantly, I'm in his consciousness. Feeling his emotions. Hearing his thoughts. Seeing the mental pictures of his mind's eye. I experience just how raw and passionate his love for me is.

With my guard down, he crosses into my thoughts, accessing my mind. Seeking out the images he's searching for. I absorb the pure bliss of being one with him before I visually relive what happened with Lord Falk. I grant him open access to all the memories, with the exception of Rulf's involvement, up until he walked in the door.

When I'm finished, I feel Asher slowly pull himself out of my head, releasing control over the recollections. I sense his emotions as they become hot with rage. I stand shaky and distraught as I watch his expression turn into pure and unadulterated hate.

Callan was right, the intensity of experiencing Asher's emotions as one being is breathtaking. I can't distinguish his feelings from mine. It's almost impossible to decipher where he begins and I end. Even with our minds separated, our connection is now open and constant. I dare to meet his eyes, filled with raw and ravenous love for me.

"I heard you," he admits quietly.

"I know. I saw. Is that part of our new connection?"

"Yes. We can hear and decipher one another's thoughts."

"That's why you threw everyone out?"

"You said your body was exhausted from the pain Lord Falk imparted. That you could barely stand," he speaks in a low voice and shakes his head.

"What?" I ask, meeting his pained eyes.

"Hearing it, versus seeing it, are two completely fucking different things, siren."

Asher's eyes squeeze shut while he calms his breathing. When they reopen, they're softer. "I'm here now." His tone is gentle, though it doesn't match his tense shoulders and trembling body. "I'm here now," he repeats. "It's over, siren."

After witnessing what I suffered, I wonder if he's trying to soothe me, or himself.

With a gentle tug, he pulls me to him, still holding my head between his strong hands. "I'm going to heal you," he whispers across my lips. "And then, I'm going to hunt down Lord Falk and end his existence for laying a fucking hand on you." His tone is smooth and calm, but his controlled rage rolls off of him in waves.

His lips press to mine but don't move. Asher stays deathly still, allowing us to just be one, connected. In this moment, his presence suffocates the room, sucking the air out of it and me.

Hot tears continue to push against my eyelids, threatening to leak out again.

Asher pulls back and his gaze penetrates through each layer of me until he hits my soul. "I was created to protect, but you've changed that. You've given me something to fight for."

"Ash—" I whisper.

"It's time to fight for us. It's time to finish this. This. Ends. Now."

Randi Cooley Wilson

16 War of Worlds

I ignore the cold that has seeped into my bones at his absence. I shake my head, determined not to reveal how truly affected I am that Asher's not lying next to me. My reaction seems childish and ridiculous. Instead, I remind myself of war, of the fact that Lord Falk and the council members need to be dealt with, and that we still need to find Deacon and Garrick, and stop the dark army.

With a determined resolve, I sit up and make my way into the bathroom to freshen up and dress. It's been four days since Asher arrived. We've been in and out of healing sleeps for three of those days. On the fourth, Asher began meeting with the clans and devising strategies for hunting down Lord Falk.

I sigh into the mirror and run my hairbrush through my

hair. Most of my outward bruises and wounds have healed. My ribs are still sore from being kicked multiple times while broken, but I'm able to finally move. I'm stronger, physically. Mentally—that's another story all together. I put down the brush and leave to seek out Asher.

As I take the last step to the first floor, I watch the commotion of the supernatural beings floating around Griffin's castle. The hum in the air is different today, purposeful.

"Good morning, Eve," Tabatha greets me at the bottom of the staircase.

"Hi. Have you seen Asher?" I question, not really needing the answer. I can feel him.

"He's in the study with the clan leaders. They're going over some plans." She lifts her chin toward a long hallway. "I've just had the plates refilled with breakfast. Help yourself."

"Thanks." I smile and head to find my mate.

My mark pulses in excitement, with tiny throbs, as I get closer to the double doors guarding the study. I push them open and slip into strategy central. Sensing my presence, Asher lifts his stare from what he's studying. He watches me make my way to him, looking over me with a prideful expression. Ignoring the other beings in the room, I stalk over to him and fold myself into his side.

"Morning, siren," he murmurs in my ear. "You're looking much better."

"I feel much better," I reply.

Asher's lips brush my neck, and in response, a dull glow emanates from my skin. The warmth of his breath ripples through me, causing me to shiver. I feel his mouth form a smile against my skin, pleased with my reaction to him.

"If we were alone, I'd throw you down on this table and ravish you," he says at my ear.

"Christ. You're not alone," Gage snaps. "You are, however, in a room full of supernatural beings, all of whom have excellent hearing."

Asher releases a light chuckle, and my cheeks turn red from embarrassment when I look up to see the watchful eyes of the rest of the room. I sigh, leaning into Asher.

We really do need our own place.

Someday, siren.

Startled at Asher's voice suddenly inside my head, I spin in his arms and stare at him with wide eyes. He offers me a sexy smirk, bending his knees slightly so we're at eye level.

"Mate connection," he reminds, using a tone that sends my stomach fluttering.

"I'm not going to lie to you, Ash. That is pretty fucking freaky," I exhale.

He laughs gently before his lips dip in for a quick peck. "Freaky, but awesome."

My eyes fall to his Adam's apple. It's so damn sexy. Who knew a man's throat could cause me to go into such a lust-filled state. A playful smile appears on Asher's lips at my thoughts, which he can now hear. *Crap.* I lift my gaze, giving him my full attention.

"I can't even begin to tell you how inappropriate and intrusive it is to read my thoughts."

He steps closer into my personal space, stealing the air around me. Air I need to breathe in order to think straight.

"You have yet to experience the level of inappropriate and intrusive things I'll be sharing with you." He smiles darkly at me. *Good lord.*

I hold his piercing stare until a throat being cleared pulls us out of our moment.

"It's always so nice to see a newly mated couple eye fucking one another with my morning coffee," Callan muses.

My skin heats at the comment, but Asher and I just hold one another's gaze. There has always been an amazing friction between us, but now, with the mate bond complete, the electrical charge flickers brighter, more powerful. Unwavering as the air between us heats and sparks with raw carnal desire.

"Well, I for one think it's romantic," Marcus, leader of the Manhattan clan, states loudly from the doorway. He sashays over to us and pulls me into a tight embrace. "Eve."

"Hi." I squeak out and pull him in tighter.

A low growl emits from Asher's chest and Marcus chuckles at the sound.

"Easy, gargoyle. As much as I love your mate, she isn't my type. You, on the other hand," he jests and reaches for Asher. "Congratulations. The ceremony was lovely and I'm happy that you two have found your way back to one another."

Asher smiles as they pull out of their hold. "Thanks, man."

Marcus rubs his hands together, giddily. "All right. I'm here. Let the war of worlds begin."

At his words, I bristle, reminded of why we are here. My stomach clenches as a dangerous foreboding sensation settles into it. Asher leans forward, placing a kiss on the top of my head before stepping away to address the room with Keegan and Callan flanking each side.

"Many of you have witnessed the foul evil Lord Falk placed upon my mate. A personal attack." Asher's eyes flick to mine, softening for a moment before becoming hard again. "Gage was just in County Kerry and has confirmed the entire council has been murdered at Lord Falk's hands. There is no doubt in my mind, Deacon and my father assisted."

"Aye. 'greed young prince," Griffin replies.

"We can no longer wait for the war to come to us. My brothers and I feel it's time to engage. The leaders in this room are responsible for our race's survival. It is our job, our duty, and our obligation, to not only protect mankind, but also our own. Over the course of the last few months, the supernatural worlds have been attacked. Realms have fallen. Kings have risen. Love has been sacrificed. It ends today. The skies will darken, but we will not run. We will fight. And if need be, we will fall to fate."

The entire room erupts in agreement and encouragement at Asher's words.

"What are you proposing?" Marcus inquires.

"A gala," Asher answers and the room falls silent, listening intently. "Celebrating love."

Keegan steps forward, addressing the room. "My brother is the rightful heir. He was to be appointed king when he fulfilled Eve's protector assignment by the council. A ruling body of which all but two members have ceased to exist. Our father, the current king, has risen from the dead. His arrogance and pride won't allow another king to be ordained while he still breathes." Keegan slides his solemn gaze to Asher. "Even if that gargoyle is his own flesh and blood."

"Dad does love a party," Callan interjects.

"I'm not following. Asher has yet to finish his assignment," Marcus adds.

Keegan looks to me, then Asher, before addressing the room again. "Technically, he has. Michael and the Angelic Council were not as forthcoming with Asher's role in Eve's protection as we had originally understood."

Abby's face pinches in confusion. "Meaning?"

Asher steps forward. "Meaning that a divination of redemption was outlined, altering our bloodlines. The request of my protection was never just about safeguarding the daughter of Heaven. Eve's existence was not designed to end the war, but instead, to combine our families' lineages, mixing the blood of Heaven with the blood of the dragon spirit. In doing so, as long as she and I exist, as one, Heaven's gates are safe from further attacks of the dark army."

"Shit," Marcus exhales. "No pressure there, huh?"

"There is no pressure. I love Eve. She is my mate. Your future queen. Our bloodlines have mixed." His gaze meets mine in resolve. "And will stay that way, forever. My assignment has been fulfilled. I have upheld my protector oaths and am ready to lead my kin," he states.

I smile at his comments.

"What o' mankind? Where dae they fit intae this divination?" Sean questions.

"Where they always do. Stuck in the middle between darkness and light. Able to exercise free will and decide which side to surrender to," Asher responds somberly.

"Without the darkness, the light can't exist. Without

the demonic legion, our race would cease to exist. Gargoyles were created to protect against evil and fight for righteousness. If the darkness faded, so would our race. It's why my father made a deal with the dark army. A misguided attempt to keep our kin in existence," Keegan adds.

Asher meets Gage's gaze. "Gage, my brothers, and I have a long-term plan to ensure future generations of protectors succeed and excel under their oaths. If you grant me royal appointment, I vow I will lead our race well."

"'N' this gala?" Griff inquires.

"Instead of hunting them down, the gala will be a well-designed ruse to lead Lord Falk, Deacon, and our father to us," Keegan explains.

"How?" I interject.

"If the leaders in this room agree to crown me king, the gala will celebrate not only our mating bond, which will interest Lord Falk, but also our coronation as king and queen. Something my father won't allow since he's still breathing, and you are human," Asher enlightens.

"And Deacon?" Marcus asks.

"The proverbial cherry on top," Callan answers. "All realms and royal courts will be invited, as well as the divine army in the event the demonic legion thinks about crashing."

"Yer sure Garrick cannae be redeemed?" Griff asks.

All three brothers become silent before Asher replies gravely. "It certainly seems that way. I've never seen him like this before. It's as if something snapped and he's lost all semblance of sanity. He's not the same protector who raised us." Asher sighs. "Or maybe he is and we just never saw this side of him. Either way, there isn't a rational thought in his actions anymore."

The sadness in his tone is unmistakable, and my heart breaks for all three protectors. After a while of silence, Griffin finally stands. "All in favor o' appointing Asher St. Michael, son o' Garrick, as our king, say aye."

Angus, leader of the Irish clan, stands. "Aye."

Marcus follows suit. "The Manhattan approves."

Gage presses his lips in a flat line before standing. "The Paris clan agrees."

Griffin turns to Asher. "Aye. Th' Scottish clan will be honored tae have ye as our king."

Asher tips his head toward me before taking a knee in front of the standing clan leaders. I watch as his demeanor suddenly becomes regal and authoritative.

"It is I who am honored to serve your clans and our kin," he responds.

"So then, it's time to attack?" Callan grins widely and Asher stands.

"It's time to attack," Asher reassures.

"And plan a gala," Abby adds gleefully.

Leave it to Abby to be excited about catering and attire at a time like this.

෴

I make my way to the kitchen in need of sustenance. The gala's strategy meeting went on for hours after Asher was elected king. Not wanting to leave anything to chance, the clans planned down to the minutest details. It was exhausting to listen to, though necessary.

My steps falter when I see Abby and McKenna with their heads together at the kitchen table. I approach slowly and salivate when I see what they're up to. Crossing my arms, I arch my eyebrow, meeting Abby's guilty glare.

"What are those?"

"Cupcakes," Abby says around a mouth full of frosting.

I lift my chin. "What's in them?"

"Sugar and chocolate," she replies, swallowing.

"Pickles?" I challenge.

She shakes her head back and forth adamantly.

"I'm in." I quickly take a seat and snatch one, devouring the yumminess. "These are amazing. When did Callan bake them?" I ask, inhaling the chocolate pastry.

Abby's sapphire eyes widen and flick to McKenna with guilt written all over her face.

I smirk. "Are you pregnancy cheating on your baby daddy with store-bought cupcakes?"

She frowns and lowers her second sweet. "You make it sound so dirty."

"Says the gargoyle who gave me the sex talk," I counter.

"Clearly you needed it," she argues.

"By the grace, you two are ruining this moment. We have about fifteen minutes left before Callan comes in and all hell breaks loose. Focus on the damn cupcakes," Kenna instructs.

I watch McKenna take a bite of her red velvet one and snort.

She sighs and glares at me. "What now, blood of Eden?"

"It's just funny that you, *cupcake*, are eating an actual cupcake." I giggle.

"There are days when I really wish Asher had brought

home a stray dog instead of you."

"Aw. I love how you sweet talk me while we eat sweets," I reply.

"Queen or not, keep this shit up and I might kill you myself today," she warns.

"Threaten all you want, but consider this. If I was dead, then who would you take out all your pent-up anger on?" I argue.

"Eves has a point," Abby adds, grabbing a third.

Rulf walks in, looking exhausted. He takes the three of us in before quickly retreating. Needing to talk to him, I hop up to chase him down, but before I leave, I turn back to the table. "As your new queen, I demand that not be touched." I point to the half-eaten baked good. When I turn back to follow Rulf, I watch McKenna out of the corner of my eye as she sticks her finger in her mouth and pushes it into my frosting.

Her immaturity knows no bounds.

After running down a few halls, I finally catch up to the protector.

"Rulf."

"Your Highness." He bows.

I cringe, placing my hands on his shoulders and pull him upright.

"Yeah, um . . . we're not going to do that." I continue when he looks at me with a blank stare. "No bowing or queen stuff."

"Eve, royal formality requires—" I cut him off.

"I know, but it's a new, younger, hipper regime. New rules. No bowing. Or . . . 'Your Highness' stuff."

"All right."

"Good."

"What can I do for you?" he asks.

"I haven't had the opportunity to thank you for saving me from Lord Falk that day and bringing me here while you got Asher, so thank you," I offer.

Rulf pales. "It's not necessary, Eve. It was my fault to begin with."

"I know," I breathe.

His expression turns surprised. "You do?"

I nod. "Helena explained. If you're concerned that I'm going to tell Asher, I won't."

He narrows his eyes in disbelief. "What is it you want?"

A ghost of a smile plays at my lips. "Let's just call it even. You saved my life."

He shakes his head. "That doesn't sit with me. Had I known what Lord Falk was planning, I never would have agreed to help him. I might have saved you, but I'm the reason you were there in the first place, Eve."

"I suppose you're right. How about you just owe me a favor at some point?"

He smiles brightly. "Fair enough."

I start walking backwards toward my ruined cupcake. "I'm going to hold you to that."

He nods. "I would expect nothing less, Your Highness."

I girlie growl at his use of *Your Highness* and turn back to the kitchen.

Randi Cooley Wilson

17 Burning Hearts

My body lies limp and helpless. The tension begins to burn deeper, thickening the air. Blazing eyes rake over my writhing body with heavy lids. Asher leans over me with his hands on the mattress on either side of my hips, his face in mine.

"You're going to make us late," I murmur against his swollen lips.

My eyes focus on his mouth, and through my erratic panting I realize I want his lips back on mine. Asher complies with soft, gentle strokes. Assaulting my heart at the same time. He takes everything I can give him with my mouth, seeking entrance into my soul.

When he finally pulls back, his eyes have darkened to a deep blue, lit with heat. Asher smiles down at me, knowingly. In this moment, neither of us cares if we're late to the coronation or not. The fate of our story will just have to wait a few more minutes.

His mouth finds mine again; ending any willpower I had left to stop him. Our kisses are intense, filled with longing and desire. He moves his body over me, his hands pulling me closer by my waist as we kiss and nip at one another's mouths.

I tug at the bottom of his white dress shirt, yanking it loose from the top of his black tuxedo pants, and slide my hands underneath the starched material, against his heated skin.

"Fuck." He sighs into my mouth, the word vibrating through me.

The tips of my fingers explore the contours of his back and the muscles etched into his stomach. Asher growls and kisses me again in a slow, sexy, tormenting way that has me breathless.

He rolls onto his back, so I'm on top of him, straddling him. I unbutton his shirt, releasing each tiny closure with a fervent need. My mouth descends back onto his with aggressive and bruising caresses. My hands release their hold on his shirt and slide into Asher's hair, gripping it tightly. Silently willing him to become one with me.

He sits us up, trailing kisses down my jaw and neck before taking my lips, holding me captive in a desire-filled state, while his fingers find the edge of my dress, toying with the hem playfully before sensually moving it up my bare thighs. His fingers climb underneath, all the way up to the lace of my black panties. With a quick tug, he rips them off me.

At the primal action, I moan into his mouth. His kiss

devours the sound. Just as I become light-headed, Asher pulls back, breaking our connection, and allowing us to catch our breaths. His large hands come up and affectionately push the hair out of my face. I smirk and bite my bottom lip at the tenderness of the gesture.

Holding my head firmly in place, his fingers tangle in my silky strands.

"I loved that pair of panties," I pant, holding his eyes.

A cocky grin spreads across his mouth. "They were between you and me, siren."

I arch a brow. "What?"

His gaze sharpens. "I plan on destroying anything that comes between us."

My tongue wets my lips at the rawness of his words. "What about my dress and bra?"

Asher's hands reach for the dress and I grab his wrists. "Wait," I say huskily.

He gives me a wry smile. "Waiting."

I suck in my lower lip. "Not the dress. Abby will kill me. It's designer," I gasp out.

Asher drops his lips to my collarbone and presses lightly, causing me to shiver. My hands curl into the hair at the base of his neck while his palms glide over my shoulders and flatten across my chest. My eyes slide closed as he caresses my breasts through the material of my dress before I hear the distinct sound of expensive silk being ripped.

"Asher!" I barely release on a breath.

"Nothing between us, siren," he reminds and tosses what's left of the material to the floor.

I try not to think of all the ways Abby is going to murder me. Instead, I focus on the back of his knuckles caressing the rise of my breast before he places a soft, deliberate kiss there.

My breath hitches, and his arms circle around my waist. With a quick move, he positions me on the bed. I'm on my back, with Asher kneeling over me. His shirt is still unbuttoned, revealing his statue-like chest and stomach muscles. The raw power he's releasing causes my heart to beat rapidly and my pulse to thrum loudly in my ears.

His eyes fall upon me with a combination of mischief and passion while he smiles against my breast. I sink into the heat of his tongue against my nipple before his lips close around it, drawing it in deeply. He continues the torture before granting my other breast the same attention.

"Oh. My. God. Asher." I groan.

"Are you wet for me yet, siren?" His voice vibrates against my chest.

A sudden animalistic need to mark him, make him mine, overtakes me. I push my way onto my knees, running my hands over his chest and hurriedly pushing the shirt off his shoulders. It falls to the floor as my clumsy hands undo the latch on his tuxedo pants, pushing them toward the rest of our formal garments, taking his boxers with them.

I see the burning indigo glow in his eyes, and I know they match mine. I reach up and cup his jaw, bringing him down for a kiss. Our lips fuse with a force that completely wrecks me from the inside out. It's perfection. Our bond makes everything so much more intense.

"Tell me you're wet for me." His mouth brushes mine and one hand clenches my hip.

I bite down on his bottom lip as two of Asher's fingers find their way under the left strap of my bra. As I release his lip, his head slides toward my bare shoulder, planting gentle kisses on the skin as he glides the material down my arm. My body arches into his chest and he rumbles his approval. His other hand mimics the motions so both straps are dangling low on my arms.

Skilled hands slide over the material, cupping my breasts before they release the front clasp. I suck in a breath as Asher pushes apart the material, letting the straps fall completely off my body. With both of us on our knees, he eases the length of his body against mine.

Warm hands slide up my bare thighs while Asher captures my mouth in another deep, searing kiss. My body jerks at the first touch of his fingers brushing against me. The harder our kiss becomes, the gentler his touch. The contrasting feelings send my body into overdrive.

Our lips part, and he brings his right hand to his mouth, licking his thumb to wet it before slipping it between my legs and pressing down in deliberate circles. I release a loud moan. Needing something to hold onto, I take him in both hands, allowing my thumbs to run over the ball portion of his piercing as my fingers run the length of him.

Asher's free hand curls around my neck, bringing my forehead to his so he can stare into my eyes as we work one another toward release. Just as I begin to feel the familiar tightening and coil, Asher grabs my wrists, pulling my hands off him.

"I need inside of you," he pants out.

Suddenly, I'm on my back again with Asher hovering over me. With one hand, he holds my arms above my head and runs his tongue over his first two fingers on his other hand, before pressing them back onto me in faster circular motions. His features tighten as he pins me to the bed and looks down at my face, pushing me toward an orgasm.

Just as I'm about to fall into a blissful release, Asher grabs the sides of my head between his trembling hands and thrusts into me hard and without warning. I cry out from the intrusion, and my body splits into the most earth-shattering orgasm I've ever had.

Asher continues slamming into me, growling and extending my pleasure as I continue to pulse around him. Burying his hands in my hair, he presses his mouth to mine and continues his unrelenting assault. Spasm after spasm of pure pleasure rolls through me until I'm so physically and emotionally spent tears threaten to overtake me.

Shadowed eyes stare down at me, watching as I continue to come long and hard. Asher's forehead drops to mine as he shudders through his own climax, releasing a few deep grunts. His eyes close, and he slows down his thrusts, riding out his orgasm before relaxing into me.

His breath is hot across my lips as we both struggle to breathe normally. My muscles are completely gooey, and my body is exhausted to the point I could pass out and be asleep for days. *Best. Sex. Ever.* Asher drops a light kiss to my lips. His features are softer, sated.

Carefully, he slides out of me, rolling onto his side and propping himself on one elbow.

I turn onto my side so I can face him, and he cups my cheek, rubbing his thumb over my bruised and painfully swollen lips.

"You never answered me," he says quietly.

I lift my hand and run the tips of my fingers along his jaw. "What?"

"I asked you if you were wet for me. Since you didn't answer, I needed to be sure."

I burst out laughing. He flashes me a taunting smile and wink.

"Well then, a job *very* well done, gargoyle."

Asher's gaze flicks up to mine. Pure admiration shines back at me as his hand drops from my face, and he runs his knuckles over the edge of my jawline.

"We'd better clean up. We're already ridiculously late. I'm sure everyone is wondering where we are," I suggest.

Neither of us moves.

He leans in so his lips are between my ear and cheek. "I fell in love with you the moment I caught you ogling me in Professor Davidson's class. Someday, this will be over and we'll have the peace we deserve. Whatever happens tonight, know this. With every breath I take, I will protect you, always." His voice is low and lost somewhere as he rumbles the words against the side of my face before I feel the soft brush of his lips.

"Ash—" I begin in a raspy and breathy voice.

He presses a finger to my lips and stares deeply into my worried gaze. "Tell me you understand what I'm saying." His breath is warm as it whispers across my face.

I study him. "Is that when you first knew you loved me, in architecture class?"

A ghost of a smile plays at his lips. "Actually, I think I fell in love with you when I caught you checking out my ass after our first verbal encounter."

I lean forward and gently rub my lips over his. "I fell in love with you when I walked out of the coffee shop and saw you leaning against your car."

His mouth kicks up in a grin on one side. "I knew it. You're just using me for my ride."

"I love you. Even if you did ruin a very, very, very, expensive runway dress, I love you with everything that I am." My voice has a tone of finality to it that I don't want him to miss.

Asher smoothes my hair behind my ear, and his breath dances along my lips. My eyes close when his lips brush over mine. "We've been in worse situations, siren," he whispers across my lips. "We'll get out of this one too."

I nod, my throat clogged with emotion. "Then we'd better get ready. Our fate awaits."

❦

My gaze roams over the girl staring back at me in the mirror. Even with the impending doom of the gala, I recognize contentment in my face. I release a light laugh at the thought. It's been such a long time since I've felt at peace, happy.

I smile into the mirror. My cheeks are still flushed from my time with Asher, and though my eyes are no longer hazel, the indigo sparkles brightly, almost playfully. The hardship and frown lines I've grown accustomed to marring my face over this past year have disappeared. This eighteen-year-old girl, she's familiar. My heart soars at seeing my old self again.

I exhale and smooth down the front of my black silk ML Monique Lhuillier spiderweb gown. I would never admit this to Abby, but this sleeveless, V-neck dress is the best thing I've ever worn. I twist to study the lace detail at the hem. It's short in the front and longer in the back, in a delicate spiderweb pattern. I cringe at the pile of expensive material on the bedroom floor. She really is going to end me for ruining the other dress.

I double check to make sure my daggers are sheathed on my thighs, then throw a second set of weapons into the hidden pockets of my flared skirt. I touch up my soft makeup and smooth out the long ponytail of my hair, giving myself one last look over.

My eyes drop to the silver necklace Asher gave to me, and I gently run the tips of my fingers over the feather laying on its side. I close my eyes and remind myself that there isn't anything to worry about tonight. We've strategized for days. All scenarios have been accounted and planned for, and while an entire supernatural kingdom gathers to celebrate Asher's coronation, and our mating ceremony, we're going to end this, once and for all.

I try to shake off the foreboding feeling as a piercing pain makes itself known in my heart. I frown and exhale. Just as fast as it happened, it's over. I straighten myself and hold the gaze reflecting back at me in the mirror.

"Everything will happen the way it's meant to," I whisper, trying to breathe easier.

I step out of the bathroom and immediately come to a standstill when I notice the gargoyle standing by the fireplace, sipping on amber liquid. I take him in appreciatively. The bad-boy look on Gage Gallagher melts panties, but Gage in a tuxedo? Holy crap, ovaries will be exploding this evening.

Gage turns to face me and presents a devastating smile that proves all things dark and dangerous ooze out of him. His gaze drops to my black Louboutins and roam up the length of me before meeting my amused stare.

"You look exceptionally lovely this evening, love," Gage compliments.

"Thank you," I reply. "Where's Asher?"

"Checking on a few last-minute details. He asked that I escort you down."

Gage throws the last sip of his drink back and places the crystal on the mantle before stepping toward me. My heart rate kicks up, and once again, I feel the prick of pain, causing my face to scrunch for a moment before it subsides.

"What's wrong?" he asks, studying me.

"I don't know. Something doesn't feel right." I rub over my heart again.

A knock at the door pulls our attention toward it, and Nassa walks in wearing the floor-length, plum chiffon Nicole Miller Hawaiian hibiscus gown Abby chose for her. She looks stunning in the sleeveless, V-neck dress, adorned with twisted racerback straps and a full skirt. *See that, I do listen to Abby when she gushes about clothing details.*

I watch as Gage's lips part. In a sharp exhale the air literally leaves his body. Hooded eyes meet the sorceress's. I smirk to myself when I notice he's stopped breathing.

A knowing smile appears on Nassa's lilac lips. "Gallagher."

"Buttercup," he wheezes out.

I bite my lip so as not to laugh. I don't believe I've ever seen Gage speechless, or bewitched.

"His Highness is requesting the queen's presence in the ballroom," she says slowly.

After a silent pause, it dawns on me that she's talking about Asher and me. I prepare to move toward the doorway, but Gage just stares, unmoving, so I follow suit and remain still.

"Gallagher!" Nassa rasps, annoyed at his lack of motion.

"Christ. You're breathtaking." His voice has dropped an octave.

At the compliment, Nassa takes a preemptive step back, looking nervous and unsure. Ignoring everything around him, including me, Gage stalks toward the shaking sorceress.

"I mean it, Nassa. You're beautiful," he says, standing in front of her.

Jade eyes widen, and her expression becomes crestfallen. "I can't," she whispers.

One of his hands darts out, and his fingertips run over the twisted strap of the dress. Nassa swallows, uncomfortable. Her pleading eyes jerk to me, begging for assistance. I offer her a small, slow shake of my head, telling her silently I'm not intervening. This is their moment.

It's clear that Gage feels a lot for her, and before tonight, she needs to know.

"W-we should go," she squeaks out in her deep voice.

I see hesitation flash in her eyes as Gage catches her hand in his. He turns it palm side up and places a light kiss into it before closing her fingers over the gesture, as if asking her to hold on to it for safekeeping.

With a curt nod, Gage steps back and holds out both of his elbows. "Are you ready?"

The question is meant for me, but his eyes never leave Nassa.

"I don't think I have a choice but to be," I mumble,

placing my arm through his.

Nassa does the same on his other side, and Gage tilts his head toward me.

"You always have a choice, Eve. That's the beauty of free will."

18 Coronation

Gage escorts us down the ancient grand staircase of the castle toward the wooded location where the coronation is being held. As we walk down the long pathway, covered in white stones, my breath hitches, and my lips part in awe as I take in the majestic forest setting.

Medieval wooden tables and cream fur-pelt-strewn chairs sit amid towering redwood trees. Garlands of white flowers hang and sway in a canopy from the trees, set amongst twinkling amber lights. It's as if someone recreated the décor from our mating ceremony and blew it up times a thousand. Tall vases filled with white hydrangeas decorate each table, and the entire woodland setting is lit with hundreds of white candles and wrought-iron lanterns.

Except for the sound of waves crashing in the distance, you would never even know we're on the coast of Scotland. Ornate banquet tables display silver platters serving the finest food and wine, giving the gala a lavish medieval feast design.

In the center of the celebration, a dark wood dance floor sits atop the dirt ground. The London clan's family crest, a dragon, is burned into the center, branding it. To the side, a platform holds musicians performing traditional Scottish folk music, complete with Highland bagpipes.

My eyes scan the surroundings with a sense of wonderment and trepidation, taking everything in. After a moment, my gaze lands on the stone stage where Asher will officially be anointed king, and our plan will be executed. I shiver at the thought.

Keegan and Asher were adamant the festivities be held outside under the evening sky. Garrick, Deacon, and Lord Falk know security will be tight. It was assumed if they penetrated through an indoor security, they would figure out this was a set-up.

The brothers felt an outdoor event security breach would appear more organic, allowing the conspirators to think they're smarter than they are. After seeing the décor, I agree. This does feel more authentic.

I'm so consumed by the beauty of everything I fail to realize that Gage has guided us over to stand with Abby and Callan. Abby narrows her gaze, focusing on my hand, which is interlocked with Gage's elbow. I immediately remove it.

Clearing my throat, I fixate on her off the shoulder gown. "Where is Asher?"

"He and Keegan are discussing last-minute security

procedures," Callan replies.

I lift my gaze to Abby's scrutinizing one. "What?"

"While you look absolutely stunning, Eve, that isn't the dress I left you in earlier," she points out. I shrug and act like I have no clue what she's talking about. After a moment of silent inspection, realization falls across her features, and she stomps her foot like an irate child. "Damn Asher and his stupid sexy piercing. How badly is it ruined?"

I take her hands in mine and offer a sympathetic look. "It's bad, Abby. Destroyed."

Her eyes widen and her shoulders sag. "It was couture. Runway. Nooo," she whines.

I avert my gaze, noticing Callan's outfit. "Are you wearing a kilt?"

Callan grins widely. "It's a Scottish gala, Eves. Of course I'm wearing a kilt."

I throw a pointed glare at him. "Please tell me you're wearing something under it?"

He shrugs noncommittally. "Real men wear kilts. It's quite freeing, cutie."

I snort. "Why do I see another apron in your future?"

Abby turns to him and places a loving kiss on his cheek. "Don't listen to her, baby. Your calves are just as sexy as Uriel's," she whispers.

"You think?" he asks, twisting his left leg, showing off his muscle.

My gaze collides with Nassa's before she rolls her eyes at the constant cuteness that is Callan and Abby. The sorceress steps away from Gage and moves toward the bar. *Smart girl.*

"Speaking of the angel," Gage mumbles as Uriel

approaches the group.

"Gargoyles . . . and human," Uriel muses. "I apologize for the interruption, but Michael would like a word with Gage and Callan before things . . . begin."

"All right," Callan agrees and places a completely inappropriate kiss on his mate's lips.

"Christ, get a room," Gage scoffs, following Uriel toward the castle.

"Maybe if you planted a few mind-blowing kisses on your girl's lips, she wouldn't feel the need to get inebriated," Callan teases, trailing after the two supernatural warriors.

"You okay?" Abby asks.

My eyes dart around wildly. "I just want this to be over."

She pulls me into a side hug. "It will be." Her brows pinch together.

"What's wrong?" I ask, following her sightline to McKenna.

Abby and I stand speechless, watching McKenna interact with a little boy near the stage.

A few seconds later, Abby breaks our astonished state. "Do me a huge favor?"

I shake off the image of McKenna being kind and face Abby. "Of course."

"Make sure Callan makes those for our baby shower." She points to a large turkey leg.

I scrunch my nose. "Really?"

She nods emphatically.

"Wait, are you saying I have to throw your shower?" I moan.

Abby's focus slides back to Kenna. My gaze follows.

Good lord, the poor child looks like he's about to pee his pants. Abby waves her hand in a *see* motion at the uncomfortable scene.

"Yeah . . . okay." I study the child's face. "Who is he, anyway?"

"That bundle of adorable is Tristan. His mom is a nature nymph. She helped me with your mating ceremony and the coronation gala décor," Abby explains.

"She's very talented. This place looks like a fairy tale."

"It does," she agrees before her gaze locks back on me.

I continue to observe the toddler. He can't be more than two. Unease sweeps through me because he shouldn't be here tonight. Not with what is about to happen. It's too dangerous.

"What is it, Eve?" Abby asks quietly.

"Nothing. It's just," I point to Tristan. "He looks familiar in a weird way, doesn't he?"

Abby looks Tristan over for a moment and shrugs. "Not really. I should go save him from Kenna before she makes him cry. I'll be back after I return him to the safety of his mom."

"They're not staying, are they?" I ask with concern in my voice.

Abby shakes her head. "No. She understands what's about to happen."

"Good." I smile and watch her make her way over to Tristan.

Abby bends down and taps his nose with her finger before tickling him. He giggles, but I notice the light behind his cognac eyes is dim. He places a small hand on Abby's belly, and she beams before taking his hand into hers and seeking out his mother. *Abby is going to make an amazing mother.*

I turn toward the castle, and my heart stops when my gaze collides with a dark set of sexy, brooding irises. The familiar squeeze of lust begins to flow through my veins at the sight of Asher St. Michael, standing in the middle of the dance floor, on his crest, in a full tuxedo.

My chin drops and I watch him through my lashes. A cocky smirk appears on his lips as his heated gaze peruses my body. He releases a low, appreciative whistle and stalks toward me in a predatory manner. Once he's in front of me, he dips his head so we're at eye level.

"It is so sexy that you are mine," he whispers the growl.

I grip the lapels of his jacket. "You clean up pretty well yourself, pretty boy."

"Do you have your daggers on you?" he questions.

I moan in a sexy manner before whispering across his lips. "You sure know how to sweet-talk a girl, Your Highness," I tease. He laughs, running his hands down my bare back and over the curves of my ass. His body goes deathly still, his hands locked on my backside.

I peer up at him questioningly. "Something wrong?"

"Where the fuck are your panties, siren?"

"My mate ripped them earlier in the throes of passion," I counter.

Asher's gaze drops to the lower half of my body. "Fuck," he draws out as if in pain. "Not only am I going to be fighting off enemies this evening, but now I have to fight off a raging hard-on from knowing you're running around without panties."

I suck my lower lip into my mouth before releasing it. "Then next time, don't rip them."

He groans. "No roundhouse kicks tonight."

"Yes, sir."

"It's nice to see you kids learning to compromise," Callan banters.

Asher turns to both his brothers as they approach us. "Everything all set?"

Keegan nods. "It is. Security is positioned. The divine warriors are watching for the dark army. Just remember, Michael and Uriel can't get involved in supernatural matters, so there will be no divine assistance when it comes to Garrick, Deacon, and Lord Falk. That said, the protector clans are in place, and we've given non-obvious breach options."

"Eve and I will make our rounds greeting guests. When the time comes for the coronation, be prepared and on guard. This shit ends tonight," Asher states with a finality to his tone.

"Where is Gage?" I inquire.

"Lurking in the shadows. Keeping up appearances," Asher responds.

"What do we do now?" I ask.

"Now, we wait for all our worlds to collide," Keegan answers.

&

I watch as the gargoyle I've declared eternal vows to graciously addresses every guest with a powerful, dominating presence. I absorb his breathtaking good looks. They cause beings to gravitate toward him. I see the tension in his shoulders and the way he observes everything. Always studying, and strategizing, ready to strike out, like a cobra. Watching him, my fears and uncertainties are replaced with renewed dedication to what I am fighting for. Him.

It's in this moment I realize that I love him with an undeniable fierceness that can never be replicated. I've fallen to fate. There will be no more running. I would fight and sacrifice everything I am and have to protect my love for Asher. Against all odds, he's wrapped himself around my heart and embedded himself into my soul. He is a part of me. The best part. I will belong to him, always.

Asher approaches our table and smiles down at me. He laces my fingers with his and pulls me into a standing position. The gala is now filled with hundreds of supernatural creatures dancing and eating, all here to celebrate the new gargoyle king and his human mate. Nerves take over at the thought. *Crap. What if they hate me?* My breathing starts to fumble and Asher picks up on my distress.

He yanks my hand so I spin in his arms, pulling me tightly to his chest. Staring into my eyes, he leans forward, placing a light kiss on the side of my mouth. His lips brush over my cheek and settle by my ear. "You're beautiful. You belong among them. They need you as their queen, more so than any of them even realize. So do I, siren."

Asher's lips part while his gaze roams over me. My breath hitches when his eyes make their slow journey back up my body and collide with mine. The depths of love in them burn so brightly that a warm blush sweeps over my softly glowing skin.

"Care to dance?" I ask breathlessly.

A cocky grin appears on his lips. "As hot as you are,

my mate is in attendance this evening. I doubt very much that she would like me waltzing with a beautiful creature such as yourself," he teases and moves us toward the center of the dance floor.

"Oh? What is she like?" I ask, playing along as he begins to sway our combined bodies.

Asher's gaze holds mine. "Beautiful. Witty. Sensual. Stubborn. An excellent shot with her daggers, thanks to months of my skilled training sessions."

I hold in a laugh. "She sounds like a very lucky lady."

Asher's face grows serious. "Actually, I'm the one who is lucky."

The rest of the room fades away as I continue to gaze into his eyes. "Humbleness is a good look on you, Your Highness."

He leans in so I'm inhaling his breath. "*You* are a good look on me, siren."

"They're here." Keegan's two words officially end our moment.

Asher nods in acknowledgment. "We'll finish this later, yeah?"

"Yeah," I exhale and suddenly my heart is in my throat.

"Head to the stage for the crowning, and be on alert, Ash," Keegan orders, walking away.

Dread fills me, and I break out in a cold sweat. My hands cup Asher's face roughly and urgently bring him in for a deep, sensual kiss. I pour my entire heart and soul into him through our fused lips, because the thought of losing him tonight guts me.

Asher pulls back, dropping his forehead to mine. "It's

almost over."

We stay like this for another moment before Sora's voice floats around the gala.

"Good evening," she says from the stage, commanding the attendees' focus. "I am honored to be here tonight with you to celebrate the appointment of Asher St. Michael as king of the gargoyle race. Our community realizes the Royal Council of Protectors normally oversees such formalities." She clears her throat. "However, due to unfortunate circumstances, the Spiritual Assembly is privileged to direct the ceremonies this evening as our young prince takes his rightful place with his newly bonded mate by his side."

Clapping and cheering breaks out across the guests, and Asher takes my hand in his, holding a little too tightly, guiding us toward the stage. A fresh wave of fear washes over me as I watch Asher's eyes dart around wildly.

We take the two steps onto the stage. Once we reach Sora, she curtsies elegantly.

"Your Highnesses," she greets.

Asher dips his head in a regal manner and I follow suit. "Sora," he replies, formally.

Keegan and Callan take their spots, flanking Asher and me with their mates on either side of them. I scan the crowd, meeting several pairs of familiar eyes.

The eccentric Sorceress Lunette offers me an encouraging smile. Next to her is Professor Davidson, the elder gargoyle and guardian of the divination of redemption. Tadhg places his heavily tattooed arm around Fiona, squeezing the shape-shifting panther into his side while her proud stare fills with water. I offer a warm expression to Rulf, Tabatha and Helena, standing in the front row.

My gaze shifts over Lord Valentin, leader of the vampire world, and his second, Stephan, who've both traveled from Romania to be here. Lucian, king of the werewolves, offers me a respectful dip of his chin with Leo, his beta, by his side. *I wish Aria were here.* I can't see them, but I can feel Gage, Nassa, Michael, and Uriel watching the stage and the crowd below, along with the gargoyle leaders: Marcus, Griffin, Sean, Angus, and Thomas.

And hidden somewhere in the darkness, I sense Garrick, Deacon, and Lord Falk lurking in the shadows of the dark army, waiting for their chance. Knowing they're watching, I lift my chin and stand taller by Asher's side. As his warrior, I'm prepared to make any sacrifice necessary for him and the throng of supernatural realms in attendance on this night.

Sora's voice brings my focus back to the reason why we are all truly here today. "Asher and Eve, please take a knee in front of me," she instructs, and we do.

Keegan hands Sora Asher's Angelic Sword. "Asher St. Michael, do you swear to uphold all aspects of gargoyle decree? Do you affirm you will lead your kin with righteousness and grace? Will you practice and instill protector bylaws of duty, honor, and protection during your rule, so long as you shall exist?"

Asher's gaze skates over the crowd, waiting for any sign of an interruption before landing back on Sora's with a lift of his chin. "I do."

She places the tip of his sword to his right shoulder, then left, and finally the crown of his head. After each motion, she chants in Gaelic. "Dieacht, honor, agus Cosaint."

Asher squeezes my hand and Sora places his sword back into Keegan's protection. Callan steps forward, offering my daggers to the Spiritual Assembly Leader.

She stands in front of me. "Eve Marie Collins, do you swear to uphold all aspects of gargoyle decree? Do you affirm you will lead your adopted kin with righteousness and grace? Will you practice and instill protector bylaws of duty, honor, and protection by your king's side, so long as you shall exist?"

"I do," I say firmly.

Sora follows the same steps with my daggers as she did with Asher's sword. After each motion, she repeats the Gaelic words, only this time, using English. "Duty, honor, and protection."

I watch as she hands my weapons back to Callan and motions for us to stand. Turning to the silent crowd, she smiles. "It is with most distinguished honor that I present to all supernatural realms, the king and queen of the gargoyle race, Their Highnesses, Asher and Eve."

Excitement ripples through the guests with applause and hollers. This should be a moment of great happiness. Instead, those of us on stage are on high alert.

After receiving a number of congratulatory wishes, we return to the table and rearm ourselves with our weapons. "What the hell is going on? Where are they?" Asher snaps.

"Something isn't right," Keegan responds. "I would have bet my life they would have interrupted the coronation."

"They're definitely here. The guards have seen them and I can sense them," Callan adds.

"So do we wait some more?" Abby asks.

Restoration

"Or draw them out?" McKenna interjects.

We all fall silent in contemplation, which is cut short by the clinking of a glass.

After the third clink, the end begins.

19 In the End

Garrick stands in front of all of us on the stage, with Deacon and Lord Falk on either side. A champagne flute in one hand, and a butter knife in the other, clanking the glass to gain attention. He smiles out into the crowd before meeting the clan's eyes.

Their father's face reflects kindness, though his body language is giving off nothing but malevolence. Nassa and Gage step out from behind the musicians. Gage turns to me, his face stricken with panic, and I know, I just know, something awful is about to happen.

Garrick patiently waits for the murmurs and rumbles to die down before he begins his speech. "How wonderful to see so many familiar faces this evening. I'm sure that my son and his new mate are pleased you've joined them tonight on this special occasion."

Asher's gaze slides to mine, his jaw clenched in anger. Keegan takes a step toward the stage, but Callan stops him. "Let's just see what Daddy Dearest has to say."

"If you all would be so kind as to indulge me, I do believe a toast to the new monarchy is in order and within my rights as your previous king and the new ruler's father." He pauses for dramatic effect. With an eerie confidence, Garrick locks eyes with Asher. "Now that you have everything, son—your mate, your title, the love of your race—would you give it up? Would you dare let it go? Are you prepared to sacrifice love . . . for your kin's existence?"

Everything around us becomes silent, unnaturally still. My heartbeat syncs with Asher's, and our combined beats slam against my ribs as we listen to Garrick.

"My bloodline, *your* bloodline, has been cursed over the years. Our race was bred by the divine for one purpose—to protect. While the Heavenly army fights for virtue, the demonic legion struggles for control." Garrick barks out a laugh. "The sad irony here is, both sides engage in an ongoing battle that neither will ever win. But you already know this, don't you, son? And during this cycle of waging war against one another, the gargoyle line continues to sacrifice their existence in order to save Heaven's precious human race." He sighs, passing the champagne flute to Deacon. "And for what? Free will?" He tsks. "How petty. It seems a shame to allow humans an avenue to continue to fuck up." He tilts his head in contemplation. "Though, perhaps that was the plan all along. Perhaps, the divine prefer mankind to stumble so they can continue to feel superior to lesser races." Asher's father passes his gaze over the group.

"What do you think will happen to the supernatural realms when it is no longer essential to shield mundanes from evil? Gargoyles were created for protection, so if there is nothing to protect, we cease to exist."

Asher seethes. "There will always be a threat. Our continued existence is set in stone."

Garrick's expression saddens. "Love blinds you, son. Isn't that right, Eve?" His gaze slides to mine and my stomach bottoms out. "For those of you unaware, my son's *human* mate is the daughter of a divine archangel, which, unlike nephilim, makes her bloodline pure. As a result of her parents' treachery, her father positioned her as a weapon of Heaven, designed to end the long-standing war. A struggle, we all know, will never end. Knowing this, Michael bound his daughter to my son's bloodline. You see, as long as Asher and Eve exist as a bonded couple, the dark army cannot attack Heaven's gates. Mankind, however, is once again left to seek protection from darkness by the gargoyles."

"That is enough!" Asher's voice bellows around the forest.

The gala's guests appear stunned and worried by Garrick's bold words.

He smiles widely. The gentleness is gone from his expression. In its place is a sadistic look. The dark army lingers in the shadows. Deacon and Lord Falk seem too calm.

Garrick releases an awkward laugh. "I realize toasts at these events tend to go rather long, my apologies," he says in a creepy, smooth voice, reaching for his glass and raising it toward Asher and me. "To the new monarchs. May Asher and Eve's love for one another continue until they take their last breaths."

My mouth hangs open at the evident warning. I seem to have forgotten how to breathe. A violent pulsation flows through my veins, and I realize I am experiencing Asher's blood boiling at his father's threat.

"Shit," Callan exhales and positions himself in front of Asher's fuming body.

Garrick throws the crystal flute into the throng. The crowd parts and the glass hits the dance floor in front of us, landing on the St. Michaels' family crest. It shatters into a million tiny pieces.

"*I* have ensured the gargoyle race continues to exist by aligning with the dark army. *I*. AM. STILL. YOUR. KING! Under my rule, *I* will lead us to everlasting existence without the burden of protecting human life." Garrick's eyes lock onto mine. "Darkness will always prevail."

In the blink of an eye, Asher is around Callan and stalking toward the stage. "NO! *You* sold your soul to the darkness for your own selfish wants!" he yells, pointing at his father. "Do not manipulate what you've done as anything but."

"WRONG!" Garrick shouts back. "I did what I had to do to save my race as KING!"

Asher stops in front of the steps. "Who are you? Where is the father I revered as a child? You had it all. A loving wife, adoring sons, and a kingdom that worshiped the ground you walked on. Instead, *you* chose to embrace and turn to darkness. The very things you taught us to rebel against our entire lives," Asher pants. "I don't recognize this self-serving asshole you've become."

Garrick's nostrils flare. "You cocky little prick." Asher jerks back as if slapped. "You know nothing of what it takes to run a kingdom, to be responsible for the success of a realm. I had everything, but I am a KING! *I* sacrificed love. *I* gave it up. *I* dared to let go, so that my race could continue to exist. My kingdom could thrive. My realm could grow. You know nothing."

Asher straightens his posture, morphing into warrior mode. I flinch, knowing he's about to attack. "I might be a cocky prick, but I'm sure my mate can attest to the fact that I am certainly not little." Asher throws a wink over his shoulder at me. In response, I give him a pointed glare that clearly says *not the time*. "Let me point out where your regime failed. Without my love for Eve, none of this matters. I don't, I can't, exist without her. So fuck you and your ideologies of what must be sacrificed to save our race. *Eve* makes me a great leader just by standing by my side. In the end, if my love for her is my downfall, then I'll be ten times the king you ever were."

"She *will* be your downfall, son." Garrick's cold stare meets mine.

I remain silent. Keegan and Callan step slightly in front of me. My light energy buzzes inside of me at the approach of the dark army. Garrick nods his head as if signaling something. The small amber light bulbs twinkling against the inky sky above us begin to pop and spark as the crowd runs to take cover.

McKenna grabs my arm, pulling me backward as Keegan and Callan disappear from my sightline.

Mass chaos erupts as the dark army slithers out from the shadows of the trees with the divine legion behind them, weapons drawn. Protectors from each of the gargoyle clans stand ready to fight. The leaders of the Royal Supernatural Court begin dishing out orders to members of their realms.

I look around and watch as the gala transforms before my eyes into a full-out war zone.

A loud crack of thunder booms and explodes throughout the night sky, shooting large shards of light into the woodland site. I flinch back and withdraw my daggers. Standing, I watch in horror as our supernatural guests engage in battle.

McKenna pushes me toward Abby. "Stay with her!" she orders before taking off toward the stage.

I look back and see the dark army already closing in on Abby. Immediately, my energy floats through my body, down my arms and out my hands, hitting the small group of demons and ending them. Abby's wide eyes turn to me, and she nods her thanks before wiggling her fingers and conjuring up a massive windstorm. The air whistles and whips around through the trees as the dark shadows continue to descend.

Michael's divine warriors appear in droves, rushing at the dark army. Shrill, heart-stopping cries break out through the commotion as his army annihilates the demons, destroying them with an ease and speed I've never seen before. Howls of pain rip through the air as the Heavenly warriors obliterate and devastate the demonic legion.

Seeing Michael and Uriel have the dark army under control, my gaze snaps to the stage, seeking Asher out. I turn back to Abby, but the wind is making it difficult to hear, so I point my dagger toward the area, letting her know that is where I'm heading.

Once again, she nods, and I take off. I try to block out the nightmare coming alive in vivid details around me as I disappear into the battling mob. The sounds of clattering blades, screams, and shouts mingle with the sounds of flesh being ripped apart and life extinguishing, surrounding me.

My hair is gripped violently from behind, my neck snapping back. I spin and come face-to-face with a demon. I clench my teeth, taking a deep breath, and engage the fiend. I slam into its chest with my foot, causing it to release my hair and stumble backwards. As it rushes at me again, I grip my daggers tighter and duck out of its grasp. I swing my right hand around and land my blade into its chest, causing it to extinguish in blue flames.

I stand straight. "Asshole," I pant out and turn, only to have another demon come at me. *Crap.* I sink my other knife into this one's throat. I don't wait for the blue flame, because when my gaze lifts, I notice that Asher has his sword across Lord Falk's throat and doesn't see the demon ready to attack from behind.

I bolt toward them, running at the dark being. It doesn't sense me coming from behind it. "No one touches my mate but me." I plunge both daggers into its back, ending it.

Asher spins, Lord Falk in his clutches. His eyes drop to the blue flame, and then back to me. "I'm not going to lie, that was damn sexy," he grunts.

"Thanks." I nod my chin at Lord Falk who is watching us with disdain. "Need help?"

"Nope. I'm glad you're here though." Asher sinks his blade a little farther into the council leader's throat, causing his eyes to widen in fright. "I'm about to painfully end this asshole's existence for what he did to you. Anything you want to say to him?"

I swallow. I'm not a cruel person, but I really hate this jerk. "Rot in hell."

In the background, I hear a loud popping noise and know Abby released her sonic boom. I keep my eyes focused on Asher. He now has the council leader on his knees, whispering in his ear. Lord Falk's face is ghostly white, and without warning, Asher whips his sword through the air in a graceful and brutal manner, landing it in the middle of the gargoyle's head. He runs it down the vertical length of Lord Falk, literally splitting him in two, before plunging the tip in the leader's heart, turning him to dust. I wince. *That was violent.*

Asher faces me, breathing heavily. "Where is Deacon?"

My eyes roam around the slowly ending battle. There are a lot of bodies on the ground, some demon, others supernatural. My stomach roils. Asher follows my gaze and sighs.

"Right here." Deacon emerges from the shadows on the stage, pulling our attention.

Gage, Keegan and McKenna are right behind the half-demon, half-gargoyle, trapping him between the five of us. Memories of what happened while being his prisoner hit me, but I immediately push them away.

"Hello, little girl." His voice is filled with malice.

"Deacon," I reply.

"Interested in some play time?" he goads.

Asher steps forward angrily, but I cup his elbow, pulling him back.

"We're mated. That means I get to follow supernatural rule. Hence, it is my right to end him," I explain to Asher.

"No fucking way," he retorts.

I ignore him, stepping toward Deacon.

"An eye for an eye," I say.

Deacon laughs cruelly. "I've taken great pleasure in your friend and mother's deaths."

I clench my teeth at the reminder. "As I will take in yours."

The right side of his lips tilt in a smug smirk. "Come get me then," he baits.

I grip my daggers and meet him halfway. We circle around one another, seething at each other for a few moments. In the background, I see the four other protectors watching, ready to attack if need be. Deacon has to know he's outnumbered. Out of respect, though, they let me try. I wait patiently, putting into practice everything Callan and my demon training instilled.

Finally, Deacon gets bored with our standoff and lunges for me, making a grab at my right arm. I feint to the left. He might be twice my size, but I'm fast. I have Asher's gargoyle speed now, and my anger. I kick at his knee, but he doesn't move. *That sucks.*

He lunges for me again. This time, his arm swings, and his fist aims for my face. I jerk back, avoiding the punch, but still getting knocked back a few steps.

Asher steps forward.

"NO!" I shout at him. "It's my right."

"Eve," he growls in warning.

I shake my head, praying he'll stay put.

He does, with a ticking jaw.

Deacon takes advantage of my distraction and dips quickly, viciously swinging his arm. I jump to the side, but not in time, and the tip on the blade of his knife slices into my upper arm, deep. I wince and release a small cry from the pain.

He offers a sinister smirk. "You are no match for me." Deacon disappears and reappears right in front of me, his fist slamming into my stomach. I double over, dropping my daggers and staggering to the ground, gasping for air. "I'm going to rip you apart, little girl."

Behind us, Asher rushes the half-demon with his sword. Just as he approaches, I kick my right leg out in a semicircle, sweeping Deacon's legs out from underneath him. He falls quickly turning onto his back with Asher standing over him.

Asher brings the Angelic Sword down on the half-demon's throat, searing the skin. My eyes widen as three of the dark army's demons charge at Asher from behind. Gage, McKenna and Keegan spring to action, taking them out quickly.

"You will never lay another hand on her again," Asher fumes.

I stand and grip my daggers, watching. Callan's words come back to me. *Demons are smart, always one step ahead. Therefore, you too must always be one step ahead, cutie.* I straighten myself and calm my breathing, knowing what Deacon will do next.

In an instant, Deacon vanishes and reappears behind me, his knife to my throat now. I remain calm, because I'm one step ahead of him. Panic falls across Asher's expression. I meet his eyes and give him a look that assures him I've got this. After a moment, he nods his understanding. We've practiced this a thousand times in training, and I'm ready.

Deacon is barking ridiculous threats at Asher. I ignore the words. Asher responds, playing into Deacon's anger. I've got one chance at this, so while he's distracted, I lift my daggers, plunging them into each of Deacon's thighs. He grunts, releasing the blade at my throat.

Using my speed, I duck and spin behind Deacon. In the process, I yank one of my daggers out of his leg and push him toward Asher, who plunges his sword into Deacon's stomach. The tip protrudes out his back.

Asher's eyes lock onto mine before he shouts. "Now."

From behind, I charge at Deacon's back and push my dagger into it, piercing his heart. My mouth is at his ear. "This is for Aria and my mother."

Seconds later, Asher violently removes his Angelic Sword and thrusts into Deacon's heart from the front. The five of us watch as Deacon begins to turn to stone from the bottom of his feet. I withdraw my blade and step around to the front, standing next to Asher.

He interlaces our fingers and violently yanks his sword from Deacon's half-stone body.

Deacon's expression is blank as he turns into a stone statue. When the marble hits his neck, his eyes narrow on me. "In life or death, Eve Collins, I will haunt you."

With those final words thrown at me calmly, the stone petrifaction finishes, and he is forever trapped in the confines of his stone prison.

Asher exhales and pulls me into a tight embrace. "Well done, siren." His lips brush my temple as he holds me tightly, sending healing energies into my body. The bleeding cut on my upper arm closes up immediately, and my stomach muscles stop throbbing from the punch. "See what we can do when we trust one another and work together, as a team?"

I nod, unable to speak. My body trembles from the adrenaline.

A loud crackle shatters through the woods, and the five of us turn our attention to the battle below. Most of it has ended. We look around the forest floor and see all of the faces we know and love staring back at us. Everyone looks rough, and tired, some bleeding, but they're all there. Alive. Breathing.

The dark army has receded, and Michael pulls his lightning bolt from the ground. Uriel steps to his side and both archangels turn their focus to the stage, taking a knee and leaning on their golden swords in front of Asher and me. Everyone has halted their movements across the gala, transfixed on the two beautiful angelic warriors.

"It is with distinguished honor we inform Your Highnesses the divine warriors have successfully ended the dark army's threat this evening," Michael says. "We are also pleased to proclaim that we have just received word from the Angelic Council. It appears an agreement has been reached, by both the divine and demonic realms. A second peace treaty has been signed."

I pinch my brows. "What does that mean?"

Uriel and Michael stand and take steps toward the stage.

"It means, Eve, that the dark army will no longer hunt you," Uriel states solemnly.

"Really?" I exhale. *Why aren't they happy about that?*

Michael's expression is crestfallen. "For now, yes.

Negotiations were set forth, and promises were made by both sides. Consider the next one hundred years a reprieve."

Asher exhales. "What happens when this treaty expires?"

Michael's eyes meet Asher's. "Your Highness, divine records are sealed. As a warrior of Heaven, I cannot share the contents with the supernatural world."

Asher bristles at Michael's answer but drops his chin in understanding.

The archangel turns his attention to me, stepping onto the stage and lowering his voice. "Eve, trust my words. When this treaty ends, the world as you know it will cease to exist."

A sinking feeling curls in my stomach and my mind reels at all the ways the Angelic Council negotiated. I study Michael's unreadable expression. After a moment, I realize it wasn't the Angelic Council. Michael has agreed to something to get a second treaty signed.

My eyes sting with tears as I meet his empty stare. "What did you do?" I whisper.

Michael smiles. "Protect my daughter."

I frown. "What?"

"Libby and I love you. We will protect you from above, always," Michael states.

Uriel steps closer to us. "Our assignment is over. We're being called back."

Michael nods and brings his hand up, cupping my cheek. "I am unsure of when Uriel or I will return. I hope you will accept this treaty as a token of my paternal love for you."

Overcome with emotion, I wrap myself around

Michael. "I love you."

A collection of light fractures the dark sky as the divine warriors take their leave, including Michael and Uriel. The supernatural creatures still here come back to life and take in the destruction surrounding us. The stench of sulfur and blue flames are everywhere.

"What a fucking mess," Keegan says, looking around.

Callan and Abby join us. "Dad is gone."

Asher rubs his face and pushes his hands through his hair. "Good."

Callan shakes his head. "No, not *gone* gone. Gone as in disappeared. Escaped."

"Fuck," Asher exhales, drawing the word out.

All of us stay silent for a while, exhausted and pondering what happened tonight.

Keegan sighs. "We should get down there and see what the damage is."

"Agreed," Callan responds.

We begin to work our way through the guests and mess. From the dance floor, I stare up at the statue that was once Deacon before my gaze shifts to Asher. He pulls me into his strong arms, and I relax against him.

"Are you okay, siren?" he asks, his lips brushing my temple.

"Yeah," I mumble into his chest.

"Not going to lie. Your fighting skills are fucking hot."

I laugh and pull back. My gaze collides with his. "You're not so bad yourself, gargoyle."

"We make a good team." He smiles brightly and my breath hitches. "I think we're going to be very happy together," he whispers before closing his eyes and meeting my lips.

Suddenly, I feel a searing pain. My eyes fly open, as do Asher's, and we both look down to see a butter knife sticking out of my chest. My blood gushes around the silver cutlery protruding from my heart, staining my dress and Asher's white shirt.

"I disagree, son." Garrick's smug voice circles us.

My eyes are wide as I stumble back in confusion. A waterfall of crimson liquid cascades onto the ground. Asher's gaze swings to my blood running like a fast river through his dragon crest. Tears begin to stream down my face. I exhale a breath and my knees go weak.

Asher folds me into his arms, gathering me close. We both drop to the ground and he pulls me on his lap, cradling my trembling body. His expression is filled with panic and horror as he thrusts his hand into my hair, pressing my face to his heart. *Shit. The earlier pain I felt in my heart was a warning.*

"It's going to be okay. I've got you. I'm here, siren. I've got you," he says over and over again while pushing healing energy into me. The dark tendrils twist between us.

My head lolls back as the blackness threatens to take over.

Asher's gaze snaps to Garrick.

"It's over, son. It's time to let. Her. Go," Garrick coos.

My lungs try to expand and drag in air, but for some reason, I can't do it. I force my eyes open and closed. My chest is on fire.

Garrick appears behind Asher, placing a hand on his shoulder. "The knife is made from an Angel Blade, son. It's destroying the divine light in her. Your healing energy won't work."

Asher's eyes widen and fill with fear as he clings to me. *Damn, the Angel Blade. The same one Jade used across my neck in the park. The only weapon Asher can't heal me from.*

"I'm sorry, Asher," I whisper as Gage comes into view behind Garrick, his sword drawn.

Asher's brows pull together in confusion. Gage looks down between us and my gaze slides to his. "Now," I barely manage to say.

In the next second, I see Gage lunge for Garrick. My vision blurs, and as if in a tunnel, I hear an odd gurgling sound coming from Asher's father as Gage plunges his sword into Garrick's heart.

"That is for Camilla, you fucking asshole," Gage seethes.

I focus on Asher's eyes as he leans over me, trying to heal my wound. With great effort, I lift my hand and trail the tips of my fingers over his jawline. I don't want him to watch his father being murdered at Gage's hand. Instead, I demand his attention stay on me.

"This is my favorite . . . my favorite part of you," I choke out.

"Siren." Tears form in his beautiful eyes.

A cold emptiness falls over my body. My heart beats at a slow and sluggish rate. My breathing is labored. My chest seizes. My fading gaze shifts to Asher's distraught face.

"Stay with me," he demands as his voice cracks.

I watch a single tear as it slowly rolls down his cheek. Using the last of my energy I brush it away before my hand slips and falls with a thud on the ground.

Asher brings his mouth toward mine, breathing into me.

"I-I . . . won't . . . I won't let go," I struggle to say across his lips.

A hard sob wracks his body. "Don't fucking let go, siren. Don't let go."

"There is beauty in darkness," I exhale on a last breath.

In the end, Asher's darkness is the last thing I feel before my light goes out.

20 Restoration

The golden rays of sunshine filter into the room, casting warmth and natural light across the bedroom as Asher watches me sleep. I can feel his eyes roaming over my body, taking in every inch of me in a slow, predatory manner. It's as if he's memorizing me, willing me not to vanish into thin air.

He reaches across the bed and caresses my face. I turn to face him. My eyes flutter open and he exhales slowly.

"Good morning, siren," he whispers softly.

I smile, cupping his left cheek with my hand. The stubble I love so much lightly scratches my palm as I whisper back.

"Hey you."

Asher leans into my palm, holding it to his face before

closing his eyes and inhaling.

"I can't believe we are really here. In a place of peace."

I lean up on my elbow, my hair cascading down my bare back onto the sheets.

"Open your eyes, gargoyle. I promise it's real."

Our intense gazes collide as Asher bends his forehead to mine. "I'm so grateful."

"I'm the one who is grateful. Your darkness saved me and protected my light," I whisper.

Sometimes, I have to remind myself to breathe because this is my life. It turns out the darkness Asher transferred to me during our mating ceremony is needed to keep my divine light. When Garrick stabbed me with the Angel Blade, he assumed the light in me would cease to exist, killing me. He was wrong. Asher's darkness wrapped itself around my soul, protecting my light. Keeping me alive so that he could heal me in stone state.

I smile, lightly grazing his lips. He cups my face and deepens the kiss, showing me what he feels his words are failing to say. His other hand brushes over my shoulder, down my back, caressing his mark. The touch sends heat throughout my veins.

Asher pulls away, his breath on my face. He lovingly brushes my hair over my bare shoulder. "Every choice I've ever made, every mistake that has come from those choices, it was all for you. This, was all for you. I love you, siren."

My throat closes up, filled with emotion as I place my hand over his protector tattoo. After a few moments, Asher brings my hand to his lips, kissing my fingers. "Don't be long."

I lie on my back; staring at the ceiling fan and

watching it rotate. My body and muscles ache in the best possible way when I stretch. I turn my head on the pillow to eye the empty spot beside me on the mattress. My hand runs over the warm sheets, and a small smile forms on my lips, recalling all the amazing things Asher and I did to one another last night.

The sound of a kitchen cupboard being shut draws me up and out of bed. I feel around the floor for my tank top and matching shorts, finding them and quickly sliding them back on. I hop into the bathroom and twist my hair into a messy bun, then brush my teeth and touch up my gloss before heading downstairs.

I take the last step of my childhood home's stairs and turn toward the kitchen, stopping short in the doorway. Silently, I watch the shirtless gargoyle pour two cups of dark hot chocolate. The muscles in Asher's broad shoulders move with him, making the dragon on his back come alive as he throws mini marshmallows in the mugs.

I release an appreciative moan, and he snaps his head up. His gaze meets mine, and he presents his full-blown signature sexy smirk. *Good god.* That smile hits me in the chest like a punch. It's intimate and affectionate, something only lovers share.

In one stride, he crosses the small room and hands me a cup. My fingers wrap around the mug at the same time his lips graze mine. It's official. I'm addicted to the taste of Asher St. Michael in the morning.

His mouth kicks up on the sides at my reaction to him, knowing what the sight of him half-naked in black pajama bottoms and bare feet does to me. I retreat a step and make my way to the couch, curling up into the corner and burying my feet underneath me. In a casual manner, he strolls over and sits next to me, tucking a loose piece of hair behind my ear.

"How are you feeling?" he asks.

I shrug and take a sip of my cocoa, basking in its warmth. "Better. It's only been a few weeks, but the scar seems to be going away," I reply, pulling down the left side of my tank.

Asher's expression instantly changes from soft to hard when he sees the tiny scar above my left breast, where Garrick stabbed me with a butter knife, of all things. The look he has is unreadable as the muscle in his jaw ticks. I feel like he's trying to see into my soul as his frown line appears between his brows.

I place my mug on the coffee table and cup his cheeks, moving closer to him. "Hey," I dip my chin and shift my head until he meets my gaze. "I'm here. I'm all right. It's over."

His finger lifts and he brushes the tip across the raised skin. "Is it weird that it matches mine?"

With a shake of my head, I lift the strap back. "Nope. It means we complete each other."

Asher shifts closer and smiles down at me. He brushes his lips across mine, and my hands find their way around his neck.

The color of his eyes becomes darker with desire, and immediately, he crushes me to him. His lips demand I open my mouth, and I do, allowing him the access he so desperately wants.

This kiss is deep, possessive. All Asher St. Michael.

"Baby, be careful." Abby's voice interrupts our

morning make-out session.

We pull apart and watch her following Callan into the kitchen. He sets down two cases of what appear to be small glass jars.

Abby turns around and her eyes widen at us. "Oh good, you're both up." She claps cheerfully. She skips over, pushing her way in between Asher and me on the couch, forcing us apart. Callan sits across from us, propping his flip-flop-covered feet on the table.

"What's that?" I point to the cases of jars.

"Callan is making organic baby food now." Abby beams.

"Really? What brought this on?" I ask, reaching for my mug.

Abby averts her eyes, and Asher covers his mouth with his palm, hiding a laugh.

What the hell is going on?

Callan smiles widely at me. "You did, cutie."

"Me?" I squeak out as McKenna and Keegan hop down the stairs at the same time Rulf and Gage come inside from the front porch, smelling like cigarette smoke.

I watch as all the large gargoyles try to maneuver their way around my small vineyard house, attempting to grab coffee and breakfast as they perch themselves in various spots between the open kitchen and living room.

"That first week after you were stabbed, you had a breathing and feeding tube. Once we removed it, I thought it would be easier to feed you pureed food." Callan shrugs. "So I did. Then I got to thinking, 'Hey, this is just like baby food. I should make baby food for my *actual* baby.'"

My mouth is hanging open before I shake my head.

"You fed me baby food?"

Abby rolls her eyes. "Eve, don't be so dramatic. Look at it as something you did for your future niece or nephew. Now we know what the baby will like and dislike," she offers while Asher and Gage chuckle.

"You're all insane," I say.

"Christ, don't knock it, love. You look well nourished to me," Gage quips.

My eyes meet Asher's playful ones. "We need our own place."

"Agreed." He scowls at the large group taking up the entire downstairs.

"No, you two don't need your own place. There is a baby coming. All hands on deck," Abby interjects. "Besides, Asher has news."

"Please don't tell me you're pregnant," I tease and bite my lip, preventing a laugh.

"As cool as that would be, I am not." He stands and walks over to the counter, picking up a large white envelope before returning to the couch.

Pushing Abby over so he can sit next to me, Asher hands the envelope to me.

"What is this?" I ask, flipping it over and studying it.

"Your re-admittance package for Kingsley College," Asher answers.

I grimace. "After all that's happened, you seriously want me to go back to school?"

Asher leans in, dropping his tone. "You made a promise too. To both me and your mom."

Frowning, I sigh. "Ash, I don't know if I can handle school right now."

"Queens need an education, Eve," Keegan adds from the kitchen.

"Yeah, what if my child asks their aunt Eve what two plus two is?" Callan asks.

I throw a pointed look at him. "Four. I went to kindergarten, Callan."

"No child of mine is being raised in a home with a college dropout," Abby argues.

"Hey," I scold. "There are amazing people who have never gone to college and still accomplished incredible things with their lives."

"I agree with Eve," Rulf interjects.

"SHUT UP, RULF!" Everyone shouts at once.

"Fuck. No need to bite my head off." He sighs and averts his attention.

"Just think about it, okay, siren?" Asher cajoles.

"All right."

"Good."

"By the way, Ash, you owe me fifty thousand dollars," Abby blurts out.

His lids slide shut before he twists on the couch to face her. "For what?"

"A beautiful little one-of-a-kind silk runway number you ripped apart in the throes of passion," she counters.

"Is it throes or throng?" I ask.

"An English degree would help with questions like that," Callan points out.

"Suck it, gargoyle," I retort.

Keegan stands. "As always, I've thoroughly enjoyed our witty banter, but it is time to head back to the manor. Eve's house is too small for all of us."

"In England?" I ask, chewing the inside of my lip. My heart sinks at the thought of leaving. This is my childhood home, where I was raised.

Sensing my internal struggle, Asher faces me and takes my bottom lip between his fingers, ending the torture I'm causing to my mouth. "We're staying in Massachusetts for a while," Asher states. "This is your home. We'll come back as often as you would like."

"Plus, it's perfect for the summer. The beach is right down the street," Callan adds.

"Ooh!" Abby squeals. "We've never had a beach house before. We should build an outdoor shower in the backyard."

"By the grace," Kenna huffs. "Eve is right, this family should come with a warning label."

Everyone stills. "Did you just agree with me, cupcake? And call me Eve?"

Realization crosses her face. "Don't get used to it, blood of Eden." She storms upstairs.

A few seconds pass before everyone shakes off the moment and leaves. Rulf takes a few steps to go back, but I step in front of him, blocking his movement.

"Rulf."

"Your Highness." His tone is cautious.

"I'm actually really glad you're here," I say sweetly.

His brows rise to his forehead. "And why is that?"

"Do you have plans to head back to Scotland?"

"I was thinking about it. Why?" he asks.

"Do you like babies, Rulf?"

He shrugs. "I guess they're cute when they aren't drooling, crying, or peeing on you."

I grimace at the image he's conjured up. "Agreed. Anyway, I think you are the perfect protector for my new niece or nephew," I state, meeting his confused expression.

"Don't take this the wrong way, Eve, but *hell* no," he scoffs.

"You owe me," I whine.

"For what?"

"Does a kidnapping incident with the council ring any bells?"

He holds my stare before his shoulders fall. "Are you telling me you are cashing in your *You Owe Me* card on babysitting services?"

"It's not babysitting, it's protecting a charge. A very important charge, because not only is the baby my niece or nephew, but technically, they're next in line to Asher's throne."

"No."

"The way I see it, the council no longer exists. You were a council guard. That means you're out of a job. It just so happens I have one for you. A royal guard to the prince or princess and heir to the gargoyle throne."

He sighs. *I've so got him.*

"You owe me," I remind.

"Fine . . . but if she or he bites me, you will pay me additional compensation."

"Deal."

"Everything okay, siren?" Asher asks, wrapping his arms around my waist.

"Yes. Rulf has decided to join us at the manor," I explain.

Rulf growls and storms around us, sulking his way out

the front door.

Asher's breath is at my ear. "What are you up to?"

I shrug innocently. "Just fulfilling my royal duties and protecting this family."

A light rumble releases from his chest. "Come on, we have to pack."

"You start, I'll be right up. I want to wash these mugs first." I point to the empty cups.

Asher presses a light kiss to my neck before stepping away. "Don't be long."

I grab the hot cocoa cups, then step into the kitchen and start washing them in the sink, cursing my mother for not installing a dishwasher.

A throat being cleared shifts my focus to the bad-boy gargoyle leaning against the doorway. One arm is crossed over his chest, and the other arm is stretched out in front of him, an unlit cigarette in his hand. Gage rolls it nervously between his fingers. He's dressed in all black, similar to the first day I met him.

I wipe my wet hands on a dishtowel and smile at him, studying his nonverbal mannerisms. My shoulders sag, and I place the towel on the hook before swallowing the lump forming in my throat.

"You're leaving?" My voice cracks.

A small smile crosses his lips. "I am, love."

I fold my own arms over my chest and cock my hip, leaning against the counter.

"Why?"

"My job here is done."

"Technically, you're still my protector. I need you," I admit.

Gage exhales. "I beg to differ."

A silent beat passes between us as I hold his gaze.

"Can I ask you something?" I question, ending the quiet.

"You can." He dips his chin in that sexy way he does.

"Did ending Garrick give you the peace you were seeking?"

Gage exhales, his gaze lifting and focusing on the window behind me. "Yes."

"It won't bring her back."

"No, love, it won't. Either way, Camilla is gone."

"What are you going to do with all your free time now that you don't have to babysit me?" I try to keep my tone light.

Gage steps forward, dropping his crossed arm. "My art studios and architecture firm in Paris could use some attention."

"So then, back to Paris it is?" My eyes meet his.

"I have a stop to make first."

I smile. "Would this stop be to the magic dimension?"

"There is a very sexy sorceress I need to see. Apparently, she feels that actions are louder than words. Therefore, love, I have some actions I need to put into place."

My hand moves over my heart. "Gage Gallagher, are you admitting that you are ready to open your heart to Nassa?" I feign shock.

"I don't know, but she's worth trying for," he admits quietly.

Tears fill my eyes. "Your story is just beginning. I'm glad you've restored your faith."

I step into his open arms and inhale his scent of cigarettes and spices one last time.

Gage drops a kiss to the top of my head.

"Thank you for being my redemption, Eve."

21 This Remains

The barista calls my name and I snatch up my café mocha before pushing the café doors open. The light breeze caresses my skin, and a small shudder runs through me. I wrap my scarf tighter around my neck in an effort to keep the cool air at bay.

"Cold?" A deep, cocky voice greets me.

A bashful smile crosses my lips at the familiar greeting. I look up to see Asher leaning against his black Aston Martin DB9. Damn if he isn't looking every bit as delicious as he always does. I cock my head, deciding to play along, recreating the recognizable scene.

"Why do you care?" I question in a light, teasing voice.

At my customary response, Asher flashes his signature sexy smirk and holds his stance while I internally melt. I inhale, basking in the burning sensation his gaze leaves on my skin as it seeps into my soul. His stare is so intense I bite the inside of my cheek and look away.

"Do I make you anxious, Eve?" he asks.

"No." I shiver, knowing what comes next.

Nodding his head in understanding, Asher prowls toward me, leaning into my space.

"You sure, siren?" he whispers.

I lift my chin and get lost in the deep layers of blue in his gaze. "Yes."

The corners of his mouth lift smugly as he moves closer. So close I can feel his minty warm breath across my lips. With each breath he releases, I inhale, breathing him in.

Chuckling quietly, he takes off his leather jacket, and my heart rate picks up. Slowly, he leans forward, wrapping his coat over my shoulders, engulfing me in warmth and his intoxicating scent.

His lips brush my ear as he whispers. "I've got you, siren, always."

"I know you do, pretty boy."

Asher drops a light kiss to my forehead and wraps his arms around my shoulder.

"Let's get out of here, yeah? We don't want to be late to your first class," he says, snatching my coffee and taking a long sip.

"Hey," I whine.

He pulls me tighter into his side. "We're mated. What's yours is mine and vice versa," he announces while we walk toward his car.

Once we reach his car, I stop moving and stand defiantly. After a moment, I meet Asher's questioning glare with a smirk. "If that is true . . ." I hold out my hand.

Asher's indigo eyes drop to my outstretched palm before his expression turns horrified.

"Siren," he drawls out in warning.

"A deal is a deal, Asher St. Michael."

A long pause beats between us before he swallows, hard, and lifts his gaze to mine. His face is serious. I wait. Finally, he reaches into his jacket pocket and produces the car keys. With a painfully slow nod, Asher lifts the keys and drops them into my waiting hand.

"Fuck," he spits out and tosses my empty coffee cup into the trash.

Giddily, I clap and all but run over to the driver's side, sinking into the seat. *Oh. My. God.* The leather seats in this vehicle are like Heaven. I could die right now. I can't help but beam watching Asher slide into the passenger seat. *Holy shit! He's actually going to let me drive.*

Placing his palms on the dashboard, he closes his eyes, leans in and drops his voice.

"Normally, once you're mine, I don't share. In this instance, I'm making an exception to keep my promise." He sighs. "No one touches her. She is the love of my life. Yeah?"

I roll my eyes at his dramatics. *Damn gargoyle.*

"She and I are connected in a very intimate way. She is my íde ámo. Protect her," he whispers sexily and opens his eyes, sitting up and meeting my hesitant expression.

I frown. "Ash, I promise to take care of your car. I know you love her."

He looks at me thoughtfully for a moment before reaching over and pulling the seatbelt across my body, then snapping it in.

"I was talking about you, siren," he says softly. "*You are the love of my life, tas ámotas.*"

Tears sting my eyes and my lips part. It's insane how much I love this damn gargoyle.

"I will protect you, always," he vows.

I hold his gaze. "I love you. That will never change."

Asher runs his thumbs under my eyes, wiping away the tears. "All things change, siren, but this," he motions between us, "this remains."

The End

EPILOGUE

Serenity...

Winter brings immense beauty into the world. There is a spiritual tranquility in the cleanliness of snow and the quietness of the world. I stare at the snowflakes as they fall and press my index finger to the cold windowpane, tracing the random patterns the delicate, untainted crystals make as they tumble out of the darkened sky.

The pure white snowfall covering the Massachusetts landscape adds a breathtaking exquisiteness to the estate, turning La Gargouille Manor into an enchanting wonderland. I've been standing here for almost an hour, watching the feathery crystals gather onto the bare, weak wooden branches of the estate's trees.

The silence is peaceful, a rare thing in our world. In a strange way, the serenity of the pure snow is perfect for this day. It's almost as if the universe knows the chaos that is about to unfold and it's steeling itself for her arrival.

I savor one last moment of peace before the velvety swishing of car tires on snow shifts my focus. I exhale and relax. *Thank God they made it in time.* I watch as the black

Escalade pulls into the driveway and all four doors open simultaneously.

A ghost of a smile crosses my lips when I see four protectors slide out of the vehicle, all dressed in black. They look just as intimidating and unapproachable as the first day I met them. Sensing my presence, a set of indigo eyes lift to the window, and my soul ignites at the sight of my mate and gargoyle protector.

Instantly, I turn to the staircase, and in record time, make my way down to the first floor just as the heavy wooden doors swing open. I don't even wait to confirm it's Asher I'm running to. Instinctively, I know it's him. I leap into his strong arms, and he pulls me tighter against his hard body, engulfing me in the scent of smoky wood and leather.

"Fuck, I've missed you, siren." His voice is ragged and heavy near my ear.

"I missed you too." I sigh into his shirt.

After a moment, I'm gently placed on my feet. Just as I touch the floor, large hands cup my cheeks, pulling me into a warm, soft, delicious kiss.

"By the grace, do you two think you could wait until the rest of us get into the manor before you attack one another?" McKenna barks from the doorway, stepping around us.

Asher and I ignore her snip, and he continues to unapologetically devour my mouth.

"You'd think it was a month, not a week, they were apart," Keegan mumbles.

A frigid wind floats over Asher and me from the open doorway, causing us to pull away. My fingers brush my bruised lips, and Asher smiles, knowing he was the cause. *Damn gargoyle.*

"Ye kids ah gonna catch pneumonia if ye don't shut dat der door," Fiona reprimands from the top of the second floor rise.

Asher rolls his eyes, and I smile at the plump woman's scolding just as Callan strolls in.

"Did I miss it?" Callan asks, looking scared.

I shake my head. "Nope. You got home just in time."

He grins widely at all of us, shutting the doors behind him. "Thank grace, my girl would have skinned my behind if I had."

I scrunch my nose. "Is that a real thing? The skinning of one's behind?"

"Yes, and it's pretty painful from what I understand," Asher adds.

"Says the gargoyle with an apadravya piercing," Keegan chimes in.

Callan visibly shivers. "Both scare the unicorns right out of me."

"What the hell does that even mean?" McKenna narrows her eyes at Callan.

"By de grace, children." Fiona sighs.

McKenna begins to make her way upstairs, mumbling under her breath about the stupidity of this family's endless discussions over insignificant topics.

"Abby is resting in her suite," I call up to her.

"No shit, blood of Eden. Thanks so much for the insight," she throws over her shoulder.

"Language, lass," Fiona warns before turning and facing the clan. "Let me be crystal clear, less der is any confusion amongst dis here royal clan. A baby is about ta be born. Foul language," her eyes dart to Kenna's retreating form before returning her gaze to the group, "and vulga' behavior won't be tolerated by me. Are we clear?"

"Yes, ma'am," erupts in a mumbling chorus.

"Good, ye children need ta learn some manners. Ye get worse as ye get oldah. 'Twill be nice ta have an age-appropriate gargoyle en da house," Fiona states wearily.

"Are you saying we act like babies, Fi?" Callan feigns hurt.

"Aye, lad. Ye especially," she replies with a sigh, heading back upstairs to Abby.

Callan steps toward the staircase, but Keegan places a hand on his chest, halting his movement. "Real quick, I just got word that it's done." He holds his iPhone up.

Asher's head lifts along with his gaze. "He accepted?"

"Gallagher is heading to County Kerry as we speak," Keegan replies.

"What's going on?" I interject.

"Now that the Royal Gargoyle Council of Protectors has been dismantled, my first royal task as king of the gargoyle race is to turn Domus Gurgulio Castle into an academy for gargoyle protectors. Those who wish to, can study there and fine-tune their protection skills," Asher explains. "Hopefully, the school will empower the next generation of protectors with a sense of duty, loyalty, and protection while they receive a top notch education."

"Professor Davidson has agreed to be the headmaster, cutie," Callan adds.

"That's amazing, guys." I smile.

"The Royal Protector Academy will be our legacy and will hopefully make up for some of the chaos and damage our father and the council created during their reign," Asher continues.

I cringe at the reminder of Garrick and what he did to all of us.

"Gallagher's architectural firm will be there in the morning to start RPA's transformation," Keegan points out, reading an email on his phone. "He thinks it will take about a year to get the building renovated and running the way we need an academy to be."

"We'll go after the baby is born and check it out," Asher says.

My hand wraps around Asher's arm. "Will Nassa be there with Gage?"

His eyes soften. "I don't know. I'm not sure if their story is finished or not, siren. We'll just have to wait and see what tomorrow brings for them."

Callan stares at the stairs. "I can't wait to meet my son."

I narrow my eyes at him. "How do you know you're having a boy?"

"It's a boy, cutie," he counters without room for argument.

"You have a fifty-fifty shot, Dad-to-be," Asher muses.

"I have it on good authority," Callan states proudly.

"What authority?" Keegan asks with a disbelieving tone.

"I know divine beings who have assured me it's a boy," Callan retorts.

I tilt my head. "What *divine beings*?"

"Uncle Urie," he says.

Asher and I both release a light laugh. "Archangel Uriel? My uncle?"

Callan narrows his eyes and points a finger at me. "He prefers Uncle Urie, Eves."

"Callan St. Michael, get your adorable ass up here this instant!" Abby's sweet, yet firm, pinched bellow floats down from the second floor.

"Shit! I'd better get up there. Can't wait to introduce you guys to Thor."

Keegan pats his younger brother on the shoulder, and they take the stairs two at a time.

"You okay with all of this, siren?" Asher asks from behind me.

At the sound of his voice, I close my eyes and inhale before turning around. I know what he's asking, yet not. He's worried that someday I'll regret this life. Choosing to be with him above all else. Giving up children of my own.

My gaze takes in the striking gargoyle. My protector. I'm filled with nothing but intense love and devotion when it comes to him. It seeps out of my soul. What he fails to understand is that he is my life.

My everything.

"I don't think any of us are ready for Callan and Abby to be parents, Asher," I tease.

"That's not what I meant." Asher's head tilts, watching me.

I step into his arms and pull him to me. "The only thing I am feeling right now is terrible for that little girl. This clan's overprotectiveness is going to follow her for life." I place a small kiss across his lips. "And we're going to love and protect her as if she's our own."

"She?" he questions.

I wiggle my eyebrows. "Callan isn't the only one with inside information."

Asher interlaces our fingers and guides us upstairs to a sitting area just outside of Abby and Callan's suite. *Who knew it took so long to give birth.* We watch McKenna pace nervously for a little over two hours before Callan reappears.

His face is ashen as he steps into the middle of the group.

"What's wrong?" I ask anxiously.

Callan swallows and just stares at us. "I-it's a girl."

"Holy shit!" Asher exclaims.

"Congratulations, brother." Keegan pulls both St. Michael boys into a tight embrace.

My gaze collides with McKenna's and we both smile brightly. After a few moments, the guys release each other and Callan wipes his teary eyes before exhaling roughly.

"What the fuck am I going to do with a girl?"

I bite back a laugh. This poor little girl is so screwed. As are these big bad gargoyles.

"By the grace." Kenna impatiently pushes past them into the suite and we all follow.

A glowing Abby is sitting up in bed, holding her tiny cooing daughter. Fiona fusses over the little bundle of joy, fixing her blanket and stroking the tiny wisps of red on her mostly bald head. Callan takes a seat on the bed, next to his girls.

Abby's sparkling eyes lift to the clan in pure happiness. "May I introduce Serena Elizabeth Vivian St. Michael," she says, with tears forming in her eyes.

I cup Serena's cheek and smile at Abby. "What a beautiful name."

"She's our little piece of serenity in the world," Callan whispers.

"Welcome to the family, Princess Serena." I fight back tears.

Asher leans down and kisses Serena's forehead before whispering to her. "We will protect you, always."

Restoration

THE ROYAL PROTECTOR ACADEMY
SPRING 2016

Thank you so much for reading The Revelation Series. So many of you have expressed how sad you are at the thought of the series ending. Though *Restoration* is the last chapter on Eve's journey, I'm excited to introduce you to the next generation of the St. Michael and Gallagher clans in the **Royal Protector Academy Trilogy**.

RPA will follow **Serena St. Michael** and **Tristan Gallagher's** story. Some of your favorites from the Revelation Series will also be making guest appearances.

Keep reading for a sneak peek of *Vernal*.

EXCERPT FROM VERNAL
SPRING 2016

My eyelids slide shut as the tiny drops of water cascade gracefully from the darkened sky. The warm droplets hit my face and trickle with effortless ease across my cool skin. I feel alive as my essence connects to the vigor the weather bestows. It seeps into me, penetrating each layer until the earth's energy flows within my veins.

Ignoring the dull ache forming in my neck from tilting my face skyward, I lift my arms and without thought twirl my body. Embracing each tiny bead of water. The storm soaks the crenulated coastline with a fierce assault. The torrential rain heightens my innate tendency to absorb weather elements, causing my core to hum with vitality.

My lips lift blissfully as I pirouette my way through the mist-shrouded, endless green hills, each rise criss-crossed by tumbledown stone walls. I loved doing this as a child. Spinning so fast I'd become dizzy and disoriented until the earth around my feet would slip away and, breathlessly, I would collapse on the soggy blades of grass waiting to embrace me.

There's something freeing, liberating, about standing in an open field with your arms extended, allowing the falling rain to wash away your inhibitions. Not that I have many hang-ups. Still, the ones I do own cling to my heart like chains. Suffocating me.

A childish laugh escapes me as my body tumbles and sprawls itself onto the soaked ground. I stretch my lean limbs across the damp blades of grass, while my long auburn locks fan out around my face. Opening my eyes, I watch the world spin around me, allowing the dizziness to rid me of who I am, and why I'm here.

My free-spirited moment ends abruptly at the sound of a throat being cleared. I release a half-moan, half-sigh, knowing my moment of reprieve has ended. I don't sit up to face the protector assigned to guard me. Instead, my annoyance overtakes the fleeting serenity I felt seconds ago.

My protector's presence reminds me of my royal bloodline, my duties and obligations. I frown. He's probably standing with his arms crossed in aggravation from my lack of acknowledgment. Well, the fucker can just stand in the rain. Serves him right for ruining a beautiful private moment. One I won't see again while here.

"Go away, Rulf," I instruct my bodyguard.

"You're naked." The statement comes from an unfamiliar seductive, masculine voice.

"Your keen ability to state the obvious is mind-blowing." I smirk at my own wit.

The guy who isn't Rulf releases a dark chuckle that unnerves me, rattling my core.

"I must have missed the *clothing optional* portion of the academy's handbook."

My stomach clenches as his silky voice drifts over my bare skin, caressing it.

"Something to work on."

"What's that?" The stranger inquires.

"Reading. It's a prerequisite if you're attending," I counter.

"Is nudity a habitual behavior of yours?" he questions with an amused tone.

I roll onto my stomach, lift my cobalt gaze and meet his. "Yes." *Holy shit. He's hot.*

A knowing smirk appears on his delectable lips and my breath hitches.

"Nice ass," he compliments, while his cognac irises run the length of my body.

Comfortable in my skin, I don't shy away from his open perusal. His eyes roam across my body, leaving imprints everywhere they caress. I blush from his heated intensity. Desire slithers inside me, crawling into the crevices and suffocating me.

I take advantage of the fact that he's lost in thought to observe his breathing, which is smooth, velvety soft. Unlike my unsolicited need to have him whisper dirty things to me in the dark, forever, he seems unaffected by me.

He runs both of his large hands through his dark blond, almost caramel hair, pushing the long top pieces of hair back in a sleek and sexy manner. The rain has soaked every perfect strand and they keep plastering themselves to his gorgeous sun-kissed face. It elicits a pang of jealousy within me, because for some stupid unknown girlie reason, I want to be the one to touch his perfect, chiseled face.

Silver and hematite rings adorn his fingers—like mine, all except his pinky finger are covered with them. I blink away the idea that our hands match and instead focus my roaming attention on his broad chest. It's hidden under a thin white long-sleeve, V-neck cotton thermal, drenched by the rain, allowing me full viewing access to his muscles.

I study the leather rope hanging low from his neck. An emblem dangles from it, sitting under his shirt. He has his sleeves pulled to his elbows, showing off the leather and chain bracelets on each of his wrists. Adornments I'm familiar with. I sigh internally and something inside of me sinks.

My gaze lowers to his black worn jeans and black heavy boots. This guy reeks of danger and trouble. The air of cockiness he emanates is one I grew up with. It matches my father's and uncle's traits, meaning this hot specimen is definitely off-limits.

I meet his powerful glare and a shaky breath escapes me. I'm startled by the way he's looking at me, like I'm his entire world. I need to get a grip on my erratic emotions. Standing, I put my entire unclothed body on display, hoping to throw him off balance.

Unfazed, his eyes lock onto mine. "Are you done assessing me?" he challenges.

"You're a protector?" I accuse, pointing to the black inked Celtic tattoo on his right forearm. The symbol binds him to the Spiritual Assembly of Protectors.

His expression falters as if my accusation hurt him somehow. He doesn't say anything but dips his chin in response. I take a step back, knowing all too well the feeling of suffocation associated with who we are and what we're meant to do.

While trying to come up with something clever to say, I play nervously with my own piece of protector jewelry, sitting on my left wrist. The silver bracelet is intricately designed with flowers and vines around the band, hiding my smaller identical tattoo.

My aunt Eve, the queen of our race, gave it to me two years ago for my eighteenth birthday. It was something that her deceased mother, Elizabeth, a jewelry designer, had made for her when she was in high school. She had my uncle Asher, her mate, and our king, add the tiny chains and emeralds, my healing stone, so they would hang off the sides in a feminine manner.

A small watch face was set on top with the hope that I would have become more responsible about time management. Not one of my strong suits. Along with rules, focus, education. . . you get the point. I despise the leather bands my family wears—they've always felt more like handcuffs to me than a required accessory.

As the only human in our clan, my aunt understands the need for me to have something that is truly a reflection of me. When she saw the band that was open, airy and less formal, she immediately had it made into something special that I adore.

Sometimes, I think Aunt Eve is the only one who understands my free spirit.

"I'm Tristan," the stranger says in a way that slices right through to my bones.

"Serena," I reply.

Tristan's gaze roams over my body in a palpable manner, as he becomes intimate once again with my every curve. "Are you always so . . .welcoming, Serena?" He smirks.

When his eyes finally meet mine again, I arch a brow. "Only to those I like."

"So you like me then?" He attempts to hide his smile.

I push my shoulders back, his eyes still locked on mine. "Don't flatter yourself."

Tristan cocks his head and crosses his impressive arms over his chest. My focus slides to the rain dripping off his face as he steps closer to me, so close that I trap a breath he's exhaled in my lungs when his bare arm brushes my own.

Slowly he bends down, piercing me with an amused expression. "And here I was, completely impressed with myself that I had a beautiful girl naked, and wet, within five minutes of meeting her," he seduces.

"That a record for you?" I offer a shy grin, not able to stop myself.

"It would seem so," he counters.

"Maybe you're just having an off year," I reason.

Tristan's eyes bore into me with an obvious sadness that stretches over us. "You have no idea just how off it's been," he retorts.

I trace his mouth with my eyes and part my lips to speak but he abruptly cuts me off when his hands lift to my face, cupping my cheeks. My body trembles at the touch. Tristan's thumb lightly brushes a drop of rain off my bottom lip. I watch with a rapidly beating heart as he brings his thumb to his mouth and sucks off the bead of water.

"It's been interesting meeting you, Serena." My name feels like a test on his lips as he releases my face and takes a step back, sliding his hands in the front pockets of his jeans.

I lift my gaze to his. "You too, Tristan."

A bright smile appears on his face. "See you around, raindrop."

DIALECT TRANSLATIONS

Tas ámotas: My love (Garish)

íde ámo: The love of my life (Garish)

Ilem jur pri tú-tim, ew tú-tim pri pos-tim ali ide in-zen, máni, vas-wís, ew ter-ort. Esta-de ai esta Ilem de, Ilem pos-tim in-saengkt pri, tú-tim: I promise you forever, and forever you shall have my heart, soul, mind and body. With everything that I am, I will protect you, always. (Garish)

Whit has become ay th' fairy, yer highness: What has become of the fairy, your highness (Scottish).

It was th' will ay fate 'en: It was the will of fate then. (Scottish)

Ye'ur askin' us tae kill one ay our own. By torture?: You're asking us to kill one of our own. By torture? (Scottish)

Ah dinnae loch it, yoong prince: I don't like it, young prince. (Scottish)

Yer wuid es noted, yer highness. When we find hem, th' Scottish clan will brin' Deacon tae ye, strugglin' fur his last breath. On our honur as protectors: Your words are noted, your highness. When we find him, the Scottish clan will bring Deacon to you, struggling for his last breath. On our honor as protectors. (Scottish)

In-zen, mání, vas-wís, ew ter-ort: heart, body, mind and soul (Garish)

Zhen pri: Family first (Garish)

Xnuk Ek': Evening Star (Mayan)

Dieacht, honor, agus Cosaint: Duty, honor and protection (Gaelic)

ACKNOWLEDGMENTS

Nothing can be accomplished without a team of amazing people around you who love and support you. This is true for this series, these characters, and me.

Dave and Maddison. You are both the epitome of unconditional love and support. It's because of you this series exists. Thank you for allowing me to follow my dreams.

Kris Kendall. Best. Editor. Ever. I truly mean that. Over 500,000 words later and we can still laugh and have fun with these damn gargoyles. I'm extremely lucky to have gotten you out of this crazy ride. I am forever grateful to you, lady.

Liz Ferry and Kristin Phillips, thank you both for polishing this story so that it shines. Danielle Simmons at Bravebird Publishing, thank you for another beautiful cover. Hang Le, who designed the swoonworthy branding. You're the best!

A special thanks to the beta readers: Sara Dustin, Maureen Switalski, Terri Thomas, Heather White, Kayla Clinton, Shari Anderson, and others. You all have made this series what it is today. I thank you.

Terri Thomas (mybookboyfriend.net) was the first person (other than Kris) to read *Revelation* and my first beta reader. She took a chance on me when most said no, and then continued with me to the end. I owe her a huge debt of gratitude. Terri's insight and direction have been invaluable to this series. Please check out her reviews if you have a chance, and her 'book boyfriend' images are hot too!

To Nichole at *YA Reads* and all the amazing bloggers who host my books with enthusiasm and love, there are not enough words to show my appreciation. I can't thank you enough.

Randi's Rebels, you all ROCK! I am blessed and blown away at your constant show of love and support. By the grace, you Rebels have no idea how many times you've helped me fight the urge to crawl under a rock. You're truly the best group of gargoyle lovers, ever. A special shout out to Rebel Whitney Downs for naming Onix in *Restoration*.

As always, my deepest gratitude to the readers, thank you for taking a chance on this series. I'm humbled that you've embraced it as you have. It's been a journey of self-discovery, love and sacrifice for not only these characters, but me as well. Thank you for allowing me to be a part of your reading library. I look forward to continuing to be part of your literary world.

ABOUT THE AUTHOR

Randi Cooley Wilson is an author of paranormal, urban fantasy, and contemporary romance books. Randi was born and raised in Massachusetts where she attended Bridgewater State University and graduated with a degree in Communication Studies. After graduation she moved to California where she lived happily bathed in sunshine and warm weather for fifteen years.

Randi makes stuff up, devours romance books, drinks lots of wine and coffee, and has a slight addiction to bracelets. She currently resides in Massachusetts with her daughter and husband.

She loves to hear from readers, please reach out to her at: **randicooleywilson.com** or via social media outlets:

Twitter: @R_CooleyWilson

Facebook: www.facebook.com/authorrandicooleywilson

Goodreads: www.goodreads.com/RCooleyWilson

Randi's Rebels: www.facebook.com/groups/randisrebels

Made in the USA
Middletown, DE
04 June 2017